About Protecting His Own

Masters of the Shadowlands: 11

From the heartbreaking first chapter to the last I dont think I ever had a dry eye during this book. This was one emotional powerhouse of a story.

~ SNS Reviews

A man protects those given into his care.

Landscape designer, Beth King survived an abusive husband and built a new life for herself with the help of Master Nolan, the strongest, most protective man she has ever known. She loves him with all her heart, but the one thing he wants, she can't give him. To her grief, the damage from her abusive first marriage means she can't bear him children.

As Beth and Nolan change their plans and pursue adoption, they're already imagining a baby girl in the nursery. But when two boys from the local domestic violence shelter see their mother taken to the hospital, they call Beth in a panic. Agreeing to care for them temporarily, Beth soon falls in love with the two adorable boys.

Now Master Nolan has a new problem. How can he protect the children when their drug-addicted mother is released—and how the hell can he keep his sweet submissive's heart from being broken when they leave?

Heads-up, my dears: the story is heartwarming…yet heartbreaking due to children in a domestic violence situation.

Protecting His Own gets a FIRM BUT TOUCHING, FIVE SHOOTING STARS! This book will leave your emotions in every which way and back again!

~ Marie's Tempting Reads

Want to be notified of the next release?

Sent only on release day, Cherise's newsletters contain freebies, excerpts, and articles.

Sign up at:

www.CheriseSinclair.com/NewsletterForm

Protecting His Own

Masters of the Shadowlands 11

Cherise Sinclair

VanScoy Publishing Group

Protecting His Own

Copyright © 2016 by Cherise Sinclair

Print Edition

ISBN: 978-0-9975529-1-1

Published by VanScoy Publishing Group

Cover Artist: April Martinez

Acknowledgments

Let's start with the usual suspects. My crit buddies, Bianca Sommerland, Fiona Archer, and Monette Michaels get warm, squishy hugs and kisses for wading through rough drafts and helping unearth the actual plot.

Many thanks go to Red Quill Editing for polishing this book into readability. They even worked on weekends to get the book finished quickly. Blessings upon Saya and her crew.

A big hug to Ruth Reid who vetted the psychology for me. You're awesome, Ruth!

In the past, three readers have (ever so tactfully) pointed out errors that escaped my various editors and publishers. Well, a job well done means someone hands you a new job, right? This time, I recruited them *before* the manuscript was published. Thank you, Lisa White, Barb Jack, and Marian Shulman, for your incredibly sharp eyes, your knowledge of grammar, and your wonderful suggestions.

To all of you who have survived abuse, as children or adults, and struggled through the aftermath, I know it can be so very tough at times. Hang in there, my dears. Get help from friends and family and therapists. And know that slowly, but surely, there *is* healing.

Author's Note

To my readers,

The books I write are fiction, not reality, and as in most romantic fiction, the romance is compressed into a very, very short time period.

You, my darlings, live in the real world, and I want you to take a little more time in your relationships. Good Doms don't grow on trees, and there are some strange people out there. So while you're looking for that special Dom, please, be careful.

When you find him, realize he can't read your mind. Yes, frightening as it might be, you're going to have to open up and talk to him. And you listen to him, in return. Share your hopes and fears, what you want from him, what scares you spitless. Okay, he may try to push your boundaries a little—he's a Dom, after all—but you will have your safe word. You will have a safe word, am I clear? Use protection. Have a back-up person. Communicate.

Remember: safe, sane, and consensual.

Know that I'm hoping you find that special, loving person who will understand your needs and hold you close.

And while you're looking or even if you have already found your dear-heart, come and hang out with the Masters of the Shadowlands.

Love,
Cherise

Chapter One

"Beff?"

In the center yard of the Tomorrow is Mine domestic violence shelter, Beth King smiled at the four-year-old boy. Each time he couldn't pronounce the "th" in her name, her heart melted. Had any gardener had such an adorable assistant? "Yes, sweetie?"

He set a tiny dandelion on the weed pile, and his little brow furrowed as he frowned. "Lamar tooked my coloring book, but Grant made him give it back."

"I'm glad Grant was there." Connor's brother was seven and as protective as they came.

"But..." Connor shook his head to show she'd missed the point. "Lamar doesn't like to color."

Ah. The problem wasn't the attempted theft, but the illogical behavior. She removed her gloves to stroke his ear-length, dark brown hair, and he tilted his head into her hand. Always so grateful for affection. "Maybe Lamar saw that coloring made you happy, and he hoped your book would make him happy, too."

Connor scrunched his face up in thought. "Uh-uh. He hates sitting still."

"He'll learn. People don't always know what makes them happy, but stealing is a sure way to get a big helping of unhappiness."

Worry gone, he giggled. "Grant yelled at him, and he runned away."

"There you go." Heart full, she hugged him. When the boy had first arrived at the Tampa shelter last spring, he'd rarely spoken. Now, in mid-July, he chattered like a magpie in his little-boy-speak.

He hugged her back and whispered into her shirt. "Beff? We going home."

She froze. "Today?"

"Uh-huh. Going back to our and Jermaine's place 'cause Mama needs to get from here. She says here is driving her crazy."

"I'm"—Beth steadied her voice—"I'm sorry to hear that, honey." Their departure wasn't a complete surprise, after all. When Drusilla McCormick's boyfriend, Jermaine, had completed the court-ordered anger management classes, he'd asked her to return. *Dammit.* With Drusilla's history of drug abuse, she'd do better to dump him and find new friends.

This was Drusilla's second visit to the shelter since May. The first reconciliation with Jermaine had succeeded until they fought over money, and he put her in the hospital. Drugs and abuse—the combination went hand-in-hand and was never good for the children.

Please, let the anger management classes have worked for the jerk. And let both of them stay clean.

She rested her cheek on Connor's head and held him close. Although still too skinny, he'd gained weight at the shelter. "Are you leaving this morning?" she asked past the lump in her throat.

He nodded and rubbed his face against her shoulder.

Darn it, she'd miss him and Grant so much.

As if conjured from the air, his big brother trotted across the yard. "Mama's ready to leave, Connor."

"Hey, you." Beth held her hand out.

He hesitated, far too reserved to push for affection as Connor did. But, when she put her arm around him, he soaked up the hug like a rain-starved plant. His mother wasn't affectionate. In fact, when the shelter had given Grant a party for his seventh birthday, Drusilla appeared only long enough to eat some cake.

Yet, from what Grant said, she had been a good mother before her husband's death in Iraq last year. Before she'd started drinking and then using meth. Beth couldn't even imagine the pain of losing the man she loved; just the thought was like being stabbed in the chest.

However, Drusilla had two children who needed her care. Didn't the woman realize what precious gifts she'd been given? Beth had spent the past year trying everything she could for the chance at *one* child.

"Beff, we gots to go."

"I know, baby." She hugged the boys harder, wishing she could surround them with a protective shield. *What if they run into trouble?* She should at least give them her phone number. Her overprotective Master would grumble, but he was so softhearted, he'd understand. And he wasn't here to fuss, anyway. "Do you know how to make phone calls, Grant?"

"Sure." He waited. Brown eyes the color of rich milk chocolate were steady on hers. He was the first-born. The tough guy. He'd told her it was his job to protect his little brother and his mother, too.

As a child, Nolan had probably been just like him. The thought of her husband brought an ache of loneliness. "I'll give you my number. If you need me or want to talk, you call, okay? Or you place the call so Connor can talk."

Connor bounced in agreement. Grant would never call to chat; like Nolan, he was all action, no words. However, if Grant dialed, Connor could get on the line and babble at her, and she'd know they were all right.

Grant considered. "Okay."

Beth let out the breath she'd been holding. "Good. My

number's easy. 555-1234. Can you remember it?"

"555-1234," he returned. To her amusement, Connor echoed him in his higher voice.

Such bright kids. "Perfect."

Their mother appeared in the door, shoving her brittle blonde hair back over her shoulders. "Connor, Grant." Her voice was like sharp ice. "Get your butts in here. Now."

Beth's eyes burned with tears. "I'm going to miss you two a whole, whole lot."

Two hard squeezes. She heard their choked sobs before they ran into the building. Their mother raised a hand to Beth in farewell before disappearing. No long goodbyes for Drusilla. Then again, the woman had spent most of her time getting off drugs, not making friends.

With blurry eyes, Beth watched the door close. Oh, she'd pine for those boys, as would Nolan.

Like many abused children, the boys were wary around men, and her Master was scarred, big, and scary. But he'd patiently worked to earn their trust. Grant used to follow him around everywhere. His own silent, little shadow.

Please, be safe, babies. Beth rose, brushed off her khaki shorts, and headed inside to do her part to achieve that goal.

In the office, the gray-haired secretary pulled up the children's file for her and grimaced. "Poor kids. Looks as if Clifford E. Price is the DCF investigator assigned to their case. I'll write his number down."

"Seriously? Price?" Beth heaved an unhappy sigh. The man should have retired or changed careers at least five years before. Burned-out, indifferent, arrogant. And lazy. A social worker who'd rather do paperwork than actually get off his rear end and check on his cases, he was a glaring exception to the caring nature of the other Department of Children and Family investigators and supervisors. Over the past year, she'd butted heads with him so often that she'd tried to have him reassigned. Unfortunately, she'd failed.

" 'Fraid so. Isn't it the kids' bad luck to get him?" Shaking her head sadly, the secretary jotted down the phone number.

"They deserve better." Beth walked out into the yard as she punched in the number.

"DCF. Price." He sounded as impatient as if she'd interrupted a call from the governor or something. In all reality, she'd probably interrupted his cigarette break.

"This is Beth King at the Tomorrow Is Mine shelter." As she moved toward the picnic area, her arm brushed the blue flowering plumbago hedge, and she remembered how Connor had danced in delight at the way the butterflies rose in the air before resettling again. "Drusilla McCormick and her sons, Grant and Connor, are on their way home. Drusilla's boyfriend, Jermaine, still lives there."

"McCormick? Hold on." The sound of typing came over the phone. "I have it. According to the file, Jermaine Hinton completed his anger management class, and Mrs. McCormick agreed to return. I don't see the problem."

No staff or resident was in the quiet area, so Beth perched on a picnic table. "The problem is Drusilla's history of substance abuse—meth, to be specific. Her boyfriend has a history of drug abuse and violence. The children are at risk." Why had the woman gone back to him? Maybe she worried she'd end up homeless or broke. She sure hadn't kept any job for long.

More tapping. "Drusilla received counseling for substance abuse while she was in your shelter. All the bases have been covered, Mrs. King."

Beth bit back a rude response. "I'm not as concerned with the bases as I am with the children. Can you, please, see your way clear to check on them?" Her words, somehow, came out more a demand than a question.

Price's tone chilled. "My time is extremely limited, Mrs. King. However, I'll attempt to fit a call in somewhere in the next few weeks."

Next few weeks? A call? "I was hoping for sooner and a visit in person. After all, this is the second time the family has been in the shelter."

"Which is why Jermaine was forced to take classes." She heard his fingers tapping impatiently on the desk. "Now, excuse me, but I have other work to attend to."

Silence.

Beth took the cell from her ear and stared at it. The bloated, self-indulgent toad of a man had hung up on her. Well, *fine.* If the children didn't call her soon, she'd simply…happen…to be in their neighborhood and drop by for a sociable visit.

After checking her watch, she jumped to her feet. The shelter's director had asked her to lead a morning session since the psychologist had called in sick. Talk about the wrong person for the job. Just because she'd donated money to the shelter didn't mean she knew anything about counseling.

She was a gardener, for heaven's sake.

AN HOUR LATER, Beth brought the session to a close. It broke her heart to see so many lives disrupted—not *ruined*, she'd never use that word. Nevertheless, these women had endured far too much pain and suffering. For some, their physical recovery would take a long time—Melody, her cheek scarred from the scalding coffee her husband had tossed in her face; Sandra, her arm broken from her husband's boot; Juli, her throat bruised from her boyfriend's big hands.

Their mental recovery would take much longer.

If only she could help them see themselves as they really were—lovely, bright, and unique, each and every one of them.

But, as she knew all too well, physical and emotional abuse could grind self-esteem right into the dirt. A few months ago, she'd believed herself completely recovered from her sadistic first husband. After all, it'd been over three years since he died.

Yet, all summer, she'd fought the return of her miserable self-loathing.

Shaking off her worries, she rose and smiled at her small group. "Marta should be back tomorrow, so today, make a note of any derogatory thoughts you find lingering in your head. In the next session, you can share and come up with ways to counter them."

All of them knew her history, and she collected hugs and thanks as they filed out the door. They were already chatting about the afternoon's plans and chores and sessions as Beth gathered her notes and bag. She had a lot to do yet today. First, landscaping plans for a bank in Carrollwood. Then she'd swing by Egypt Lake where a newly constructed B&B required a front yard makeover.

As she stepped from the air-conditioned room into the heat and humidity, she felt herself wilting like an unwatered violet. Honestly, she'd been in saunas that were less intense than Florida in August.

The children in the grassy square enclosed by the shelter buildings didn't seem to notice. In the sandbox, two giggling toddlers were filling red plastic pails. Older children played happily on the playground swings and monkey bars.

As Beth entered the administration building's foyer, she spotted Jessica with her baby perched on her hip.

"Hey, Beth, I was hoping we'd see you." Her friend's blonde hair had been pulled up on top of her head—and undoubtedly, her four-month-old daughter was the reason most of it was now in tangles.

Another friend stood behind Jessica. Holding her son's

hand, Kari pointed. "Look, Zane. It's Beth." The toddler let out a high scream of delight and danced forward to be picked up.

So, so cute. Beth couldn't help but think that a child of Nolan's would probably have dark hair like Zane's—and be every bit as adorable. *Please, give me the chance.* She bent to hide her face and scooped the toddler up. "Who's a big boy? Who's the best boy in the world?"

"Me, me, me." His certainty was a bittersweet joy; for most of the children in the shelter, their answer would never be "me."

"Exactly, my boy." She raspberried his neck.

His infectious belly laugh made her lips curve upward. Settling him on her hip, she offered a finger to Jessica's baby. Sophia had a grip like steel, which wasn't surprising with Master Z as her daddy. "What are you and Kari doing here?"

"We dropped off a bunch of donations from the last fundraiser." Jessica waved her hand toward the storage room.

Those boxes stored in Kari's garage had been huge. "You hauled everything here by yourselves?"

"No way," Kari answered. "It's Dan's day off, and Jessica talked Z into a long lunch break. They carried; we supervised."

"Sure, you did." Who would dare boss around Master Z or Master Dan? The men were two of the most powerful Dominants in the Shadowlands club.

Jessica rolled her eyes. "Okay, we opened the doors for them and motioned them through."

"Now that I believe." When Zane squirmed, Beth set him down.

Crowing in delight, he made a beeline for the children's corner where three other kids were playing. After snatching up a plush dog and a fluffy cat, he plopped down to conduct a meowing-barking dialogue.

"Just listen to him." Beth sighed as the other very quiet children stared at the toddler in wonder. It was far too obvious that

Zane had never been slapped for making too much noise. "He's so happy."

"Hey, girlfriend." Still holding Sophia, Jessica rubbed her shoulder against Beth's. "Remember why you kept this place open—so others could be safe and happy."

"True." Beth offered a small smile and turned as a door opened.

Master Z walked out of the storage room. "Elizabeth." The smoothness of his deep voice didn't decrease the power underlying it. Dark haired, leanly muscular, he strolled across the foyer to join them. His *I'm-a-psychologist* attire had been adapted for hauling boxes. The sleeves were rolled up on his white, button-up shirt; the silvery gray tie that matched his eyes was loosened. "It's good to see you. Has Nolan returned?"

"No. The roofing material was delayed. His postcard said he'd be there another week." Why couldn't Sir have volunteered somewhere with decent—or any—phone service? Postcards weren't any substitute for a real person. Each day felt interminable without him. They'd never been apart more than a few days in the three years they'd been together.

Z's gaze sharpened. "Are you getting any sleep?"

The Dom could probably see every long, endless night she'd experienced. Her fair skin certainly didn't conceal the dark circles under her eyes. Unfortunately, dodging a Master's question was an exercise in futility. "Some. You know how it is after you've been married a while. It's hard to sleep alone."

"Indeed." His gaze didn't waver. "Nolan didn't want to leave you—not after what happened to Anne."

Last May, a woman's abusive husband had wanted his wife back and attacked Beth's friends to get the location of the shelter. The women had won the fight, but it left everyone pretty shaken. Beth hadn't even been there, but…hearing about it and tending their injuries had resurrected old memories. Maybe because she knew exactly what a fist to the face felt like.

She brightened her tone. "I had a few nightmares at first, but I'm fine now." Except on the nights when being all alone in the big house got to her. "So, are you guys going to the Shadowlands tonight?"

"Absolutely. We're going to actually have time to visit with people and even do a scene." Jessica made a glee-filled sound. "Linda's spending the evening with Sophia. In fact, she demanded babysitting time since she misses having babies."

"With her babies in college now, I'm not surprised." Beth smiled at the adorable baby. "And hey, who wouldn't want to hold Sophia?"

"Hear that, little one? You're popular." Z lifted his daughter over his head, and she squealed in delight, kicking bootie-covered feet.

Oh, I want a baby.

He tucked Sophia into the curve of his arm before touching Beth's shoulder. "Nolan will be home soon, I'm sure. Until then, I want you to call me if you feel unsafe or worried."

"I'm fine. Really."

"Kari." Dan joined them and gave Beth a smile before telling his wife, "Boxes are stacked. Time to get going, sweetheart."

Little Zane abandoned the stuffed animals and toddled across the room to be picked up and swung in a circle by his father. As with Z, Dan's hard expression turned gentle. The tough Masters of the Shadowlands sure were softies when it came to their children.

Nolan would be like them if he had a child. He was born to be a father and should have lots and lots of children. *Please, please, please.*

Kari hugged Beth. "Teacher planning days are in a couple of weeks, so let's get together before I'm inundated with students."

Where had the summer gone? "Yes, let's." She glanced at

Jessica. "Have fun tonight."

Jessica gave her a squeeze. "Just because Nolan isn't here doesn't mean you can't come to the Shadowlands. Come early, and we'll chat, watch the scenes, and eat munchies. Okay?"

"I…yes. Thank you." It was hard to be alone. Even though her Sir could take taciturn to new levels, just his presence was enough. When he was gone, the house echoed with loneliness. "I'll come early." She'd also leave soon enough that Jessica and Z could have their playtime.

When the group left, she picked up her gardening tools and returned to the center yard. Once she finished here, she'd grab lunch before starting her afternoon projects. If she rushed, there would be enough time at home to assemble a new client packet for tomorrow's early morning appointment.

After tugging on her bright blue gardening gloves, she weeded the St. Augustine grass from the flowerbed until the scent of rich, moist earth hung in the humid air. A low rumble of thunder drowned out the sounds of the children, and contentment seeped into her soul. Flower gardens were a visible assurance that the world held far more color and beauty than pain and ugliness.

Her phone rang.

Seriously? She scowled at her filthy hands. Was some demon lurking nearby and coaching his cohorts? *"Wait…wait…yes, her gloves are covered in dirt. Put the call through now."* With a huff of exasperation, she worked her gloves off and swiped ANSWER. "This is Beth."

"Mrs. King, this is Dr. Thompson." One of their fertility specialists.

Her heart skipped a beat. He'd have her results. "What did the tests show?"

"I'd like to make an appointment with you and your husb—"

"No." All the moisture in her mouth disappeared. Doctors

might share good news over the phone but would insist on delivering bad news in person. "He's not available right now." Nolan didn't even know she'd tried this final treatment. "Tell me. Now."

"Mrs. King, it would be good to—"

"Spit it out, doctor." Her ragged tone was unrecognizable. "My uterine lining still isn't…thick enough? Even with the hormones?"

His sigh was one of concession. Undoubtedly, he was telling himself she'd already guessed the results. "I'm afraid the endometrium didn't respond as well as we'd hoped. There simply isn't enough for implantation."

Oh God. No. She closed her eyes. Even though she knew the answer, the question still broke out. "What's left? What else can I do?"

"Mrs. King." His voice softened. "Beth. It's time to consider using a surrogate mother or pursuing adoption."

The thick air clogged in her throat, smothering her. The laughter of the children on the playground sounded harsh and shrill. "Of course." She roughly swiped her T-shirt over her wet cheeks. *Foolish Beth.* Then again, her period had started yesterday, and her emotions were already messed up by the hormone shots. That's why she was crying. Not because all her hopes were now dead.

Nothing had worked.

Outraged accusations and anger rose…and she swallowed them back down. The doctor's unhappiness emanated through the phone. Not his fault. "Well, we knew—you told me—success wasn't likely."

He hadn't even wanted to try, but she hadn't been able to give up. Not if there was any chance at all.

"I'm sorry, Beth."

He was, she knew. Just because he'd smashed her dreams

didn't give her license to take her unhappiness out on him. Despite the enveloping grief, she kept her voice steady. "Thank you for calling. I appreciate that you didn't make me wait, even though it was bad news."

As she said goodbye and shoved her phone into a pocket, she concentrated on breathing. *In. Out.* Tearful meltdowns weren't unusual in a domestic violence shelter, but she was a volunteer, not a resident. Not a survivor.

Only she *was* a survivor. A scarred...damaged...*blighted* survivor.

Damn you, Kyler. Damn *her* for being so young and stupid when she'd met him, for thinking she was marrying a Dom who'd cherish her. Instead, she'd wed a sadist—and psychopath.

Scars marked her body, others her soul. Perhaps the worst wound had been losing her unborn baby. She'd always wondered if he'd deliberately chosen to beat her that day. It'd been too early for the baby to live, too late for a simple miscarriage. Staring down at her fingers, she felt again the panicked realization when something inside her had...broken and blood had pooled between her legs.

Her hands fisted in the dirt as grief seized her—along with the enduring shame that she hadn't somehow shielded her baby.

After losing the baby, she'd continued to bleed, and the necessary D&C had caused some ghastly *syndrome* where her uterine lining became so thin that no egg could latch on. *Asherman's Syndrome.*

Even if she got pregnant, the doctors doubted she'd carry to term. Nolan hadn't wanted her to try, hadn't wanted to risk her. But it was *her* health and *her* life. After much discussion, they'd compromised. He'd supported her through the medical treatments and, at the same time, they'd gone ahead with adoption and foster care classes, inspections, and certifications.

When they'd brought up using a surrogate to carry their fertilized egg, Nolan had refused completely. He had good reasons, actually. A cousin, bearing a surrogate child, had died in labor. Another surrogate friend had committed suicide. Too aware of the risks of pregnancy, Nolan wouldn't hire a woman to endanger her life in such a way.

So no surrogacy.

Adoption it would be. Since many children lacked parents, she and Nolan had always planned to adopt. Eventually. But first, she'd wanted to give him a baby—a child they created together. And…to know she wasn't really broken.

But she was.

She laid her cheek on her knees. How could she ever tell him about this failure? He didn't even know she'd attempted the risky treatment. He'd be furious. But the horrible cell reception at his third-world construction site had made it impossible to explain—let alone argue. Considering how much stress he was under, what with late deliveries and untrained laborers, she couldn't stand adding to his worries.

What could she have said anyway? How could her man understand her longing to bear a child for him, to cradle a baby with his black eyes and beautifully bronzed skin?

He wanted children. He'd grown up surrounded by brothers and sisters, wanting the same for his own future. He'd designed his house big enough to hold a large family. Now, she had to tell him she couldn't give him his dream.

That he'd taken a wife who was…barren.

Maybe she really was as worthless as Kyler had always said.

Chapter Two

IN THE PARKING lot of the Shadowlands, Tampa's most exclusive BDSM club, Nolan King turned off his truck and opened the door. The humid Florida air wrapped around him, plastered his white shirt to his torso, and turned his jeans to fucking cling wrap. With a grunt of exasperation, he slid out of his pickup. At the jarring movement, his shoulder set to throbbing as if someone was hammering masonry nails into it.

Crap. The long hours on the plane hadn't done him any favors. He braced his good arm against the pickup and waited. The pain would eventually subside...as would the gut-twisting memory of how he'd gotten hurt.

The night sky was erased by the noon sun that'd turned the African roof into a frying pan. The older carpenter working with him had stood up abruptly and staggered backward. One step. Another. Nolan had lunged forward, stretching to catch the guy. Brushed his boot. So close. But the man had toppled over the roof's edge without a sound.

Off balance, Nolan had almost followed. *Sliding, sliding. Desperately rolling sideways. Falling through the unfinished portion, hitting a rafter. Fingers closing on the wood, his weight almost ripping his shoulder from the socket.*

Nolan had lived, but the old guy was dead. Turned out the fall hadn't killed him—the heart attack had. *Couldn't have saved him.*

He still felt guilty.

The hum of a car passing on the lonely country road returned him to reality, and he slammed the door shut then headed toward the three-story mansion. Time to get his life back in gear—and to find his wife. He'd hoped to surprise Beth at home, but she wasn't there. *Shouldn't make assumptions, King.* Still hoping for a surprise, he'd texted Jessica to see if she knew where his wife was, and Z had responded. Beth was at the Shadowlands—and had been looking stressed.

The thought of his Beth being anything but carefree was a boot in the gut. He should never have left her, never have let Raoul talk him into supervising construction in a third-world country. He'd known the job would be a can of worms. Relying on volunteers and a put-together crew with unreliable sources of materials? *Yeah, no.* It'd been a goat-fuck. True, the medical clinic building was now up and looked fine but at the cost of a month longer than he'd calculated. His own construction firm here in Tampa had suffered.

Beth had suffered.

He hauled open the heavy oak door and stepped inside. Behind the security desk, Ben saw him. "Hey, King." The craggy-faced guard's pleased expression faded. " 'Bout time you got back. Your girl's wasting away—and you don't look much better."

"Screwed up my shoulder. It's why I ended up returning early." But what was this about Beth? His little subbie must look like hell. Nolan frowned as worry knotted his guts. "Is Beth inside?"

"Yep. You know, she didn't even put on fetwear."

"That's not good." Beth loved dressing up in fetish clothing—something he sure enjoyed. His tough little woman didn't possess many girly traits, so he'd come to cherish the few she had.

He studied Ben for a second, noting the guard's relaxed demeanor. Being in a relationship was good for him. "How's your Mistress doing?"

"Got herself tired out today, so she's staying home and taking it easy." Ben patted his flat gut and grinned. "She's finally showing a baby bump. It's cute as hell when she frets over how her clothes fit."

"I'd give money to see that. Tell her hi for me." When Mistress Anne, former Marine, former bounty hunter, and the most renowned of the Shadowlands' sadists had become pregnant, everyone was amused—and delighted. Giving Ben a two-finger salute, he headed into the clubroom.

Inside, as the raspy-voiced music and brutal rhythm of Coil's "Heartworm" scraped against his skin, he paused to let his eyes adjust to the dimmer light of wrought-iron sconces. Good crowd tonight. The clubroom encompassed most of the mansion's bottom floor, and every scene area down the length of the room was filled.

In the right corner, dancers writhed on the small dance floor. Fancy latex and leather gear vied with the classic choice of bare-ass naked. Past them, in a roped-off spanking bench area, a Domme smacked her whimpering blonde submissive with a paddle. Erratic screams farther away were probably from someone using a cattle prod.

On the left, the food and drink buffet corner held small tables and chairs. No Beth.

In the center of the room, unoccupied submissives had a sitting area where they hung out. No Beth.

Doms and their submissives clustered around the massive oval bar, which was tended by Cullen and his submissive, Andrea. Someone there would undoubtedly know where his little rabbit had holed up.

"Hey, welcome home, buddy." Cullen's voice boomed out as he reached a long arm across the bar top to grip Nolan's hand. "Didn't think you'd ever get back."

"I was beginning to wonder myself." Nolan accepted a Corona from Andrea. Cold brew—one of life's finer pleasures and one he'd been missing lately. Making love to his woman was another. "Where's my wife?"

Three years ago, *wife* had been a four-letter-word; Beth had transformed the word into one that meant *miracle*.

"She and Jessica wanted to watch Vance and Galen co-top." Cullen motioned toward the far end of the room. "Good you're back. Beth's not looking good."

"So I hear." Nolan's mouth tightened. She was probably having nightmares brought on by those fucked-up assholes who'd broken into Anne's house. Thank God, Beth hadn't been there. Kim had suffered a few flashbacks from the attack, but Raoul, her Dom, had seen her through them.

Nolan hadn't been around to help Beth.

Cullen's thick, brown brows drew together. "You look almost as bad as she does. You okay?"

"Yeah. Banged up my shoulder a tad."

As he headed for the back, other members greeted him. He spotted other Masters here and there. Olivia was with a new subbie—a blonde this time. Jake had restrained Rainie to a St. Andrew's cross and was adjusting the lighting to show off her colorful tattoos.

In a gold-trimmed dungeon monitor vest, Dan watched a newbie trying to flog a pretty brunette. From the cop's displeased expression, he'd soon take the flogger away and send the young Dom home to practice on a pillow.

In the back corner, Z had roped off an oversized area for the whip enthusiasts. Chains from an exposed ceiling beam restrained Sally's arms over her head. In front of the little brunette, Vance teased her breasts with a small deer hide flogger. Behind her, Galen was using a single-tail to crisscross her back and buttocks with thin red lines.

From the way her head rested on her upraised arm, Sally was deep into subspace. Not surprising. The two Doms did a damn fine job at double-teaming their submissive wife.

Nolan checked the chairs outside the area...and found Beth and Jessica. He set his unfinished beer on a table for the staff to pick up, crossed his arms over his chest—winced at the pain—and studied his woman.

Curled into a corner of a leather couch, his little subbie wore jeans and a plain white T-shirt. No makeup. Her long, red-brown hair was yanked back with a scrunchie. Jesus, she'd normally dress up more than this to pull weeds.

When she jumped at a man's shout from a nearby scene, Nolan knew her nerves were shot. Yet the few times they'd managed to talk, she'd insisted she was fine.

She'd lied to him.

As he was swallowing that unpalatable fact, she glanced around the room. Her gaze went past, stopped, and snapped back to him. Her hand went to her mouth. "Master?" And then she tore across the space and slammed into him so violently he rocked back on his heels.

Fuck, that hurt.

Didn't matter.

He wrapped his arms around her and pulled her tighter. *Finally.*

"You're here!" She squeezed him with arms that were too thin, but beautifully muscular, and he bent down to inhale her strawberry-lemon scent. His own sweet, spicy treat.

Her lips were soft, urgent, and giving as she pressed up against him so closely not a hair's breadth of space remained. Damn, he'd missed her.

As footsteps moved away, he realized Jessica had tactfully left them to their reunion.

Eventually, he pulled back…and frowned. His friends had nailed it. Although Beth's face was flushed with excitement, the dark circles under her eyes showed clearly.

Not noticing his study, she patted his short beard. "What is this? I almost didn't recognize you."

"Didn't take the time to scrape it off when I got home." With Native American ancestry, he didn't grow much of a beard. Shaving at the job site had been too much trouble for what was mostly scruff.

She traced the beard's edge along his jaw. "I kind of like it," she murmured.

"I'll leave it for another day for you."

Her hand paused, and her forehead furrowed. "You look awfully tired, my Master."

"Long flight." As he ran a finger over her cheek, he noted how the bone was more pronounced, and he tilted her face up. She'd always been slim, but she'd dropped several pounds. She hadn't had it to spare. Concern edged his voice. "Little rabbit, what's going on? You look like hell. How much weight have you lost?"

Her flinch conveyed he should have gone easier. Maybe so, but every time they'd managed a connection, he'd asked her how she was. And every time, she'd said, *"I'm doing okay. No problems."*

"I'm fine." She lifted her chin. "Working outside when it's this hot kills my appetite."

"Does it now?" *Aaaand that would be lie number…something.* She was just piling them up. He'd swat her ass, but she lacked the padding now to take a good spanking. "Instead of doing a scene, I'd better feed you."

"I… Okay." Her eyes held disappointment—and relief.

Relief? His eyes narrowed. First, he'd get some food into her and then he'd take her home, and it'd be come-to-Jesus time. A long talk was overdue, one where she'd be nice and close. She might have evaded his questions over the phone, but her body couldn't lie to him.

Putting an arm around her, he guided her toward the bar.

HE WAS *HERE*. Her husband and Master. Her life.

Yet, even as Beth's heart danced with happiness, her worries kicked in. Because, tired or not, Nolan was devastating. Over the summer, his dark tan had deepened. His arms were corded with muscle, and his shoulders had grown even broader. His postcards had mentioned he'd done a lot of the work on the project in addition to supervising.

A leather tie bound his shoulder-length, straight black hair. With the rough beard, black T-shirt, and black jeans, he looked like a dark warrior. A deadly one.

She looked "*like hell.*"

It was true, too. Darn it. And he didn't like skinny females. Submissives always gossiped about the Doms, especially the Shadowlands *Masters*, so over the years, she'd heard everything about Nolan. Like the fact that all his numerous women before her had been lushly curvy with big boobs and wide hips— everything she wasn't. Her weight loss made it worse. Instead of a fertile valley, she resembled a rocky ridge top, unwelcoming and dry. *Barren.*

No, don't start down that path. She'd never been "abundant" and he loved her anyway. Now he was home, she'd regain the weight she'd lost.

However, she could never regain the hope of carrying his babies, and grief was a cruel wind through brittle grass. *No. Not now.* Her Nolan was home. With a shake of her head to dislodge the despair, she ran her hands up his chest just to reassure herself of his reality.

He flinched.

Shocked, she stepped back. The brighter lights of the bar

area revealed harsh lines beside his mouth. His eyes were tired...and haunted. She set her hand on his arm. "Nolan, what's wrong?"

A corner of his mouth edged up. "Guess we can talk about that later, as well. First"—his tone held the iron edge of command—"I want you to go fetch a plate of food. If it's not as much as I think you should have, we're going to have words."

A shiver ran through her. Oh, she'd missed the rumbling authority of his voice. Missed *him*. "Yes, Master." Her voice came out husky, and the corners of his eyes crinkled.

"Once you're fed, I'm hauling you home. After we talk, I figure on fucking you all night."

The way his black eyes turned to molten lava made her insides flutter. Then she remembered and bit her lip. "I... It's the wrong time."

Disappointment dimmed his gaze. "Hell. Wrong time of month? Did I lose track of the days?"

He hadn't. She was off-schedule because of the hormone treatments. "I'm sorry." While flowing, she was always uncomfortably tender down there, and he wouldn't hurt her in such a way.

"I'm sorry, too, sugar."

She licked her lips, contemplating alternatives like giving him a blowjob and indulging in the sheer intimacy of kissing and licking his thick cock. "Instead, maybe I could..."

"Mmm." He ran a finger over her lower lip as if considering putting her mouth to good use, but then he traced the hollows below her eyes. "You need a good night's sleep, I think."

Even with the joy of his return, she could feel tiredness dragging at her limbs. He hadn't missed it.

He, too, was exhausted. She lifted her hand and repeated his gesture, touching the dark circles under his eyes that showed despite his tanned bronze skin. Odd. Nothing usually wore him out like this. "So do you."

"Yeah. For now, go find some food so you'll have enough strength to survive tomorrow." As he turned away, she noticed how stiffly he moved. He started to lean on the bar, winced, and straightened.

This was more than exhaustion. "You're in pain. What happened?"

"Just pulled my shoulder."

Just? More than just. If he'd banged himself up, he'd make a joke about it, not look…haunted. "I think there's more to it."

His shrug obviously hurt, and the lines beside his mouth deepened. Her name came out a growl. "Beth."

She put her hands on her hips and scowled. "Nolan."

His lips twitched. "The rabbit takes on the lion."

She waited. He'd taught her how effective silence could be.

"Hell. Thought li'l rabbits were supposed to be timid, not ornery." Fatigue thickened his Texas drawl. After a second, he sighed and gave in. "We were on the roof. One of my crew had a heart attack. I tried to catch him. Failed."

The single word held a wealth of anger and guilt. Carefully, she put her arms around him. "Oh, honey. Is he badly hurt?"

"The heart attack got him."

Oh, God. "Oh, no. I'm sorry. So, so sorry." She flattened her hands on his back, trying to give comfort, helpless to fix this kind of pain. Of course, he was hurting; her tough Dom thought he should be able to save everyone. "There was nothing you could have done about a heart attack—and you still feel guilty, don't you?"

His silence answered her question. She stood quietly, holding him, her face against his chest, and after a minute, he rested his cheek on top of her head, taking the comfort she offered.

To help him in any way was a joy. "You got hurt then, too?"

"Yeah. Caught hold of a rafter and messed up my shoulder."

"Caught hold of a rafter." How close had he come to falling? Her heart skipped a beat as shock chilled her skin. He could have died down there. Without her. She shoved away her first reaction—to yell at him—and her second—to burst into tears—and settled for holding him and feeling his tense muscles relax. Thank goodness, he was home where she could watch over him. "I'm so glad you're all right."

"Me, too." Eventually, he kissed her head, pulled back, and tapped her cheek. "Go. Fetch some food before you disappear altogether."

"Yes, Sir."

She put a sandwich on the plate, added Nolan's favorite peanut butter cheesecake bites, and realized she was actually almost hungry. As she walked back, she felt lighter. After she ate, they could—She jerked to a halt.

Her Master, her husband, was hugging a woman.

When they broke apart, Beth's happiness was ripped right out by the roots. The woman was a walking, talking example of lush fertility. Around five-eight and all curves. Her fire engine red corset made the most of her voluptuous breasts, and her matching red stilettos were so sexy that Ben, the door guard, had let her keep them on. A thick mane of mahogany-colored hair hung long and loose. Her heavy makeup accentuated wide, dark brown eyes and plump lips.

Somewhere, a *Playboy* magazine was missing its centerfold.

"Alyssa, it's good to see you." Nolan still held the woman's hands.

Fear seeped into Beth's thoughts like a cold mist as he continued. "How long's it been? Five years?"

"Six. We moved to New York six years ago." Alyssa's lips quivered. "Last month, Master u-uncollared me."

"Ah, hell, sugar. I'm—"

"Hey, Beth," Cullen called from the bar. "I see Nolan found

you."

As she smiled a shaky greeting for Cullen, Sir turned and saw her. Releasing Alyssa, he held out his hand. Feeling scrawny and ugly, Beth let him draw her forward. "Beth, this is Alyssa. She used to be a member here."

From the devouring—and familiar—way the woman gazed at Nolan, she'd scened with him. Enjoyed him. And she'd recently lost her Dom. Uneasiness sprouted next to Beth's sympathy.

"Alyssa, this is my wife, Beth."

"*Wife?*" Alyssa's flush showed she realized the rudeness of her incredulity. "Uh, congratulations, Master Nolan. It's a pleasure to meet you, Beth."

If Beth felt green-tinged, no one in the world needed to know it. "It's nice to meet you."

Nolan glanced at the plate of food Beth held and nodded in approval before popping a cheesecake bite in his mouth. "Thank you, sugar."

His pleased hum might have warmed her if a chill hadn't been edging through her defenses. "You're welcome, Sir."

After taking the plate from her, he stretched to set it on the bar top—and winced.

"Bad Master." Frowning, Beth took the plate back from him. "Stop using your arm."

He snorted.

"Are you all right, Master Nolan?" Alyssa asked in a soft voice.

"Just strained my shoulder at work."

"May I check it, please, Sir?"

"Sure."

Alyssa ran her fingers over Nolan's biceps and up over his shoulder, probing gently. "There is some swelling and tightness. It would be my pleasure to work on it if you would permit."

"Work on it?" Beth asked carefully.

"I'm a physical therapist. I can get it loosened up and healed faster."

Nolan leaned against the bar. "Aren't you here on vacation?"

"No. I came down for a class at the college." Alyssa's eyes filled. "I needed to get away from New York."

Fresh sympathy tugged at Beth's heart. She couldn't imagine a world without Nolan in it. "I'm so sorry, Alyssa."

"Thank you." Alyssa turned to Nolan, and a desperate need leaked into her voice. "*Please*, Master Nolan. I miss being able to serve."

He shook his head. "No. I don't need—"

"I think it's an excellent idea." Beth had to force the words out. But Sir was hurting, and maybe, if a *therapist* ordered him to take it easy, he wouldn't overdo and strain his shoulder further. "If therapy would help, that's what should happen, Master."

His frown turned gentle, and he ran a finger down Beth's cheek. "I've missed your bouts of bossiness."

The warmth in his gaze sank deep inside her, melting the icy worry.

Turning to Alyssa, he nodded. "I'd appreciate the assist."

"Wonderful." The therapist's face brightened. "Do you still live in the same place?"

Beth stiffened. This submissive had been to the house? *Their* house? Like coarse sand, anxiety grated along her nerves.

"Yeah," Nolan said.

"Tomorrow is Sunday. Why don't I visit and see how your shoulder is doing?" Alyssa said. "If nothing else, I can give you some exercises to help keep it from freezing up."

"Sounds good." He turned Beth toward the bar and tapped the plate. "Eat it all, sugar. Cullen, could you get her a glass of milk?"

Beth frowned. "I don't—"

"Yes, you do." Nolan's firm voice silenced her protest.

Dammit. Her appetite had disappeared again, but if she didn't eat, he'd be unhappy with her.

"It was nice meeting you, Beth." Alyssa gave Sir a quick upward—yearning—glance. "Master Nolan, I'll see you tomorrow." As she walked away, head down, graceful and lovely in her submissive posture, every Dom at the bar turned to watch.

With a groan of disgust, Beth picked up her sandwich and scowled at it. A therapist was an excellent idea—but why couldn't Alyssa have been a guy? And why did second thoughts always arrive too late to act upon?

FUCK, IT WAS nice to be home. Nolan followed his wife inside, breathing in the light scent of the cinnamon candles she liked to burn. As usual, everything was spotless. Between his housekeeper and Beth's own tidy habits, no mess survived long.

She stopped in the foyer. "Can I make you something to eat? Or get you a beer?"

"Nope." He closed and locked the door, set the security system, and put a hand on her abdomen. It was more concave than convex, and his worries resurfaced. He should never have left her. Guilt added harshness to his already rough voice. "What I want is you in my arms in our bed."

He hadn't realized she'd been tense until he saw her muscles relax. Hell, exhaustion and pain had thrown him off; he was missing too much. The length of time they'd been apart was adding to the problem, making things off-key. Making her hesitant. But this wasn't the time to pursue what was bothering her. He'd need to be careful and observant. Not half-dead.

He bent to scoop her up and realized he couldn't carry her. His shoulder already throbbed like a son-of-a-bitch. *Fuck.* With a snort of exasperation, he tucked an arm around her and steered her across the house and into the master suite.

The small nightlight illuminated the muted golden walls and shadowed the tiered trey ceiling. His boots thudded on the hardwood floors, and the noise disappeared as he reached the Oriental carpet at the foot of the king size poster bed. The elaborately carved headboard had once anchored bondage chains, but before the adoption and foster care home evaluations had begun, he'd retired the dungeon room along with any visible BDSM gear.

No matter. He didn't want restraints tonight anyway.

Right now, he needed to hold his woman, to refresh the connection between them. To simply enjoy the intimacy of sleeping together. Fuck, he'd missed her.

There were times he wondered at how abruptly he'd changed from a guy who'd happily sampled an infinite variety of women into a firmly married man who was profoundly happy with just one.

Then again, his one was *Beth*.

Chapter Three

THE NEXT MORNING, Nolan discovered he was alone in the bed. When he sat up, his stiff shoulder screeched like a squeaky door. Smothering a groan, he worked the immobility out of it while he listened for Beth.

The house was silent.

Because she wasn't home.

Right.

Last night while snuggled up against him, she'd talked about her work and mentioned having an early Sunday appointment with a new client. Damned if he hadn't nodded off while she was talking.

He hadn't even heard her leave. Despite his aching shoulder, he'd slept like a rock. It was the first time he'd gotten a whole night's sleep since the old guy died. Apparently, having Beth in his bed was what his subconscious needed.

It'd sure been a long summer. He scrubbed his hand over his face. For both their sakes, he would keep any future separations real damn short.

After donning his jeans from the floor, he headed for the kitchen. He'd better suck down some coffee, or he'd bite the little rabbit's head right off if she came home her usual cheerful self.

But would she? As he plugged a pod into the coffeemaker, he frowned. At the Shadowlands, her exuberance at seeing him had faded before they left. In bed, having her in his arms had been good, but she'd still been…subdued. The bond between them was different.

What with his exhaustion and pain, his ability to read her yesterday had been fucked up, and he'd been wise not to push matters. But he was home now and on the mend. Whatever was messing up their relationship would be straightened out.

He'd see to it.

GRANT MCCORMICK EASED the bedroom room door open far enough to hear what was happening in the house. He was really hungry and so was Connor. They hadn't had much to eat yesterday after leaving the shelter. If it sounded…safe, they could go into the kitchen and get some breakfast. His stomach made a growling noise like it agreed.

"…strike him out." The noise of the television came from the living room. Baseball. His stomach got tight. Mama didn't like sports, but Jermaine did, so he must be here. He didn't like seeing Grant or Connor in the kitchen. He said they ate too much.

Having Jermaine at home wasn't safe.

The sound of glasses clinking was another warning sign. *Booze.* They always drank booze if they were watching sports. Mama said alcohol made the stupid games easier to stand.

A familiar, icky smell drifted down the hallway, like the scent of candles, only not, and he closed his eyes in despair. He knew what the smell meant.

At the shelter, she'd cried and promised she wouldn't do the drug stuff anymore. She'd *promised*. His stomach and chest felt funny, like he was gonna throw up…or cry. This morning when she'd pulled her glass pipe and lighter out of the cupboard, he'd wanted to throw the pipe across the room. To stomp on it and break it into pieces.

No, Mama, no.

But she didn't listen to him. He couldn't make her stop. Daddy could've. She wouldn't do the drug stuff if he was home. But Daddy had gone off to be a soldier and died being a hero. He'd never come home. Angrily, Grant hit the doorframe with his fist. Daddy should have stayed. When Daddy was here, Mama had liked her kids. She'd hugged them and played with them and cooked. She'd laughed like she was having fun. Now her laugh was all screechy and crazy.

Because when she smoked stuff, she turned different…like a monster in a cartoon. She got mad—scary mad. Like once, when Connor'd asked for supper, she'd screamed and thrown her cup at him, and it'd busted on the floor, sending glass everywhere.

She'd promised she'd stop smoking the drugs.

Grant shivered as she started laughing, the sound sharper than any broken glass. Jermaine was talking, too, his words crashing into each other all funny.

Soundlessly, Grant closed the door.

Half asleep, Connor huddled in the corner, waiting for Grant to decide what to do. "Did Mama leave?"

"No," Grant whispered. "And Jermaine is out there, too."

Connor's forehead scrunched up. "They're smoking the stuff?"

"Yeah." *No breakfast for us.* Could he sneak into her bedroom and get a dollar from her hiding place? She never noticed if they only took one bill. He and Connor could crawl out the window and buy food from the gas station down the street.

But she or Jermaine might go to the bathroom and see them. Getting caught in Mama's bedroom would be…bad.

Silently, Grant pulled a pillow and a loose blanket off the bed.

Connor's face fell, but he pulled a suitcase out from under the bed. Pushing the blanket and pillow before him, he squirmed behind the jumble of suitcases and storage boxes to the narrow space beside the wall.

As Grant followed, his shoulders caught painfully on the bedframe. What would happen if he kept growing? If he couldn't hide under here any longer? He shivered as he curled up next to Connor and shared the pillow. His stomach growled again.

"*Grrr, grrr*," Connor whispered like a lion and giggled.

So did Grant. But he *was* hungry. "Check the box. Is there anything to eat?"

His brother opened the battered lunch box they'd found in a trashcan. Two crackers were left from last night.

Grant grimaced. Before Mama had taken them to the shelter, Jermaine had realized Grant and Connor were sneaking food from the kitchen. He'd been really mad and tried to whip them with his belt.

Last night, knowing they had to be careful, Grant had only grabbed a handful of crackers out of the box on the coffee table. Two were left. He handed both crackers to Connor. "You go ahead and eat them."

Connor shook his head and handed one back.

Why couldn't crackers be bigger? With a sigh, Grant took a small bite, hoping to make it last.

Then he pulled the suitcase back in place, closing them inside their small cave of safety.

UNABLE TO SLEEP longer or eat breakfast, Beth had left home before dawn. As the sun rose into a clear blue sky, she'd weeded the flowerbeds for one of her bank clients and then a realtor. A few hours later, when her energy had faded, she'd swung by Starbucks for a caramel apple Frappuccino.

Coffee for breakfast—actually, it was getting close to lunch. Her Sir wouldn't approve. But, hey, it had apple in it. Very healthy.

Sipping her drink, she detoured past some of her residential clients on the way to Hyde Park. Her yard crew was doing a good job of staying ahead of the summertime growing season. A block off North Hines, she slowed to study one of her first landscaping projects. The foundation plantings were excellent and the grounds immaculately groomed; however, the effect this month was…blah. A seasonal splash of color was needed. She pulled over and made a note in her planner before resuming her drive.

After her appointment, she could go home. To Nolan. Her lips curved. The mere thought of him filled her heart. Honestly, she'd never known she could love someone so much.

Thank you for being you, Master.

Loving him made her world complete, although it was a bit worrisome how much she'd missed him. For heaven's sake, before he'd entered her life, she'd managed quite nicely, thank you very much. She'd lived on her own during and after college until marrying Kyler. But, *okay, admit it*, after escaping Kyler, she hadn't felt safe. Not until Nolan pushed into her life.

This summer, all the time Sir had been in Africa, she'd felt so much on edge it was almost like being cold. Face it, Nolan was her sun, and she didn't do well when his warmth disappeared.

But he was home now, and she should feel better. Really, everything should be fine.

She wrinkled her nose. Everything would be fine after they got past a couple of snags.

The big problem—her Master was hurting. Seeing him so weary and in pain made her want to cry. Made her want to beat on Master Raoul for sending Sir to such an unsafe, uncivilized location. Her mouth firmed. She'd have to make sure he didn't overdo. He'd be stubborn about wanting to return to work. Too bad for him. She'd get a chance to pamper him up a little.

And the other glitch in their happiness...was her.

She was a stupid, emotional mess.

Yes, she sure was.

Should she tell him about the final treatment she'd tried? And how the doctors had...had given up on her? She pulled in a pained breath. Normally, she'd never keep anything from Sir, but...this? The news would hurt him worse than his injured shoulder. Because of her. He knew how much she wanted to have his baby.

She thumped her head on the headrest in annoyance. Why couldn't she get past this...obsession...that her life wouldn't be complete without children? It was stupid. Not everyone had children. Not everyone wanted children.

However, both she and Nolan did, and she couldn't give them to him because she was damaged. Broken.

He needed to know, though. He'd want to know. And she would tell him.

She would.

As she drove through historic Hyde Park, she frowned as she considered scenarios. Perhaps it would be best to delay the disturbing discussions for a while. She was too emotional, and he was hurting. So today, she'd go home and be cheerful and let things get back on an even keel. In a few days, she'd sit him down and explain how she couldn't ever give him beautiful dark-eyed babies.

Stupid tears.

Blinking hard, she checked the house numbers and pulled into a curving driveway. Her client's home was a beautiful three-story, nineteenth century, Italianate house with asymmetrical lines and a square tower in the center—one of the older homes in the city. And absolutely beautiful.

Time to be a professional. She wiped her eyes, pulled in a

few restorative breaths, and grabbed her bag.

From the street, she studied the cream-colored house with its dark red, tile roof. The tall windows were twice her height, which meant the inside would get plenty of light. Excellent bones.

In contrast to the beautifully restored exterior of the house, the yard was simply pitiful, filled with dying shrubberies, patchy grass, and weed-filled beds. Dr. Drago had mentioned that the previous owners had completed the extensive remodeling, but the husband was transferred to New York before they'd started on the grounds. It appeared she could begin from scratch if she wanted. She walked up the white brick sidewalk and considered various landscaping styles. Would her British client prefer something formal?

She stopped dead, realizing Dr. Alastair Drago was sitting on the lovely, white-pillared porch. Darn it. Had he seen her imitation of a waterfall in the car? Were her eyes all red?

He rose and, cup in hand, strolled around to the portico to meet her.

Long and lean and muscular. She'd seen him in passing in the darkly lit Shadowlands. Now, in the full light of day, she'd say the man was a perfect match for his gorgeous house.

In tailored khaki slacks and green button-up shirt, he was perhaps an inch or so taller than Master Nolan. His black hair was as short as the perfect beard outlining his strong jaw. His sharp, greenish-hazel eyes were eerily beautiful against his flawless brown skin. Yes, the man was jaw dropping in a classically handsome way—and he was *Doctor* Drago, as well. She'd bet the physician attracted women by the droves.

Not her. She'd be perfectly happy to avoid any and all doctors for a good decade. "Good morning, Dr. Drago."

"It's Alastair." His resonant voice held a crisp English accent. "What's wrong, love?"

Oh, honestly. Visiting a Shadowlands Dom when upset was a major mistake on her part. Of course, he'd noticed her tears and red eyes. "Nothing." When his eyes narrowed, she revised. "I'm having a crummy morning, but it has nothing to do with work. Shall we—"

"We shall go inside and have a cup of tea—or coffee—and chat." He invited her to precede him with a smooth motion.

With a silent sigh, Beth straightened her shoulders, walked through the front doorway, and stopped to admire. His home was lovely. High ceilings with traditional crown molding, gleaming hardwood floors and Oriental carpets, pastel walls, sparkling chandeliers, antiques. Despite the formal decor, the living room's white sofa and chairs were comfortably sturdy, and the statuary, art, and brightly patterned woven goods from all over the world provided quirkiness.

On the way through the small breakfast nook beside the kitchen, she noted boxes stacked against the walls. Spare chairs, tables, and shelves were bunched into corners. "Didn't you move in a couple of months ago?"

"I did." He set his cup on the table and seated her with an easy graciousness. "Tea or coffee?"

His cup held tea. "Tea will be fine."

After getting another cup, he poured from an antique china pot, placed the drink in front of her, and slid over the silver-serving tray with cubed sugar, tongs, and sliced lemon. "I have milk in the refrigerator if you like."

"This is fine, thank you." As he took a seat across from her, she sipped the tea, enjoying the subtle flavor. "You have a beautiful home, and I have a few ideas already as to landscape styles that might suit you. We could—"

In the kitchen light, his unwavering eyes were more brown than green. "Perhaps we could first discuss your unhappiness."

"What?" Her tea almost spilled, and she set the cup down

carefully. "I'm fine."

"I'm afraid I don't believe you." His perceptive gaze swept over her, and the concern in his expression deepened. "I know your Master returned yesterday. Perhaps, you should take the day to be with him. And talk. We can reschedule this appointment."

"That's nice of you, but he's sleeping late this morning. And he's exhausted. He doesn't need to know I had a...moment."

Alastair leaned back in his chair, stretching long legs out in front of him. "May I call you Beth?"

She blinked and nodded.

"Beth, I have heard your Master speak of you, his wife who is also his submissive. There is no doubt in my mind he is extremely protective of you. Am I in error?"

"No."

"Wouldn't he want to know of your...moment?"

Stubborn, stubborn Doms. As the landscaper for the Shadowlands' Capture Gardens and Master Z's private gardens, she'd picked up many clients from the club. She'd quickly learned that even outside the club, Doms could be awfully persistent—and they didn't sidetrack worth a darn.

And this was a very experienced Dominant. The minute he'd told Master Z he was settling permanently in Tampa, Alastair had been nominated for "Master," the honorific awarded to the most powerful, skilled, and ethical Dominants in the Shadowlands. And he was a doctor, too. Of course, he'd be both caring and observant. *Dammit.*

Unfortunately, he was correct. She breathed a sigh of capitulation. "Yes. He would want to know. I'll tell him today."

"There's a good girl. Thank you."

Something inside her relaxed as she realized her decision had been made for her. No more worrying about *when.*

He took a sip of his tea, watching her closely.

When she picked up her own cup, he smiled. "Very good."

She gave him a wry look. "Are you going to be this obstinate about your landscaping?"

His grin was a brilliant white in his dark face. "Not unless the flowers start moping."

The laugh that escaped her was heartening.

"You were wondering about the boxes and furniture," he said in a tactful change of subject. "My cousin Max moved in last month, but his furniture only arrived last week. We haven't had a day off at the same time to decide what to keep and what will be stored or sold."

"I bet pediatricians have horrible hours." *Hmm.* How hard would it be to talk him into volunteering time at the shelter? "What does your cousin do?"

"He's a detective with the Tampa Police Department." Alastair set his cup down. "You'll meet him one of these days. If not here, then at the Shadowlands."

Was Max a Dom like Alastair, or would he be a submissive? "Is he—" *Sheesh, Beth. Have some manners.* "Ah, how nice. I look forward to meeting him."

Alastair huffed a laugh. "He's a Dominant, and we play together much as Vance and Galen do. Or we used to before our paths parted."

Beth barely concealed her surprise. Like Galen and Vance? The two did co-top together—and had also married her friend Sally, which was unusual. Although two Doms might occasionally share a scene, two heterosexual men sharing a submissive in a full-time relationship was pretty rare.

Alastair rose with a grace that belied his height. "Since you're back on your game, let us assess the yard."

TWO HOURS LATER, Beth shook hands with Alastair. To help her plan a smooth transition from inside to outside, her camera held shots of the house interior as well as the grounds. "I'll have a detailed conceptual drawing along with a project description for you in a few days. Before the final drawing and proposal are created, we'll revise depending on what you like and don't like about it." She hesitated. "Since your cousin lives here, it might be good if he was present, too."

"That was the plan. He'd hoped to meet you today, but got called into the station unexpectedly." Alastair frowned at the barren front yard. "You have your work cut out for you, I fear."

"It'll be fun. And you'll enjoy how quickly plants grow in this climate."

She couldn't stop smiling as she hopped into her truck. At one time, she'd planned to follow in her father's footsteps and own a nursery business, but a couple of years ago, she'd realized she loved landscape design. With Jessica's accounting help and Nolan's management expertise, she'd expanded her yard service business and hired a small crew, giving her time to take on design work.

Each new project felt like a child's unopened box of crayons—a gift filled with the potential for creating beauty. And utility. And fun.

As she headed back, she felt...normal again, and her anticipation rose. Nolan was *home*.

Maybe she should start by cooking a good Sunday dinner and feeding both of them up; she wasn't the only one who'd lost weight. Afterward, she'd tell him about the treatment and the results. They could talk—something else she'd missed.

Two months apart was too long, especially when the phone service didn't allow long, chatty conversations. Then again, chatty and Nolan was a contradiction in terms.

She grinned. Her Master was comfortable with people, but talkative? Hardly. In his opinion, anything more than the bare facts was overkill. But he listened like no one she'd ever met.

When they talked, she had all of his attention, and his focus was as sexy as it was amazing.

Oh, she was glad he was home and that he was all hers today.

As she walked into the coolness of the house, she stopped and sniffed. Rather than cinnamon, the air smelled of a rich and musky perfume. Someone had visited.

Nolan wasn't in his office, the kitchen, or the great room. She found him outside, sleeping on the patio, wearing swim trunks. Two glasses sat on a nearby table.

The physical therapist. Alyssa had said she'd come by today.

Nolan's tanned skin gleamed with oil. That lush, big-breasted submissive had touched him. Rubbed oil into his muscular back. Pain stabbed Beth's heart, as unexpected as when a thorny rose would pierce her leather gloves.

Stop, Beth. Jealousy is beneath you. Alyssa had seemed nice. Beth bit her lip as she watched her husband sleep. Maybe a little too nice. And too beautiful. And uncomfortably needy.

Nonetheless, having Alyssa come by was best; Sir certainly wouldn't take the time to get a referral to a regular therapist, let alone go to any appointments.

I can handle a little jealousy. For Nolan.

Of course, she could handle it better if she had some nice big breasts like the therapist's. Beth rolled her eyes. Now, there was a goal.

What do you want in life, Beth?

World peace. A large family. Huge tits.

Talk about silly. Aside from giving her Master something fun to grope, huge knockers would totally get in her way, would probably make her shoulders ache—and, with her luck? Some bus door would close on them.

Go, girl. Take a shower and try not to think about Alyssa touching Sir.

Chapter Four

HIS LITTLE RABBIT was taking a long time in the shower.

In jeans and T-shirt, Nolan leaned against the kitchen counter, drinking iced tea. When he came in from the patio, he realized she was in the bathroom. Odd. Normally, she woke him up if he was sleeping when she left or when she got home.

What was going on with his Beth?

Her exhaustion and weight loss, although worrying, weren't unexpected. The distance between them though, this was new. Fuck, he wished he'd turned Raoul down and stayed home for the summer. Of course, after hearing about the conditions, his softhearted Beth had been adamant he should go. And the village *had* needed him. He'd seen the piss-poor shelter they'd been using, seen the sick and injured lying in the dirt, suffering from heat and insects.

Now, he needed to find out what had happened here while he was gone.

He glanced at the fridge and considered making lunch. She didn't need to miss more meals. But perhaps a better strategy would be to catch her right out of the shower.

In the bedroom, he sat on the bed and worked his shoulder as he waited. Alyssa had good hands, and the pain was better. A pity she'd broken up with her Master, though. Some submissives did poorly after being uncollared.

As he stretched, Nolan monitored the sounds from the bathroom.

The shower stopped. Drying off. Lotioning. The door opened.

Hair wet and tangled, Beth emerged with a towel wrapped around her body. Seeing him, she stopped dead.

Nolan smiled. Funny how sometimes she struck him as gorgeous, other times simply heartwarmingly pretty. He had to say, though, her big turquoise eyes were always the most beautiful he'd ever seen. Her skin was lightly tanned, her face, arms, and shoulders freckled, and her breasts were a flawless white. "Come here, sugar."

When she hesitated, he studied her carefully. With the abuse in her past, he was cautious of frightening her; however, he did enjoy raising her anxiety a bit. It was part of the push and pull in their relationship. Just as his clever Beth wasn't a blindly obedient submissive—no matter how much she loved to serve him—she preferred the reins in his hands, but would still give a tug now and then.

And they both enjoyed the fact he didn't loosen his grip.

When he took her hand and pulled her between his legs, she bit her lip nervously. Heat rose from her shower-warmed skin along with the fragrance of her strawberry-scented shampoo and soap.

Mmm. Ever since meeting her, the scent of strawberries would give him a hard-on.

With one finger, he traced the velvety skin above the top of her towel. Several shiny white scars bore evidence of her previous husband's torture. It'd be a pleasure to kill the bastard again and, this time, go about it slower. When he realized his gaze had lingered on her scars, he looked up.

Distress showed in her eyes. Her puffy, reddened eyes. *What the hell?* "You've been crying." He curved his hands around her waist, securing her in front of him. "Tell me why."

Her head gave a shake, and she covered the scars with her

hands.

Hell, he'd fucked up. She was sensitive about the marks of past abuse, partly because of the memories, partly because of the marring of her skin. And he'd rubbed in the fact that she had scars, damn him for a fool.

Talking would have to wait. Good thing he was just the Dom to get her to mellow out. "All right. We can talk about the tears later."

Under his palms, her muscles relaxed.

"Is your period finished, little rabbit?" The same syndrome that rendered her infertile also gave her extremely short periods lasting hours instead of days.

She nodded, her gaze averted.

"Are you achy? Tender?"

"No," she whispered.

She hadn't been this insecure since they'd first gotten together. He needed to find out why. And he damn well would. Carefully.

"I'm glad to hear it." He tugged her towel downward, ignoring her half-grab as her breasts were exposed. Mercilessly, he tightened his legs, trapping her in place so he could use his hands.

He loved all of her body, but, yeah, he was a breast man and hers were amazing. So small and firm. Her solid muscles beneath held them up as if she were in her twenties rather than early thirties. Enjoying the pure white skin, he ran his knuckles underneath each one, and the small raspberry-colored nipples puckered. He leaned forward and traced his tongue over the pebbled sweetness, flicked the tips, and felt her start to tremble.

She tried to step back.

MISTAKE, BETH THOUGHT, when Sir lifted his head and pinned her with his black gaze.

"Do you think I'll let you back away from me today?" he asked, ever so quietly. His sable hair was loose, brushing his broad shoulders, and he hadn't yet shaved. The jagged scar over his cheekbone and the dark, short beard gave him an edgy menace.

Her mouth went dry as her knees wobbled. She shook her head.

"We're going to make love, little rabbit." His hard lips curved, reminding her of the relentless Master he could be when he decided on an action. "Do you remember your safeword?"

Her eyes widened. It had been a long time since she'd even thought about a safeword, but that he needed to remind her meant he was going to push her...now, when she was feeling so off. When she didn't want to talk with him or—

"Beth?"

"Red. It's red, Sir."

"Good." Holding her in place with his legs, he deliberately resumed his actions, twirling his tongue around and around each nipple and licking over the top. So wet and slick and warm.

Shivers coursed down her body. *Oh God.*

His teeth closed on one peak, compressing to the very point of pain, before pulling it into his mouth and sucking.

A slow pulse of arousal awakened in her pelvis.

As he alternated breasts, he rubbed his short beard against the sensitive sides in an erotically unfamiliar sensation. He nipped. He sucked. Teeth. Tongue. Lips. Beard.

Her breasts swelled. The skin tightened. And a lovely heat bloomed beneath her skin.

"Now, kiss me, subbie." He didn't wait for her compliance, but curved a hand over her nape and pulled her head down. Her cold, wet hair spilled forward, slapping over the heated skin of her breasts.

When he teased his lips over hers, the beard made him feel

like a stranger, and she stiffened. His hand closed tighter. But, as he nibbled on her lower lip, her mouth softened, letting him take possession. Nothing was unfamiliar about the insistent, confident way he kissed, and a sigh escaped.

He took her mouth deeply, possessive and demanding, continuing as he rose to his feet and bent her back, pressing her pelvis against him with one steely arm. His erection was thick against her stomach, his body rock hard against hers.

And he kept kissing her until every thought disappeared right out of her head, and her body melted into his.

When he released her mouth, her legs had turned to jelly, and only his arm kept her upright. Amusement lit his eyes as he waited for her to find her balance again.

Once she could stand alone, he stripped her towel completely off and opened a drawer on the nightstand. "Since we removed the bondage hardware from the bed, let's use this instead." He lifted out a dark red leather harness and started fastening it around her torso.

"Where did this come from?" Vertical straps running down her front and back anchored two horizontal ones. One went around her waist. The other went around her neck like a collar. Beth shivered as he buckled it on.

"Before I left for Africa, a sales rep visited the Shadowlands when the Masters were meeting. He showed us his stock, and I liked this one." He took his time, tightening and fitting, before adding ankle and wrist cuffs as well. Finally, he wrapped a wider cuff around her right thigh above her knee and did the same on the left.

Although the harness wasn't as...carnally comforting as the rope Sir preferred, the leather warmed to her skin quickly.

"It isn't rope, but sometimes faster is good." The dark simmer in his eyes promised pleasure...and other more ominous things...and her body reacted as if it was onboard all the way.

He clipped her wrist cuffs to the collar and played with her breasts some more, deliberately showing her she couldn't stop him.

Her resistance, her worries were slowly melting away under his confident control.

He straightened and patted the mattress. "Up here and on your back."

Without the ability to use her hands, she was forced to wiggle her way onto the bed and roll over clumsily. *The meanie.*

His appreciative chuckle for the show was low and gravelly, and she felt herself flush.

After dragging her to the mattress's edge, he clipped the left ankle cuff to the back of the thigh cuff, pressed her leg toward her chest, and hooked the front of the thigh cuff to the side of the waist belt. When he did the same on the right, her bent legs were splayed out on each side of her body. He'd always liked having her pussy available for anything he wanted to do.

The knowledge sent a pulsing desire swirling through her pelvis.

He pulled more items from the nightstand. More new stuff. Good God, she needed to check the drawers on his side of the bed more often.

The first toy was a small anal plug with two attachments—a wired remote and a hose with a bulb on the end.

A hose? "What is that?" Her heart rate increased. They did anal sex occasionally, but...it'd been a long time. And he didn't use toys often.

His level gaze met hers, held hers, and said she'd pushed her limits. "I'll let you know when you can talk...or make noise. Clear, sugar?"

Oh God, he was going to insist on his damn protocols. "Yes, Sir," she whispered.

"Good." Without any more talk, he lubed the anal plug and

pressed it firmly in, past her unhappy rings of muscle. It lodged in place with a tiny plop. The slight burn and discomfort was outweighed by the erotic sensation of his callused hands on her body, the determination in his gaze. She was his, to do what he wanted with, and the knowledge filled her. Turned her on.

Completed her.

He picked up the other toy—a tiny rubber triangle with thin straps. "Remember this? Haven't used it in quite a while." It was a wearable vibrator called a butterfly. He'd made her wear one the first time he'd taken her.

The air around her seemed hot enough to scorch her skin; perhaps the air-conditioning had failed.

He put the butterfly on her, seated the supple rubber part right over her clit, and turned it on low.

As the tantalizingly faint vibrations hit, she jerked, and her whole lower half rapidly wakened to need. Since he didn't like her indulging without him, she hadn't gotten off in an awfully long time.

"Now, let's have us a little chat." He smiled and slid a finger inside her.

"Wh-what?"

He adjusted the vibrator so it pulsed against the right side of her clit and stimulated a new area of nerves. "You're unhappy. Stressed. Not eating. I'm worried, darlin'." With his other hand, he cupped her breast. "Are you having nightmares about Kyler again?"

His gaze roamed her face, her shoulders, her arms, reading her in his dangerously skillful way. From the stern set of his jaw, she couldn't evade his questions this time.

"The nightmares have mostly died down. Now you're home, I'm sure they'll go away completely." Her lips quivered as guilt raised its ugly head. "I'm sorry to be so…so needy. I didn't realize I'd have trouble with you gone, and—"

He snorted. "I don't sleep good without you either, sugar. If you told me you did fine without me, I'd be pissed."

"Really?" Her hands unclenched. He slept better if she was with him. That had to be one of the nicest compliments she'd ever received.

"You like hearing I need you, yeah?" His deep masculine chuckle let her relax...and then he slid two fingers inside her, filling her, and bringing her right back to need. To serious, serious need.

"Master," she whispered. Her hips wiggled uncontrollably.

He lightly slapped her inner thigh. "Don't move, subbie."

The sting sank down, past her skin, sending an erotic burn right into her core, and his merciless order sent desire singing through her veins.

Slowly, he rotated his hand, and his expert fingers rubbed so firmly on her G-spot that her toes curled. "Fuck, I love your cunt." His voice got lower. "I'm home now, and you're still looking off. What's eatin' at you, sugar?"

She tried to think through the fog of arousal. Answer him? But this was their special time, the first time they made love after being so long apart, and she didn't want to ruin it for him. If she told him about losing any chance for a child, he'd be unhappy. Hurt. But he wouldn't accept a "nothing is wrong."

However, she could give him something else and still be truthful. "Connor and Grant went home with their mother yesterday."

"Oh hell. I'm sorry, baby. I'll miss them too. It's not good how fucked-up their home life is." He'd met their mother a couple of times and commented later on the telltale signs of a meth user—the emaciation, the rotten teeth, and the way she appeared a decade older than she was.

"Maybe it will improve. Drusilla might stay off the drugs, and Jermaine took an anger management class." She offered up the hopes, not certain she believed them.

The hard line of his mouth rejected the easy answer. "I think we should wander by and check, don't you?"

God, she loved him. "I'd planned to wait a day or so and stop in. They…" Her voice faded away when his face went still.

"Before you knew I was back?"

"Uh…"

"Uh?" He growled. "You know my thoughts on unescorted visits to abusive assholes."

She had no answer; she did know. *Oops.*

His face softened. Bracing himself on his good arm, he bent and nuzzled her temple and cheek before kissing her ever so gently. He lifted his head an inch, his gaze penetrating. "Is their leaving the only thing bothering you?"

When she flinched, she knew she'd incriminated herself.

"I figured. Give me the rest, sugar, before we move on to other things."

"It's nothing. I don't want to talk about it." Not now. Not when she'd end up crying. He deserved better from her than a sobbing hot mess.

"Not the answer I was hoping for." His dark brows pulled together, his lips tightened, and his unreadable gaze sent her right into *worry* mode. Oh, she was in trouble. Without speaking, he flipped the anal plug switch.

The low vibrations from the anal plug and the ones over her clit met low in her core. The not-quite-enough pulses were enough to drive her crazy…and his questions flew right out of her head.

As she lifted her head, planning to beg, he undid his jeans and released his cock. He was so, so gorgeous. The opened jeans revealed the flat muscle of his lower abdomen. His shaft was so much like him—purely solid and powerful.

He set the head against her entrance and pressed in…one

inch.

Oooh, the feeling. The promise of more made her hips squirm and earned her another light slap and growl. She grew even wetter.

But he didn't move. His gaze moved over her, dark and hot and…mercilessly determined.

"Sir. Master. My beloved Liege," she whispered, try-ing…trying not to move as the vibrations drove her up and up. She wanted him *inside*. "Please."

"Easy enough to fix, sugar. Just be honest with me."

Honest. Her breathing turned ragged. Her legs trembled and strained against the unyielding cuffs. He hated lies—and evasions. But to tell him now—would hurt him. Would wreck this coming together. What could she say? Frustration and need kept derailing her thoughts.

Like clouds heralding a storm, worry was followed by darker sorrow, even as her body sent zaps of needy lightning through her. She couldn't *think*. "If I tell you…" A tear escaped. She needed him, his arms around her, him deep within her—their special togetherness. Talking would ruin it.

"You *will* tell me." The determination was there in his voice.

He didn't understand. "I need to be with you first. Please…I need this…you and me, first." She closed her eyes, unable to think. "If I promise to explain after, can we…"

"Look at me."

Her gaze met his dark, steady eyes.

"I get it. We've been apart a long time." He touched her cheek. "Afterward, while you're in my arms, you'll tell me everything."

"Yes." A sigh escaped her. He'd never want to be shielded. Even if it hurt him, he'd want to know. "Yes, Master."

His hard lips curved in approval and satisfaction. "Good girl." His cock pressed in, not brutally, but steadily, filling her wonderfully full. Thick pleasure flowed up her center in a long, sweet stream.

But he kept going. *Too much.* It'd been too long. Her legs jerked in protest. With a whimper, she pulled at the wrist restraints—uselessly.

He slowed only a little. "Take me, Beth," he said gently...ruthlessly...for he knew exactly how much she could take. Knew her strengths, her weaknesses.

And he still loved her.

Her body surrendered, giving up the instinctive need to fight, and he thrust in until his warm thighs pressed against her buttocks.

Her eyes closed as she pulled in long breaths, fighting the helplessness that terrified her yet fulfilled her, the loss of control she hated, and required. Only with Nolan could she let go completely—because she trusted him with her mind and heart and soul. With all that she was.

I love you.

Watching her closely, he caressed her breasts. Each time he rolled a nipple between his fingers, her pussy contracted around him. And finally, he started to move, short in and out strokes at first, then longer and harder.

Oh, oh, oh, so wonderful. A short, unexpected orgasm shook her.

His grin was a flash of white in his tanned face. "Nice." He eased in and out as the spasms diminished. His erection was still thick and heavy inside her as he turned off the vibrators. "But you can do better."

"Do better?" Her voice came out slow. Husky.

"Yes, little rabbit, I want more." His cheek creased. "I haven't heard you scream in a long time."

More? She didn't scream unless she was...gone. Unless he pushed her to the point of mindlessness. *Oh God.*

Under his amused, searing stare, she felt her nipples harden to tiny points and her insides tighten around him. "But I've already come." She already knew his answer.

"Oh, I don't think it'll be a problem." Bracing himself on his good arm, he leaned down and took her mouth, slow and devastatingly thorough. She'd never found anyone who kissed like him, patiently continuing until she gave him everything he wanted. Just as he planned to do to her now.

The knowledge was frightening—and carnal.

He straightened and slowly thrust, in and out, driving harder, even as he flipped on the butterfly. The vibrator woke to life, back to a low hum. He frowned. "Let's kick the action up a notch."

More? She shook her head no.

When he upped the speed on the vibrator, her already sensitive clit swelled and hardened as she spiraled back into need.

To her dismay, he pulled his cock almost out.

"Master," she whined and closed her lips belatedly. She wasn't supposed to speak.

His grin came so quickly she almost didn't see it. "Now didn't that sound nice? Let's have us some serious begging." To her alarm, he gripped the hose coming from the anal plug and pumped the rubber bulb at the end.

The anal plug in her back passage began to enlarge like a balloon. "No!"

" 'Fraid so, sugar." With each squeeze of the bulb, the thing grew inside her. Too much. Too full. Ignoring her protest, he turned on the plug's vibrator as well.

Nerves jumped to life with a painful intensity, feeling so strange, so good. "Oh God, please…" Did she want him to stop…or to increase everything? She needed to come…*now.*

His chuckle was rough and sexy, and she shuddered with the pleasure of having him home. Having his hands on her. Having him in control.

"Better. Let's go for a scream."

The inflated anal plug filled her already, so the entrance of his cock into her pussy made her gasp. He was impossibly large, and all the vibrations intensified as if they raged back and forth, shaking her from the inside out. Her legs trembled and fought against the restraints without success. She was powerless to prevent anything he did. She stared up at him, panting, excited, and anxious, as the need to come built higher and higher.

He pulled out, pressed in. "Fuck, you feel good. You'd better hang on, pet."

Seriously? There was *nothing* she could do, not even hang on. Her glare made him laugh.

Then he took her, hard and fast and relentless. He paused only long enough to dial up the clit vibrator. The vibrations from the anal plug somehow merged with those from butterfly, until even his cock seemed to be vibrating as he hammered into her,

Every ruthless thrust drove her up and up.

Every stroke seemed the pinnacle of exquisite pleasure.

Her breathing stopped, the world stopping with it, as she hung there, every muscle tense as the pressure built and built.

He ever so slowly withdrew, drawing the torment out with a sadistic finesse. His gaze held hers for an eternal moment... With a hard thrust, he sheathed himself to the hilt.

Her nerves ignited, sending pleasure blasting through every cell. Glorious fireworks sparkled upward through her body and danced in her vision. The sensations soared higher and higher until her entire world went white, and a cascade of screams broke from her.

As all her muscles went limp, her Master gripped her hips, lifting her ass up for greater penetration as he took her, hard and fast. Burying himself completely, he came, leaning into her, pinning her to the bed with his weight and his cock.

Warmth filled her—the wonderful heat of his seed. Yet...nothing would come of his gift. As she stared into his intent night-dark eyes, pain slashed into her heart. There would be no baby with his beautiful skin, his dark eyes. Not from her.

"Oh, Nolan." She wanted to touch him. Couldn't. Her voice broke, as shattered as her heart. "It...it won't happen." Her breathing hitched, and tears filled her eyes.

"What won't, sweetheart?" His warm hand cupped her cheek.

The first sobs felt as if they would crack her ribs—oh, they hurt—and more followed, as she drowned in sorrow. She felt him slide out. Felt him remove everything. Felt his careful hands undo the restraints. She cried harder.

Then he was beside her on the bed, holding her in his strong arms.

"N-no!" She struggled. "Your shoulder, you'll—"

He gave a hard laugh. "Fuck, I love you, Beth." He pulled her closer, lying on his side, half on top of her, restraining her with his size alone. As he smoothed the hair from her wet face, she realized tears still flowed from her eyes. "Now, tell me, sugar."

Her throat closed, trapping the words, choking her.

"Beth." The growl pushed past her grief.

"While you were gone, I went in for the last treatment." Her words were barely audible. "It didn't work. The doctor told me to find a surrogate or adopt."

"Ah, sugar." Despite his Dom's face, his emotions were obvious. Anger that she'd acted without him present. Sorrow...for her.

"I'm sorry. *Sorry*." She dissolved into tears again, wanting—needing—to apologize. *My body is worthless. I'm hopeless, never good for anything, not—*

There was a crack of sound and pain scorched her bottom.

The shocking sting splintered her thoughts into fragments. Jerking, she met his annoyed dark gaze.

Oh, God, she'd been speaking out loud.

"If I hear any more of the crap Kyler shoved in your head, I'll lay you across my knees, and you'll get yourself a spanking session that'll leave you unable to sit down for a week." His voice was a low rasp.

She closed her tear-swollen eyes, grateful he'd broken her free of the spiral. With a shuddering sigh, she pressed her forehead against his shoulder, tangling her fingers in his loosened hair. "I'm sorry."

"You be sorry for letting that bullshit into your head, Beth. For the rest…" His sigh echoed hers. "I'm sorry, too. I do know how much you'd hoped for a different outcome. But, sugar, the doctors said it was doubtful a fetus could come to term even if you did get pregnant."

"I know." She sniffled. So many hopes. Gone. She needed to say the words, accept their truth: "Master, I can't give you a child of your own. Of your blood. There won't be—"

His snort stopped her. "At Christmas, did you count how many nieces and nephews I have?"

It had appeared there were hundreds of children running around. "A l-lot."

"They are all my blood, so to speak. The King bloodline isn't in danger of dying out." His hand was warm against her back. "Yours, either. Your mother has brothers and a sister in the Midwest, and they have children."

"I guess."

"We'd already planned on adopting, sooner or later, hadn't we?"

She nodded, as her muscles started to relax. So many children needed a home that she'd felt guilty about wanting to bear Nolan's child first. "Are you sure you don't want a baby of your own?"

"Beth, any child coming into our family will *be* my own."

As he cradled her against him, she rested her head against his chest and listened to the slow thud of his heart—one big enough to love any number of children.

SITTING NEXT TO Beth on their screened, covered patio, Nolan drank a beer and watched the best show on Earth—a noisy, pounding, late-afternoon storm. Rain sheeted down so hard he could barely see the lake. On the banks, the grass was being pounded flat. A streak of brilliant white turned the world to high noon, and seconds later, a crack of thunder shook his bones. A chill breeze wafted past, carrying the scent of green vegetation and lake water.

Fucking great entertainment. It was even better when a man had someone with whom to share. He gave the fingers twined with his a slight squeeze and turned his head.

In the chair beside him, Beth had her legs pulled to her chest, her chin resting on her bare knees. Her expression as she gazed at the roiling clouds was…peaceful. She was something. His wife. His submissive. His love.

When he'd met her mother, he'd tried to convey his appreciation for the strong foundation Beth had received. How, despite the damage Kyler had done, she'd kept moving forward. Lisabet had laughed and said her child had been born resilient. In fact, when Lisabet's husband had died, Beth had supported her distraught mother.

The two shared a hell of a lot of traits. Like how they'd straighten their shoulders when facing down a problem. How careful they were with others, managing a graceful honesty rarely seen in this uncivil world.

But, unlike Beth, Lisabet didn't bury her emotions. She cried easily and often. Nolan remembered when he'd called her from the hospital to say Beth had been rescued from her abusive husband. Lisabet had burst into tears.

Undoubtedly, Beth had been more open before she'd suffered two years of abuse. Counseling had helped her work out her issues, but the therapist had warned them both that during times of stress, Kyler's destructive programming might resurface.

And so it had.

It broke his heart to hear Beth call herself worthless. She had to be the finest woman he'd ever met, and it pissed him off she couldn't accept how amazing she was. He'd never met anyone as generous and spirited, as strong and caring. Hell, even now, her heartbreak wasn't for herself, but because she couldn't give *him* a baby.

He took a sip of his beer. Next time they visited Texas, he'd point out all his relatives who were adopted...assuming he could remember which of his cousins they were.

Dammit, she'd taken that last treatment without him present. The fucking hormones the doctors administered always shoved her onto an emotional rollercoaster. At least he was back now and could keep an eye on Little Miss Independent.

Leaning forward, he pulled the low footstool closer, annoyed when his shoulder blasted a painful objection to the movement. Damn injury. He'd ignored the pain while holding Beth in bed, but it'd been aching ever since. Settling back, he put his feet up and put the beer to one side. "Come here, sugar."

She rose to stand beside him, barefoot, dressed in her pale blue cover-up, and smelling faintly of chlorine from her swim in the pool. Taking her hand, he tugged her into his lap. Just the right size for him. Taller than Z's Jessica, shorter than Cullen's Andrea. Average, she called her size. Fucking perfect, he'd say. Big enough he could be rough with her and she'd hold her own, small enough she fit perfectly in his arms and on his lap.

Even better, they were on the same wavelength again. He could feel the tie between them, strong and open, no more tangles or knots.

He understood her desire to give him a baby who looked like him, since he'd love to see a little girl with Beth's eyes…and her stubborn, sweet personality. Using a surrogate to carry a child with both of their genes would work, but, damn, he couldn't put a woman at risk like that. Friends of his had hired a surrogate—another friend—and had a beautiful son. Their happiness was destroyed when the surrogate tried to keep the baby herself, and failing, fell into depression and committed suicide. And there was Fawn, his cousin who'd loved being a surrogate and had died in labor with her third contract. Twenty-four years old. Not more than a baby herself, dammit.

Beth had understood why he'd refused. His little submissive had the courage to step into someone's shoes and empathize. Braver than he was in many ways.

He rubbed his freshly-shaved chin on the top of her head. "We'll call the social worker tomorrow, the one we worked with when we were getting the adoption certifications. We'll call the private adoption lawyer, as well."

Her shoulders tensed and relaxed. "Yes, Master." Her resigned exhale said she was with him, and she recognized it was time to move on. "Did you want to try the foster care route?"

According to the state's priorities, a child's relatives topped the list…but foster parents were second. However, until parental rights were terminated, children could—and often did—return to their parents. Although he and Beth had completed the foster care licensing, he didn't want her subjected to any more disappointments. Not right now. "Let's save fostering as a last option."

"Okay." As a rain-laden wind whipped her hair back, she rubbed her head against him like a small cat.

"What we didn't kick around last spring"—because she hadn't been ready to give up—"was our specs."

"Specifications? You're not ordering lumber for a building, Sir." Her husky giggle was muffled by his shirt. There was his Beth. She might cry if the world fell apart, but then she'd throw her shoulders back and survive—and make sure everyone around her did as well.

"Although any child would be a gift, the adoption agency will ask if we have any preferences." He ran his knuckles over her chin. "For me...although boys would be nice, I'd like a girl first. If she had red hair like her mama-to-be, I sure wouldn't object."

She tilted her head, as if she'd never thought about choices. Probably hadn't since she'd been so damned set on bearing a child herself. "A little girl..." She smiled. "Yes. Absolutely yes."

"What about you, Beth? Do you have a preference?"

"Um..."

"Spit it out, sugar. I'll only beat on you if I don't like the answer."

A laugh appeared in her eyes. Yeah, she was feeling better. Moving ahead was the right thing to do. "I'd like a baby if possible. To feel like we're starting from scratch." Her arms moved to form a cradle.

"Makes sense. One baby girl. We got a plan." A baby girl. He could almost see her tiny face. Snuggling Beth closer, he kissed the top of her head. "You ready for this?"

Her nod was firm. "We're not getting any younger, and"—a real smile appeared—"if you want to fill all those rooms upstairs, we'd better get moving."

When he'd built the house, he'd planned for a big family. Although adoption might be less straightforward than getting Beth pregnant, it didn't matter. What mattered was filling their home with noise and laughter. Bickering and broken dishes and pranks. Homework on the table and artwork on the fridge. Girly shit and giggles. Add some boys and there'd be frogs in the bathtub and football on the lawn.

Fuck, yeah. "Have I mentioned recently how much I love you?"

Her lips tilted up. "I think it's been hours and hours." It filled his heart to hear the easy way she added, "I love you, Sir."

Chapter Five

O N THE COUCH beside Connor, Grant watched a movie on television. The little lion cub was stuck on a cliff, and his daddy was trying to save him. Connor had been giggling, but now he was silent. Scared of what was coming although they'd both seen it before.

Grant was tense mostly because he was hoping Mama and Jermaine would be done fighting when they returned.

Since leaving the shelter last weekend, Mama kept getting worse. This morning, she'd been mean to Connor. Then she'd screamed at Jermaine, telling him to get the stuff or she would, and they'd yelled at each other all the way out the door.

Why couldn't he and Connor have been lions? They'd be fast and could hide in the grass and…would have a daddy like Mufasa.

But Simba's daddy died, too.

On the television, Mufasa fell and fell and fell, and the big animals ran over him as if he wasn't there. As Connor started sniffling, Grant's eyes filled with tears, and he shook his head hard. Boys didn't cry. But he knew how Simba must be wailing, *Daddy, come back.*

A car door slammed outside the duplex. Another one. Rubbing his arm over his wet eyes, Grant turned to see Mama stomp into the house. She didn't look…right. Her yellow hair wasn't combed and the top was dark. She hadn't put on the makeup stuff that made her eyes bigger or her mouth red.

Jermaine followed. He was almost as tall as *Nolanman*, but was skinny—more bones than muscles. His greasy, black hair hung in his eyes, and he hadn't shaved for a few days so an ugly, patchy beard covered his lower face. Slamming the door behind him, he pointed at Mama. "Told you, bitch, don't set up buys here. Can't afford a cop on my ass right now."

Mama made a pffffing sound. "Don't be a dick. No one knows Python's a dealer. He's an asshole, but he'll be in and out before anyone notices, and I'm not going to wait until you think it's safe. That taste he gave me won't last long."

Twirling around and around, she spotted Grant and Connor and danced over to the couch. Up close, her brown eyes had turned blacker and twitchy. She ruffled Grant's hair so hard it hurt, and he pulled away, but she didn't notice. "Aren't my boys the prettiest boys you've ever seen? Just like their daddy." She bounced on her toes, like when Connor waited too long to use the bathroom.

"I don't give a shit about the little brats, but don't you fucking call me a dick." Jermaine kicked the footstool across the room. "Bitch, if I toss you in the ditch out back, the gators'd make your body disappear, all neat and tidy."

"Oooo, I'm scared now." When Mama spun to face him, her face changed to the crazy one. "I'll call you any fucking thing I want. Dickhead."

"Go," Grant whispered to his brother. They edged off the couch and started real quiet toward the hallway.

Jermaine stepped in front of Grant. "I don't like you sneaking around, you little bastards. You look guilty as shit. You get into the food again?"

Grant swallowed. "Uh-uh. We watched television."

Mama turned, and her face went mean. "Then why're you running off? You're always in your rooms." With an arm, she swiped the magazines off the coffee table. "You don't like your mama no more?"

"Hell no, they don't. Fucking beggars, eating all the food when our backs are turned. I'm sick of it. Of them." When Jermaine swung his arm, Grant tried to dodge.

Wham.

The backhanded blow knocked Grant into the coffee table and onto his back. His head went all fuzzy. He couldn't stand, couldn't even roll over. A warm trickle ran from his nose, and his cheek hurt. *Hurt.* He sobbed once before he could stop.

His mama heard him, and her face changed. Got soft. When she whispered, her voice was soft, too. "Oh, Grant."

Jermaine laughed and repeated in a high voice, "Oh, *Grant.*"

Mama's mouth pinched together; her eyes turned crazy again, and she slapped Jermaine right across the face. "Leave my kid alone, *dickhead.*"

"You cunt." He shoved her so hard she tripped. Her shoulders hit the wall with a loud thud.

Scrambling up, she lunged toward him with a screech of fury.

Grant managed to roll onto his hands and knees before Connor started pulling at him. "Hurry, Grant."

Teeth gritted together, Grant crawled toward the bedroom. His ears hummed funny, and his mouth tasted bad, like when he'd taken a sip of Mama's booze.

Mama was crazy-swearing, her words tangled up, her face the color of Superman's cape. She grabbed stuff around her, throwing at the wall, the floor, Jermaine, anywhere. Just...throwing, not aiming. A picture landed on the floor between Grant and Connor, sending glass everywhere.

Jermaine yelled at her.

Grant pushed to his feet. The room whirled for a second, and he staggered before it all settled. "C'mon," he whispered to Connor. But where could they go? Hiding under the bed wouldn't work. Jermaine would see them go in the bedroom. He was awful mad—he might search for them.

A dish slammed into Connor's back. Screaming in pain, he fell to his hands and knees.

Blood. Blood showed on his brother's white T-shirt.

"No!" Fear pushed Grant forward, bit at his heels as he dragged Connor up, through the kitchen, and out the back. As he yanked the door shut behind them, something heavy crashed against it. Running, he pulled Connor across the yard, pushed him through the hole in the falling-down fence, and followed.

They stopped beside the fence. Wiping his eyes roughly, Grant checked for gators. The low, muddy ditch was full of water from the last rain. Two gray shapes sunning on the far bank raised their heads to study the boys. One was bigger than Grant, and he held his breath. Jermaine said gators ate little kids—bit into them and tore their legs off and made them scream and scream.

Grant grabbed Connor's hand and held on tight. Nothing would get his brother. "Let's go."

As they ran down the bank, he could still hear Mama calling names and swearing, Jermaine yelling. Things crashed and broke, and he was a big boy, but he couldn't stop crying.

A WAILING SIREN woke Grant up. His eyes were puffy and sore as he gazed around the empty lot. The sun had crossed so far to the other side of the big tree that he and Connor were almost out of the shade. They'd been asleep for a while.

The lot was filled with man-high, sharp-leaved plants called *palm-something-toes.* Nasty, mean things, which meant no one came here. Only him and Connor, because while exploring, they'd discovered a winding path to the humungous tree in the center of the lot. Even in a downpour, the leaves kept most of the rain off. They'd named it Father Tree.

Still curled in a ball, Connor yawned. It'd taken forever to get him to stop crying. To stop bleeding. His SpongeBob shirt—the one he'd gotten from the shelter—had blood all down the back. Grant's T-shirt had Iron Man on the front, and the blood barely showed.

Neither of them had wanted to go back home—not right away—so they'd used sticks to build fences around beetles, and watched ants carry stuff to their mounds, and eventually they fell asleep.

Connor sat up, moving carefully.

"You okay?" Grant asked.

"I'm hungry. And firsty." Connor's chin quivered. "Is Mama gonna still be mad?"

"Dunno." They'd been here a long time, but was it long enough? Grant was hungry, too, and his mouth was so dry he couldn't swallow, but he could wait longer. Connor couldn't; he was still a baby.

Before Daddy got dead as a hero, he'd said Grant's job was to protect his little brother.

Sometimes it was awful hard. "Let's go back."

Keeping a wary eye out for bad guys or gators, Grant led the way along the water-filled ditch, past the neighbor's chain-link fence, to their wooden fence. After peeking through the gap in the boards, he squirmed through and into the backyard.

Connor followed right after.

Moving to the center of the yard, Grant listened for a second. No shouting. No screaming. Nothing. Maybe Jermaine and Mama had left? "Stay here and wait for me."

"No." Connor took his hand in a determined grip.

"You need to…" He frowned and glanced at the hole in the fence. Could one of the gators get through the hole? What was more dangerous for Connor—Mama and Jermaine or a gator?

"Okay." Grant went up the two sagging steps, opened the backdoor a crack, and listened.

Silence.

Jermaine was never quiet. Even when he slept, he snored. Maybe he wasn't here. That'd be good.

So quiet. Maybe Mama wasn't here either, 'cause when she got wild, she was always muttering and slamming stuff or laughing at nothing.

She'd been scary crazy this morning.

Grant squeezed Connor's fingers and let go. "Stay here while I check inside." When Connor nodded, Grant edged through the back door. In the kitchen, he stopped in shock.

Connor appeared and his eyes got big.

Grant couldn't seem to move. He'd seen a TV show about earthquakes that destroyed towns, and the houses had looked like this. Food from the cupboards was scattered across the counters and floor. The dishes were busted. The fridge door was open, and milk pooled on the floor beside shattered bottles of booze. The booze stank worse than the ditch water.

Connor took his hand again, swallowing hard. "Mama was really mad, wasn't she?"

"Yeah." Walking through the mess, Grant hung on tight, his stomach wanting to throw up.

In the living room, the coffee table lay on top of the smashed television. Tears burned Grant's eyes. No more TV. No more Simba or the shows with the little girl who lived in the country and had pigtails and did funny stuff.

"I gotta pee," Connor whined. His breathing hitched as he backed away from the mess.

"Me, too. C'mon." Grant led the way to the bathroom where they both used the toilet and then drank so much water their stomachs bulged.

"What's that?" Connor lowered his glass and pointed.

A stripe of funny red and blue lights danced on the wall.

Weird. Grant turned. The lights came through a gap in the curtains. After clambering up on the toilet seat, he peeked outside. An ambulance and two cop cars with flashing lights sat at the curb. A bunch of people were bent over someone lying on the ground. "Mama?"

"Is Mama there?" Connor jostled for position beside him.

Was she hurt? Bad hurt? She didn't move, not even when they rolled her onto a long thing and put her in the ambulance. And drove away. Fear choked his throat, and Grant's hands fisted on the curtains. *Mama.*

"Where'd she go?" Panicking, Connor started to get down from the toilet top.

Grant grabbed him. "She went in the ambulance. To see doctors."

"Is she sick?"

Grant didn't know. "I guess. But she'll come back as soon as they give her a pill."

Another man lay kind of twisted on his back, and the sidewalk beneath him was all red. Even though his eyes were open, he didn't talk or get up. Didn't look right.

A cop in a uniform walked over to some people who were watching. Their neighbor from the other half of the duplex— Jermaine called her a *nosy bitch*—talked to him and pointed toward the house. The cop started toward their door.

That was *bad.* Jermaine said cops would drag Connor and Grant away, put them in horrible houses apart from each other, and big, mean boys would hurt them. Cut them up. Even cut their tongues out if they cried.

"We got to hide." With Connor behind him, Grant dashed into Mama's bedroom and, for the first time, hoped Jermaine was home, was sleeping or something.

The room was empty.

The front door handle rattled.

Daddy wouldn't want the cops to get Connor. "*Bed.* Now." Pushing Connor in front of him, he ran to their bedroom. They skidded under the bed, and he shoved the suitcase back in place, enclosing them in.

Hands over his mouth, Connor was trying not to cry.

Grant wasn't crying, but he was shivering so hard his bones hurt, and he wasn't even cold.

ON THURSDAY, IN the beautiful upstairs office Nolan had remodeled for her, Beth printed out an alternative design for Alastair's property. The first draft was her favorite, maybe because she'd put in a tranquil koi pond to help him de-stress from his job. She wondered if his cousin, the cop, would use it.

She looked forward to meeting Max. When she'd stopped at an array of photos on the fireplace mantle, Alastair had pointed out one of him and Max—two teens crossing rapiers. Both in identical protective gear yet very different. Black and white, sophisticated and rough, streamlined and powerful. But both young men had devastating smiles.

Another photograph showed Alastair as a child beside his tall, aristocratic black mother in front of a stately English manor. One showed Alastair hugging a lean white man in a cowboy shirt, jeans, and boots. His father. Alastair said his summers were spent at the Drago family ranch in rural Colorado, winters in London with his neurosurgeon mom. Talk about culture shock.

But, travel or not, families were a blessing. She couldn't imagine not talking with her mother every week or two. All of Nolan's huge family called and visited and expected return visits to Texas. She'd enjoyed last Christmas there, although the delicate hints about children had been…painful. When the quiet pressure had abruptly stopped, she knew Nolan had explained and put his foot down.

Her knight in shining armor. On Monday—after insisting she have a snack—he'd held her hand when they called the social worker and the lawyer about pulling their applications out of the HOLD files.

Full speed ahead.

In fact, she had better assess what was needed to convert the downstairs guest bedroom into a nursery for a baby girl. She trotted down the stairs and past the kitchen to the guest room. *Hmm.* The two queen beds should go, but the shelves were fine. They should buy a crib and changing table. A rocking chair for feeding and snuggling. She could almost feel the baby in her arms. Oh, yes.

Vibrations hit her upper thigh, and she pulled her cell phone from the pocket of her khaki overall shorts. *Unknown number.* It was probably one of her yard workers calling in sick. Honestly, didn't they know she was daydreaming here?

"This is Beth."

A short silence. "Beth?" The whisper sounded…childish. Scared.

Beth frowned.

"Is that Beff?" another voice whispered.

Beff. "Is this Grant? And Connor?"

The gulping sound was from a little boy fighting tears. Her hand tightened on the phone. Oh God, what had happened? "Honey, are you hurt? Are you safe?"

Connor answered. "Mama, she outside and 'medics tooked her. And there are *cops* here." He emphasized "cops" the same way someone else might say "serial killers."

"Are you with the police now? Or with someone?" She forced her voice to stay calm despite the alarm screaming in her head. Wasn't there anyone caring for the children? A neighbor?

"Uh-uh. We're under the bed."

Under the bed? "Because Jermaine is there?"

"Beff, there are *cops* here."

"You can trust the police, honey. They're—"

"No." Grant's voice came over the phone.

Dear sweet heavens. "You're at home in your bedroom, right?"

"Uh-huh," Grant said.

"I'm coming to get you, honey. You stay put and I should be there…" Thank goodness she'd gotten their address from the shelter files. Drew Park wasn't far away. "Maybe fifteen minutes or so. Can you two wait that long?"

"Yes," Grant whispered, and the relief in his voice made her eyes sting.

"Yes, Beff," Connor agreed. "I'm hungry."

She always carried treats for the children at the shelter. Children responded to food. But these boys—they'd been scared and called *her*. She didn't have words for how their trust filled her heart. "I'll bring sandwiches, baby."

HOMICIDE DETECTIVE MAXIMILLIAN Drago jotted notes on a pad as he walked through the empty duplex. Removed from the front yard, the male victim, street name Python, had been bagged and tagged and was on the way to the coroner. Considering the smashed skull and the bloodied, concrete pelican statue upended in the yard, the cause of death was pretty straightforward.

Drusilla McCormick had a hell of a swing.

The renter on the duplex's other side had reported hearing screaming and shouting. It seems the dealer had demanded a blowjob as well as money. When Mrs. McCormick had turned him down—loudly and with insults—he hadn't reacted politely. The fight had turned physical as he attempted to take what he

PROTECTING HIS OWN   71

wanted. Another neighbor saw Mrs. McCormick flee out the front. Python caught her, tried to drag her inside, and McCormick had nailed him with one of the neighbor's garden statues.

A pelican.

Fuck. What a way to go.

Mrs. McCormick had collapsed immediately afterward. Before she'd been transported to the hospital, the EMTs told the responding officer her blood pressure was through the roof and they suspected a stroke.

Crystal meth had some real unpleasant side effects.

Shaking his head, Max resumed his study. Aside from the uniformed cop checking the duplex for the children, no one else had been in. Nice intact crime scene.

"Max, you got anything interesting?" Dan Sawyer crossed the living room. The dark brown eyes were cold, his jaw hard. Max's new partner didn't like drug-related deaths.

"Besides the place looking like a war zone and stinking like a city dump?" Jesus, he hadn't seen such a mess since viewing the aftermath of a meth lab explosion. Drug paraphernalia was scattered among all the broken crap littering the room. Blood had spattered one wall next to a fist-sized hole in the drywall. "Nope. The neighbors say McCormick and her boyfriend had been fighting earlier—sounded like a fucking tweaker rampage. The boyfriend took off by himself about an hour before Python showed up."

"The dealer picked the wrong time to visit." Dan glanced at his notes. "Boyfriend is a Jermaine Hinton. McCormick's two kids are four and seven years old."

"Hinton didn't have them. No one's seen them." The sound of an argument outside drew Max to the open door.

A woman in bibbed overall-type shorts and a form-fitting blue T-shirt had ducked under the police tape. Maybe five-seven and weighing one hundred and fifteen pounds, thick auburn hair with the freckles to match. The pretty little thing was trying to push past the officer minding the perimeter.

"That's one determined woman." Reminded him of his mama's terrier, all fight, no surrender. She didn't resemble any reporter he'd ever met, and if she wanted in that badly, maybe she had something interesting to tell them. "Officer, let her pass."

When the uniform stepped aside, the redhead hurried through the door. Early thirties, he'd guess, with beautiful blue-green eyes and a flush on her freckled face.

"Can I help you, ma'am?" Max asked politely.

"Yes, you can." She glanced at the trashed living room. Rather than disgust, worry filled her face. "There are two—"

"Beth. What are you doing here?" Dan stepped past Max. "Not a good place for you right now, pet."

Pet. Max studied her more intently. His partner was a stickler for confidentiality, both in police work and in BDSM. By using the "pet" designation, he'd quietly let Max know that Beth was club member—and submissive, despite the determination in her stance. Interesting.

"Dan, I'm glad you're here." The little redhead's smile turned to a frown. "But it would help if you guys were a lot shorter and smaller. And female."

Well, there was a hell of an insult. "Why's that, ma'am?"

She tilted her head. "I bet you're Alastair's cousin, aren't you?"

"Guilty as charged."

"Ah, right, introductions," Dan said. "Beth, this is my partner, Detective Max Drago. Max, Beth King. Her husband's a friend."

"Pleased to meet you," she murmured before turning to Dan. "Grant and Connor are here, Dan. The kids from the shelter."

"What shelter?" Max asked.

"The Tomorrow Is Mine domestic violence shelter." Dan's face darkened. "Seems like they barely left the place."

"Mrs. King," Max said gently. "There is no one here. Ms. McCormick was transported to the hospital. Jermaine's location is unknown. No one knows where the children are."

"I do." Without hesitation, she sidestepped Dan, assessed the house layout, and strode into the narrow hallway leading to the bedrooms. She walked past the master bedroom into the smaller one. The empty one.

Stubborn, wasn't she? "Ma'am, they're not here."

"Yes, they are." She went to her knees beside the ratty-looking twin bed. After dragging a suitcase out from under the bed, she bent and called, "Hey, guys. It's Beth."

A couple of puppylike squeaks sounded, and two skinny boys squirmed out. Ear-length brown hair, brown eyes, lightly brown skin. He'd guess a Hispanic/Caucasian mix. They hurtled into Beth's arms, almost knocking her over.

"Well, damn," Dan muttered.

"No shit." The uniform had checked the rooms. He and Dan had checked the rooms. But the bed was so fucking low and so packed with shit under it, no one would have fit. No adult.

He should've searched more carefully.

"I'll have children's services meet us at the station." Dan pulled out his cell.

"Mrs. King, how did you know they were there?" Max asked.

"Make it Beth." She had an arm curled around each child, and the boys clung to her so tightly, it was a wonder she could breathe. "They phoned me."

Dan tucked his phone away. "The uniformed officer called for them since the neighbor thought they might be in here."

Worry carved lines into his hard face. "Were they unable to answer? Are they hurt?"

HURT? THE IDEA made Beth freeze. She hadn't even checked. Connor was clinging to her too tightly to dislodge, so she kissed the top of his head and asked Grant, "Are you guys all right, honey?"

Grant nodded and stood up, although he stayed close to her. All seven years independent, he watched the two men with wary eyes. Understandable. The detectives were both over six feet, and Max was as power lifter, muscular as Master Raoul. With jackets off, they had all their police regalia—weapons and badges—on full display.

Actually, even without the gear, Dan was a bit scary with his coldly detached cop-expression. And his new partner was equally intimidating.

"Guys, this is Connor"—she rubbed her cheek on brown hair soft as kitten's fur—"and his brother, Grant."

As he studied the cops, Grant wrapped his hand around her wrist as if to ensure she wouldn't leave them—and her heart hurt for him. Children older than toddlers should be bold little explorers, filled with the courage that came from knowing they were loved and adorable and amazing. This little boy shouldn't be afraid of a couple of detectives.

She squeezed Grant's shoulder. "My boys, meet Detective Sawyer and Detective Drago."

"Decktives?" Connor's head lifted from her shoulder, and he stared at their badges with open fear. "Beff, they're *cops*."

"Yes, they are. But they're also friends of mine. It's okay to talk to them." She tucked him against her side and did the same with Grant, making it clear to everyone they were under her protection. "Don't worry, honey. If they scare you, I'll yell at them."

Dan's mouth quirked. Although the other detective's face rivaled Dan's for hardness, his eyes lit with laughter.

But Connor gasped in unfeigned terror and put his small hand over her mouth. "Shhh. They'll hurt you."

The detectives lost any trace of amusement.

Dan sat down on the bed, instantly appearing less threatening.

Max took two steps back and went down on one knee, resting his forearms on his thigh. Interesting how much his face resembled his cousin's. Both had squared-off chins, sharply carved cheekbones, and straight noses. But Alastair's mother had bequeathed him the chocolate-colored skin, fuller lips, and slight Oriental tilt to his light hazel eyes. Max had sharp blue eyes and light skin, despite an outdoorsman's tan. Alastair moved like a big, lean cat. Max was powerfully muscled—and his rough and tough attitude matched Nolan's.

When Max smiled at her, she had to say both cousins had incredibly gorgeous smiles. "Beth, can you give us a rundown on what you—and they—know?"

"Sure, but there's not much." Snuggling the two boys against her, she hoped the detective proved as nice as his cousin was. "They told me how the paramedics took their mother away and that they were under the bed."

The men stayed silent, probably trying to find a nonthreatening way to ask why the kids hadn't come out before. "How come you hid from the cops, Grant?"

He looked at her as if she were an imbecile. "They take kids away. And don't let them stay together."

"They'd send us to places wiff mean boys and knives, and the boys'd hurts us," Connor confided, his brown eyes earnest.

"If we're not together, I can't watch out for Connor," Grant whispered.

Beth hugged him. *Best big brother ever.* "I can see why you'd worry. But these are good cops. And I won't let anyone split you apart." If Dan and Max couldn't protect the boys, darned if she wouldn't.

"Can you tell us what happened today, guys?" Dan pulled out a notepad.

When Grant didn't speak, Connor said, "We were watching TV, and Mama and Jermaine came home, and they were mad at each other, and then they were mad at us."

"He called us fucking beggars and said we stole food. He hit me." Flushed with anger, Grant touched his bruised cheek and nose. Dried blood still showed on his lip and chin and the stains trailed down the Iron Man T-shirt.

The memory of how much a man's big fist could hurt would never go away completely, Beth knew. She tugged him a little closer.

"Mama called Jermaine a name, and they fighted, and she throwed things." Connor's waving hands showed someone grabbing anything and throwing anywhere.

No wonder the living room was a disaster zone.

"A dish got Connor," Grant said.

Connor craned his neck to look over his shoulder where the back of his shirt was stiff and sticky with blood.

Beth touched the hem. "May I see?" When he nodded, she pulled it up, turning him so the men could see as well. A nasty gash was no longer bleeding, but purple bruises were forming around it.

Fury lit Max's blue gaze, but his tone was mild. "I bet that hurt. Your mom didn't give you a Band-Aid or anything?"

"We ran out the back." Grant's hand clamped down on Beth's. "Did Jermaine hit her 'cause we ran away? Is that why she had to go to the hospital?" His voice shook. "Is it my fault?"

"Oh, no, Grant." Beth shook her head.

"No." Dan's voice deepened. A Shadowlands Master in full

dominant mode sounded much like God. "She wasn't injured, Grant, she was sick. That's why she lost her temper. That's why she went to the hospital."

Sick or overdosed? Crystal meth could be bad if a person had too much. Beth caught Max's gaze and raised her eyebrows. He understood and the grave shake of his head answered her question.

As Beth looked down at the little boys, worry nagged at her. What would happen to them if Drusilla remained in the hospital or rehab for very long?

Chapter Six

WITHIN AN HOUR, Beth sat between the two boys in a small interview room in the Tampa police station.

Fidgeting uneasily, Connor had pulled his chair right next to Beth's. Before leaving the house, she'd used Max's first aid kit to bandage the boy's gashed back, and he was comfortable enough to lean against her, almost in her lap.

Grant had a chair on her left, also pulled as close as it could get. Although the investigator from the Department of Children and Families had shown up, the children weren't about to leave Beth's side.

She couldn't blame them—she wouldn't sit anywhere near Price either. The DCF social worker sat on the other side of the metal table. His unbuttoned suit coat revealed a beer gut, and his light brown hair had been combed over in an unsuccessful attempt to hide a bald pate. The jerk hadn't concealed his boredom as the two detectives quizzed the boys about the day's events.

Arms folded over his chest, Max leaned against a wall. Using a laptop, Dan sat beside Price.

A tug on her arm made her bend down to Connor. He whispered, "I wish Nolanman was here."

Nolanman. The name made her smile. When she'd met the children, she'd called Nolan her *Iron Man*, her hero who'd saved her from a bad guy, and the boys had dubbed him Nolanman. Sir was uneasy with being elevated to hero status, but in her opinion, that was where he belonged.

"Nolan is coming as soon as he can." She'd phoned him before leaving Drusilla's house.

"He needs to hurry," Grant told her solemnly.

"I think we're about done here." Dan pushed the laptop back, then glanced at her and Price. "Do we have a next-of-kin for Drusilla?"

Darn it, Drusilla. Why didn't you stay clean? For the boys' sake, if nothing else. When Price didn't speak up, Beth answered, "According to the shelter records, there are no relatives. Their father died serving in Iraq. Jermaine Hinton moved into the apartment last spring and he was a"—she remembered the children—"wasn't nice to her."

"Why the hell did she go back to him?" Dan asked.

His ruddy face darkening, Price shot Beth a look of dislike. "Mr. Hinton had completed the court-ordered anger management class. Mrs. McCormick felt she and the children would be safe."

"Guess not," Max muttered.

"You ready to take charge of them?" Dan asked Price. "They'll go into foster care?"

The small bodies on each side of Beth went rigid.

"Foster care," Grant whispered with the same terror as he'd uttered cop.

"You'll keep them together, right?" Beth asked quickly. "They need—"

"I will, of course, try." Price's indifferent tone said he wouldn't try. The lazy bum would do whatever came easiest.

Beth hardened her voice. "I want to know you'll do more than just try."

"No need." The deep, rough voice came from the doorway behind her. "Beth and I are licensed." Nolan strode into the room, his black T-shirt, jeans, and work boots covered in dirt.

The boys turned, saw him, and squealed in delight. They hit him so hard he actually rocked back a step.

"Hey, men," he said in his guttural growl that to her always meant safety. The children obviously felt the same. When he went down on one knee, they burrowed against him like puppies.

He winced when Connor's head bumped his shoulder, but being Nolan, he'd push through the pain to give comfort.

As Beth watched, she tried to pull her thoughts into order. Foster care. Why hadn't she remembered that she and Nolan had obtained a foster care license? Would the certification allow them to care for boys who weren't up for adoption?

And…should they? Beth bit her lip. Her heart wanted to take them home, keep them safe, feed them, and give them everything they'd been missing. But Drusilla wouldn't be in the hospital forever and she'd take her boys back. They'd return to a place where they weren't safe, and Beth wouldn't be able to save them.

Max gave her an understanding look and pushed off the wall. "Hey, guys. Come and help me buy some drinks. I think Beth is thirsty."

Two pairs of worried, young eyes studied her. Afraid she'd leave them.

"Nolan and I will be right here when you get back." She made herself smile.

Reassured, the boys took Max's hands. Connor told him solemnly, "Beff always brings us juice. We can get her something this time."

So sweet.

Once they'd left the room, Dan started a low-voiced conversation with Price.

Beth turned to Nolan. "Sir…"

"No reason not to help these two out while we're waiting

for our own, is there?" His dark gaze moved over her face, and understanding filled his eyes. "Ah, that's not what you're worried about. It's because it'll break your heart to give them back. Not be able to keep them safe."

She nodded.

"Can you handle the pain?" His expression didn't change as he rested his hip against the table and waited for her to decide. Not pushing, not ordering. Her Sir, master of patience.

She remembered how Connor's tiny hand had twisted in Nolan's shirt. Holding on. They were terrified of what was to come, where they'd go. Jerkface Price might very well split them up.

She pulled in a slow breath. Losing them after loving them, guarding them, having them close would surely destroy her—and that didn't matter. Not when weighed against the welfare of two little boys. "Yes. We'll take them."

Nolan nodded as if he'd known her answer already.

"I'm sorry, but the children need to be placed quickly." Price's mouth pinched as if he'd sucked on a sour lemon. "I don't have time to review and inspect your home."

"Inspections were done already," Nolan said.

"Nonetheless," Price snapped. "There are procedures, protocols, other—"

"The boys know us," Nolan said. "Placement with us would be in their best interest."

Because of past altercations, Price didn't like her. And one time, Nolan had gotten in his face about not moving faster to help a battered mother, so he didn't like Nolan either. She wasn't surprised he was putting up obstacles.

"I'm sorry, but—" As Price blathered on, Nolan pulled out his cell phone and punched in a number. "Z? Could use your help here."

Beth blinked. *Well.* Master Z—Zachary Grayson, the owner

of the Shadowlands—was an extremely wealthy, child psychologist as well as a powerful force in Tampa. Talk about bringing in the big guns right away. Poor Price had no clue what he was in for.

BETH AND THE children ended up in Dan's office while the war was fought.

Dan set them up with toys and blankets scrounged from somewhere. Max showed up with a bag of fast food and drinks. He told them in his universe, everything got better after a burger and fries.

Now she was sitting on the pile of blankets on the floor with two well-stuffed boys sprawled across her lap. Her feet had fallen asleep, a toy was digging into her hip, and she wouldn't have moved for the world.

If only she knew what was going on…

Then she heard a familiar, smooth, baritone. One that conveyed almost as much safety as her Master's did.

"I appreciate your help, Mrs. Molina." Master Z entered the room accompanied by a short, middle-aged woman in a boxy, magenta suit. Nolan and Dan followed them. Price wasn't in the group, thank goodness.

Z's silvery-gray gaze swept over her and the children. "I see they have piled onto their preferred caregiver, ensuring she won't get away."

The woman beside him lifted her eyebrows. "So they have."

"Up you come, sugar. You need to meet Mrs. Molina." Smiling, Nolan slid the children off and pulled Beth to her feet. As she crossed the room, she heard Connor's piping voice. "Nolanman, we gots toys."

Z said, "Mrs. Molina, this is Beth King, Nolan's wife. Beth, Mrs. Molina is a supervisor with the Department of Children and Families. She came to settle the children's arrangements."

"It's a pleasure to meet you." Beth held her hand out.

"And you. Apparently, you and Mr. King know the children from their stay at Tomorrow Is Mine?" The woman's grip was firm, her brown eyes steady. She glanced at Nolan who'd gone to one knee as Connor showed him their Happy Meals toys before asking Beth, "Did Mr. King have family there? Know one of the clients?"

In other words, how had a man breached the shelter's No Men Allowed rules? "No. My husband is a contractor and helps out with repairs."

Mrs. Molina still appeared puzzled. "A man? But—"

"The shelter was falling down and on the verge of closing when Beth donated the money to keep it open," Master Z said.

His explanation sounded so altruistic, when she thought her reasons had simply been logical. Her very rich, very abusive husband had died without a will, and she'd inherited a wife's share, despite his relatives' attempts to cut her out. Since the money was an ugly reminder of him, she'd enjoyed donating it to domestic violence shelters.

Kyler's family had been appalled.

Z tilted his head. "Both of the Kings help at the shelter. People who know Beth usually wind up volunteering there—and that would include my wife."

Dan snorted. "And mine."

"I...see." Amusement danced in Mrs. Molina's warm brown eyes. "For one woman, you have a most effective—and long reach."

Beth frowned. "Long?"

"Quite. Although I agreed that placing the children with you would be beneficial, obtaining all the required signatures would have been impossible without"—she actually snorted—"the pressure brought to bear from above." Her glance at Z was both annoyed and admiring.

Beth stared at Master Z. "What did you do?"

He gave her a faint smile. "When my influence wasn't enough, I did what any smart man does—I called my mother."

Beth's mouth dropped open. She'd met the terrifyingly rich and refined Madeline Grayson. "You didn't."

"I believe she spoke to the mayor."

"She did," Mrs. Molina said in a dry voice.

Well.

"Tell Madeline thanks." Nolan joined them, Connor securely settled on a hip, Grant beside him.

"Hey, guys, you're going home with us," Beth told the boys.

In response, Connor bounced in Nolan's arms, and Grant curled his arms around Beth's waist.

And Mrs. Molina smiled.

AT HOME, NOLAN helped Grant and Connor out of the social worker's car and made a mental note to pick up child booster seats for his and Beth's vehicles. As the children took his hands and walked with him down the flagstone path, he felt a tightness in his chest. Yeah, he wanted children.

Soon, it'd be their little girl holding his hand. Hopefully, more would follow her.

Meantime, they could give these two waifs a safe home until their mother was well and able to care for them again.

"Here we go, men." Under the portico, he pushed open the front door and heard noises coming from the kitchen. Since he'd held his speed down so Mrs. Molina could follow, Beth was already home.

When the social worker reached the door, he drew the children to one side. "Ladies go through doors first." His pa had been quite firm about how men should treat women and started his sons' lessons right about birth. Nolan agreed.

"Come on in," Beth called from the kitchen. "Would anyone like some water or lemonade or milk?"

As they walked through the great room, the boys stared around with wide eyes.

Nolan considered the Spanish-influenced decor from a child's viewpoint. Boring creamy stucco walls, tan-colored leather furniture, and hardwood flooring. Minus five points. He added two points for the colorful hand-painted tiles over the arched windows, doorways, and stone fireplace. Removed another couple of points since the room was spotless. No toys. No pets.

He frowned at the dark red vases in the recessed niches. Two active boys. Might be time to redecorate for indestructibility. Besides, he had a sudden craving to play catch in the great room.

His lips twitched. Beth would kill him. "I have a hankering for something to drink. How about y'all?"

Grant managed a nod, but Connor's hand was cold and trembling. The mite was scared shitless and no wonder. "C'mere, little man." Nolan picked him up and settled him on one hip as they entered the kitchen. The boy should weigh more, dammit. "Got any good snacks in there, Beth?"

"Sure." She saw the boy on his hip and gave Connor a tender smile. But the sweet look in her eyes was all for Nolan. Fuck, he loved her.

"Let's see." She pulled the cookie jar closer. The big ceramic jar had been a wedding gift from his mother—along with all his favorite cookie recipes. The container had never been empty. "Since Nolan likes sweet snacks, we have cookies in here. Me, I like crunchy snacks, so there are also potato chips. Connor, what would you like?"

Connor buried his head in Nolan's shoulder. Grant was silent.

Mrs. Molina spoke into the silence. "I'd like a cookie,

please."

"You got it." As Nolan and the boys took seats at the kitch-en island, Beth gave Mrs. Molina a cookie and handed one to each boy. "Start with these, and there are more if you're still hungry." She set out cookies on a plate and dumped chips into a bowl as well, setting everything within reach.

The boys got milk. Mrs. Molina chose iced tea.

When Nolan lifted an eyebrow, his underweight, little rabbit dutifully took a cookie and milk for herself.

While the children enjoyed their snacks, the adults worked through a stack of paperwork and another quick evaluation. The children's bedroom was approved. The locked gate in the screened cage enclosing the huge pool got a pleased nod. Nolan had thought the foster care regulations overly strict, but when he remembered his youthful adventures, he realized he'd been wrong. Pools and lakes attracted kids like bees to honey.

Good thing the lake had been fenced off. After an intruder had gained access to a friend's lakeside home by boat, Nolan had installed a perimeter fence and security alarm for his entire property. He wasn't gone often, but his woman should feel safe, no matter what. Now the boys—and eventually their baby girl—would be safe, as well.

"I'm finished here." Mrs. Molina sorted her paperwork. "Depending on how quickly Mrs. McCormick recovers, you might need to make plans for the children to enter school. It starts near the end of August. I think you'll be in kindergarten, Connor?"

The boy returned a silent nod. Pissed Nolan off some. To-day, the words had been scared right out of the talkative kid. From what Dan had said, Drusilla had gone into a tweaker tantrum in front of the kids.

Fuck, what a world.

The boys were making inroads on the food—checking for Beth's approval before each new cookie. She'd quietly kept their glasses of milk filled.

Finally, Mrs. Molina tucked the paperwork into her hefty briefcase and rose. "Beth, Nolan, I'm pleased to have had a chance to meet you both as well as the children."

"What happens next?" Beth asked.

"Mr. Price will call and arrange follow-up visits."

Price, huh? Seeing Beth grimace, Nolan chuckled. Good thing the supervisor had already turned away and didn't notice.

After Mrs. Molina was gone, Beth held out her hands to the boys. "Guys, I put your backpacks in your bedroom. Let's go see about getting your stuff stowed away."

Beth and the cops had filled trash bags and backpacks with the children's possessions. Two garbage bags and two knapsacks sat in the center of the bedroom. Nolan remembered all the shit he'd had as a kid. Ample clothing as well as bats and balls, skates, a bike, footballs, toy soldiers, rockets, planes and trucks, Legos and building toys, coloring books, weird puzzles, picture books. His childhood belongings would have filled a hell of a lot more than a couple of garbage bags.

They should be comfortable in here though. Since his siblings had taken to heart the "be fruitful" command, the big room was already set up for kids. The two queen beds had slept up to six exhausted, small-sized munchkins.

The matching armchairs were upholstered in a sturdy, dark red to match the red-and-white floral bedspreads. A long table and chairs were stationed under the south window. Beneath the other window, white shelves held picture books, puzzles, and a batch of toys left by his nieces and nephews.

Connor and Grant should do well in here. And they'd be together. Dan had mentioned their fear that the cops would separate them and force them into homes filled with knife-wielding, *mean* boys.

A snarl rose in Nolan's throat. Probably Jermaine or even

Drusilla had used the threat to keep the kids isolated and prevent any chance of the police hearing about drugs in the home.

"This is *our* room?" Grant touched the quilt on the bed as if someone would take it away.

Nolan had to clear his throat before he could speak. "Yeah. You can share a bed or not. Up to you." He pointed to the lidless wooden boxes of toys. "Toys to play with, books to read. Go ahead and put your toys on the shelves, if you want."

After another tentative glance at Nolan, Connor took a stuffed animal and a truck out of one pack and set it on the shelf.

Grant had an airplane. And a ball.

That was the totality of their toys.

Seeing Beth's eyes swimming in tears, Nolan motioned her out of the room. "I'm going to take a shower while Beth cooks supper. Can y'all play for a bit in here?"

Two more nods.

He closed the door partway behind him.

When he got into the kitchen, Beth was crying. "It's not fair. They're the sweetest children. They should have everything. Not n-n-nothing." Her voice broke as he pulled her into his arms.

If the lack of toys sent his softhearted submissive into tears, what'd happen when the boys went back to their mother?

There hadn't been any choice of not bringing them home—not for him or Beth—but it would be fucking difficult to see his Beth hurting when the time came to let them go.

"WAIT, CONNOR." GRANT squirmed all the way under the bed, finding plenty of room, although it'd be better if there were boxes and suitcases to hide behind. When he emerged, Connor stood, waiting. Grant checked out the closet next. "This is cool, too." Big enough they could both hide in it if they needed to—

although he didn't like dark rooms much. He came out and saw Connor hadn't moved. "What's wrong?"

"I want to go home."

"Me, too." The funny feeling in his stomach made Grant's eyes burn, and his voice come out all shaky-weird. "We can't. Mama is sick." He rubbed his wet cheeks. "Jermaine is there. I don't want to be there with him. Not without Mama. Do you?"

Connor shook his head hard. "He's mean."

"He's a *douche*."

Hearing the bad word they'd learned at the shelter, Connor giggled.

Relieved, Grant opened the last door. "C'mon."

It was a bathroom…a really cool bathroom. It had *two* sinks so white they were shiny. The shower curtain had bright fish swimming on it. They looked…happy.

"Hey, Grant." Connor pointed to the walls. "We's at the beach."

Grant stared. A big wave split the wall into a sky and ocean. The bottom showed yellow and blue fish in the sea, and the top had clouds in a blue sky. The towels and fuzzy rugs on the floor were the same blue as one of the fish. "It's pretty."

Back in the bedroom, Grant paused to stand at the door and listen to the low voices of Nolanman and Beth. They didn't sound upset or anything. He stood for a minute, letting the sounds of the house wash over him. Quiet…the house was even quieter than home in the early morning before anyone got up.

He could feel Connor right behind him; he'd learned not to back up suddenly. "Let's see what kind of toys are here."

Connor stood for another second, listening. " 'Kay."

Bending over, Grant scoped out the top shelf. "Got lots of books." And puzzles. The wooden boxes on the bottom shelf were even more interesting.

Connor let out a sound, dropped to his knees, and pulled

out a dinosaur. And then another one.

Eyes wide, Grant checked out the next box. A *train* set. Holding his breath, he pulled the box off the shelf. No one yelled at him. He glanced at the door.

"Nolanman said we could," Connor whispered.

A *train*. Grant's fingers shook as he chose pieces of the track and snapped them together. Beside him, Connor was making growling noises for the dinosaur.

More pieces. A whole curve.

Big feet appeared beside the tracks.

Grant froze. The thumping in his chest hurt as he tensed, waiting for the yelling, the blows.

"You got quite a bit done there. Nice work." Nolan squatted down between him and Connor. His black hair was loose and swung forward as he picked up a weird-shaped piece. "This part makes a bridge. Want to put it together?"

Grant stared, unable to talk.

Nolan didn't move. Just waited.

"Say yes, Grant. I want a bridge." Connor waggled the dinosaur.

"Yes," Grant whispered.

"Figured. I always liked the bridges, too." Nolan selected another arched piece and handed both to Grant. "Put those together while I find the braces. Bridges need support so they don't fall down."

After some consideration, Grant got the two pieces snapped together to show when the man looked over.

"Good work. Here's another to add to it."

Connor crawled closer and set a shiny black train engine on the track. "*Choo-choo. Choo-choo.*"

Grant's chest felt all warm as he took the next piece—and his lips curved up in a smile.

Chapter Seven

IN THE MORNING, Beth woke to the lovely scent of coffee. Yawning, she turned over to snuggle against Nolan. But he wasn't in bed, which she should have known if she smelled coffee. She must have slept late. Not a surprise since her sleep had been rather broken up last night.

At bedtime, snuggled down in the same bed, the children had seemed so young, so lost. Exhausted from playing in the pool, they'd fallen asleep before she finished reading the second story. But, walking out of the room, she'd felt as if she'd left her heart behind with them.

All night, she'd worried they might wake up and be afraid and had kept checking on them. Somewhere around four a.m., when she'd started to slide out of bed again, Nolan had growled at her—half-laughing—and gone himself. Returning, he told her if she got up again, he'd spank her. And as long as she was awake, he might as well take advantage of it. He'd fucked her senseless.

Afterward, she'd slept like a log.

Sitting up, she stretched long and hard and smiled at the sounds of giggles from the kitchen.

All her worries seemed to have dissipated—for the moment—like fog on the water. The low rumble of Nolan's laughter joined the children's. Could anything sound lovelier? Obviously, everything was under control. Of course, with her Master in charge, what wasn't?

As she slid her legs out of bed, she realized the coffee scent was so strong because a steaming cup sat on her bedside table…along with two donuts.

Picking up the coffee, she took a sip and sighed happily. "I love you, too, Master."

AFTER BETH HAD eaten breakfast, Nolan spent a few hours at work. He was stuck doing paperwork rather than visiting job sites since he'd promised his worried little submissive that he'd take it easy for another day or so.

He scowled at the piles of paper on his desk. Invoices, orders, and new hires. Jesus, had his office staff saved up this shit for him all summer?

By midafternoon, he'd convinced himself Beth would need backup. When he told his secretary he was leaving, she'd laughed and announced it on the intercom. From the happy screams from down the hall, the front receptionist had won an office pool on how long the boss would last.

Jesus. He pointed a finger at his silver-haired secretary who'd been with him since he started the company. "You are fired."

She only grinned. "Yes, sir. I'll make a note of that."

Shaking his head, he grinned back and headed home.

At home, the house was quiet. While munching a peanut butter cookie, he listened to a message on the blinking answering machine, then headed in search of his young crew.

High shrieks led him to the pool, and he paused to enjoy the sight. Yeah, this was what he'd envisioned when he'd built the pool and patio. The screams of excitement, the trills of laugher, the water fountaining high in the air from a scooped hand.

In short cut-offs and a blue halter-top, Beth was teaching the boys to dog paddle. Excellent.

"Nolanman!" Welcoming cheers and his submissive's happy

smile greeted his arrival.

He sat on the edge, laughing when Connor came over to hug his leg. "Beth, did you go over the safety instructions again?" They'd been too tired last night to listen.

"Yes, Sir." She pointed to the children. "Can you tell him what we covered?"

Grant started. "Never go by ourselves to the swimming pool."

"Or lake," Connor chimed in. "Gotta have a grownup."

"Good." Nolan motioned to the concrete around the pool. "Great place to play tag, isn't it?"

"No," Connor told him, eyes wide. "It's slick and too hard. It's a no-no."

Beth had made a good start. "Good job, men. You learned well."

"Come 'n' play wiff us," Connor invited.

Fucking tempting, but he'd get sucked into playing *toss-the-munchkin-in-the-air*, which was how he ended up overusing his shoulder yesterday. But, damn, when they giggled uncontrollably, it was a fucking kick. "Not this time, but tell you what, when you're done playing, we'll make a run to pick up some fried chicken. Save Beth from having to cook."

She gave him the stare a million mothers had undoubtedly perfected. One that said she knew he was using her as an excuse to indulge in junk food.

He grinned at her. "I'll even fetch someone some extra biscuits."

"Oh, well then." Her gorgeous blue-green eyes lit with humor.

She was something, his woman was. Despite all she'd been through, no matter how many times she was knocked down, she struggled back to her feet. The way she savored life's essentials showed she'd learned what was important. Maybe her gardening career—a life spent tending to beauty and immersed in nature—had given her that resilience. "I almost forgot. You have a message on the machine. Andrea hopes you'll come back to the self-defense class on Monday."

She looked away, pretending to watch the children.

Ah-huh. She'd told him the lessons made her feel more capable and stronger. Why had she quit? When the boys started tussling for the floating ball, he held his hand out. "Come here, pet."

She put her hand in his, but still didn't meet his gaze.

"You enjoyed the lessons. Said they helped," he prompted.

Her sigh was resigned. "I stopped when I was feeling...off...because of the medicines I was taking for the treatment."

His teeth gritted together. She'd gone through hell without him. Yet...since when had Beth let physical weakness slow her down? "And?"

The next answer came slower. "I was having some nightmares, and the class made them worse."

"Because I wasn't home."

Her steady gaze met his. "You can't babysit me all the time."

He could damned well try. "I don't consider being with my wife babysitting." He considered her for a moment. "Since I'm home now, what about returning?"

She glanced at the children. "I think I'm going to be kind of busy."

"I can take a long lunch on Monday."

"Well..." Finally, her nod came, firm and heartening. "Okay. Yes, I'd like to go back."

"Go where?" Grant stopped playing, and worry drew his brows together.

"Fighting class," Nolan said.

Grant's eyes lit. "I can fight." The boy threw a sloppy punch and almost nailed his brother. "I can kick ass."

"I see," Nolan said solemnly. From Beth's concerned frown, he had a feeling the kids would eventually have to curtail their more colorful language. *Hell.* He should, too. "Shall we have our own fighting class while Beth is at hers?"

"What?" His sweet little submissive stared at him in alarm. "You can't teach them to fight. Connor isn't even in school yet."

"Best time to learn. My pa started us off right about his age."

"Beff, we're going to kick Cass." Connor beamed at her before asking Grant, "Who is Cass?"

"Oh my God, I'm outnumbered," she muttered and shot Nolan a glare. "There's way too much testosterone in this house."

Yep. Hell of a deal.

As the kids lunged after a foam noodle, he heard "The Yellow Rose of Texas" wafting from the house. The doorbell. Last month when visiting, his brother had programmed in the tune as a joke, and Nolan hadn't gotten around to changing it. Besides…he'd always liked the song.

"You Texans." Beth snorted. "I guess I should be grateful you don't decorate with dead animals, antlers, and cowboy lamps."

"You are a lucky woman." And he'd make sure she never visited his Uncle Bubba's place. He rose. "I'll get the door. Were we expecting someone?"

"Alastair was going to come over."

Alastair Drago. Now why was the new Shadowlands Master visiting?

He opened the front door to two men. One was a tall black man attired in a button-down, white shirt, and tan slacks. The cavorting puppies on his tie meant he was in need of psychiatric help—or he was a pediatrician. Nolan nodded. "Good to see you, Drago."

"And you, as well." Shifting his doctor's bag to his other hand, Alastair indicated the man in jeans and T-shirt beside him. "I believe you met my cousin Max Drago the other day at the station He works homicide with Dan Sawyer."

"We met." Nolan studied the man as they shook hands. An inch taller than Nolan, thickly muscled, cobalt blue eyes. His military bearing was accompanied by the intense focus of someone who'd learned the need for constant situational awareness. Probably a war vet. "Appreciate your help in the interview room."

"I'm glad you saved them from the dumbass social worker." Max had a firm grip. "Since Alastair was coming, I butted in. I wanted to see how the boys are doing."

"The little men get to you, don't they? Come on in. They're in the pool." Nolan led them through the house, pleased to see scattered toys in the great room. That was the way a living room should look.

Wrapped in beach towels, Beth and the home crew were in chairs on the patio.

"Alastair, it's good to see you." Beth smiled at him before turning to Nolan. "I didn't get a chance to tell you. Z asked him to check the gash on Connor's back."

"Here?" *Why not at the doctor's office?*

"Z said the children would feel more comfortable in a less clinical setting." Noting the boys' wary glances, Alastair took a chair across from Beth and set his bag beside him.

"Why is that cop here?" Grant whispered to Beth with his gaze on Max. "Is he going to take us away?"

"Nah. I'm not here for you guys. Don't even have a weapon." Max nodded toward Alastair. "The doc there is my cousin. After he checks you over, we're headed for the beach to get supper."

When he dropped into a chair, both boys relaxed. "You've got a nice place here, King. I like the lake."

Nolan leaned his shoulder against a pillar. "Me, too. It's quiet, something to be savored after a day at a construction site."

"I bet."

"Nolanman builds houses," Connor announced. "Big ones."

"So I hear." Max raised his eyebrows. "Nolanman? Like Iron Man?"

Connor nodded firmly. "He saves people."

"And he's better than Iron Man, 'cause he doesn't need armor." Grant bounced in his chair, obviously ready for Nolan to start performing incredible feats of rescue.

Jesus.

As the boys regaled Beth and Alastair with their favorite Iron Man scenes, Nolan told Max, "They'll figure out soon enough I'm no superhero."

A corner of Max's mouth lifted. "Maybe. However, I'm still pretty sure my father is close kin to Superman." The laughter died from his eyes. "He had a cancer scare this year. Shocked the hell out of all of us that he really might be mortal. But when the time does come, I figure he'll show me how to pass on with grace and style."

"Mine is like that." In fact, when he had a family, he hoped to be as fine a role model as his pa was. "Although, I wasn't much impressed with his style when he was tanning my ass."

"Same here." Max's hearty laugh caught the attention of the boys, and he said, "I see you've been swimming. Is Red here treating you all right?"

Connor's face screwed up in indignation. "She's not red. She's Beff."

"Ah." The cop smothered a laugh. "I stand corrected. My name is Max." He nodded to his cousin. "And he's Dr. Drago."

Alastair smiled at the boys. "I'm a kid doctor. I hear Connor's back got banged up?"

Grant shifted uneasily. "What are you gonna do?"

"I won't know until I see what's wrong." Alastair motioned to Beth. "Can you and Connor come over here?"

Smart. Best if the big doctor stayed sitting. Since Connor would be standing, he wouldn't feel trapped. And Beth would be right there.

When Beth took Connor's hand and pulled him out of his chair in a matter-of-fact way, he obediently followed. The tyke would probably follow Beth right into hell if need be. Nolan sure as fuck would.

"Let's do it this way." She hugged the boy to her and pushed his towel down to bare his back to the doc.

"Ouch," Alastair said mildly. "You have a nice gash with bruising around it, Connor, but it's healing." He glanced at Beth. "There is no sign of infection. Swimming is fine, for short periods. Stay too long and the scab will become water-logged and scrape off too easily." He caught Connor's over-the-shoulder gaze as he pulled a stethoscope from his bag. "I brought this to prove I'm a doctor. Can I listen to your heart if I let you listen to Grant's?"

Connor studied the device, decided it wasn't a needle, and his lips tilted up. " 'Kay."

"Excellent. Take a big breath."

The doc had some serious kid skills, and the exam—for both boys—went smoothly. Grant even answered questions while Alastair checked his bruised face.

As the doc stowed his medical gear away, Nolan realized Beth had deliberately gone swimming with the boys. They were wearing only shorts, and their battered torsos were easy to assess. The myriad of yellow and purple bruises created a vivid testimony of how they'd lived.

Max's face had gone so deadly that Grant was giving him

worried glances.

Nolan cleared his throat, caught the cop's attention, and nodded toward the boy.

Catching the hint, Max stared at his feet for a second, and when he looked up, all anger had disappeared.

Relaxing, Grant returned his attention to where Alastair and Connor were playing a counting-fingers game.

"Any information you can share about Drusilla?" Nolan asked the cop quietly.

"Not much. Found the boyfriend. According to him and the neighbors, she'd been bingeing on crystal meth since leaving the shelter."

"We heard she's still in a coma," Nolan said.

"True. The docs aren't giving any percentages there. Might still recover, might not. She's all of twenty-seven and could well die of a stroke." Max's mouth twisted sourly. "I hate that fucking drug."

"Yeah." Twenty-seven. After talking with Grant, he knew she'd been a decent mother before life—and meth—twisted her. Now, her sons would live with the ugly memories of her addiction for the rest of their lives. *Dammit.*

"My professional opinion is that you both are healthy lads." Alastair rose and picked up his bag.

"Good to hear," Nolan said.

Alastair nodded. "They need to see a dentist soon. And their immune systems are probably not up to par, so you might have more than the normal number of kid illnesses."

Beth stood and smiled at him. "The house call is very appreciated, Doc."

He looked down at her, the tenderness and worry in his gaze obvious. "You still appear a bit off, love. Don't make me lecture you again. You should pamper yourself as well as your menfolk."

Her lips curved up. "Pamper *myself*? And what kind of Domly advice is that?"

"Mine."

What the fuck? Feeling more than a mite uneasy, Nolan frowned and put an arm around Beth's shoulder in a deliberate claiming gesture. His voice came out cold. "Where did y'all do this...*lecturing*?"

With a frown, Max glanced between them, then walked back to the children. A second later, Connor's giggles were joined by Grant's quieter laugh.

Alastair's puzzled gaze turned toward Beth. "We talked when she was at my house."

His *house*? Nolan stiffened. "When was this, Beth?"

"The day after you came home from Africa. I told you I was seeing him." Beth's eyes narrowed in thought. "I do remember you were half-asleep while I was talking. Maybe you missed it?"

"Missed *what*?"

"I'm doing the landscaping at his house."

Well, fuck. "A client." The new one she'd gotten up early to meet.

She giggled. "Precisely."

"Beth." Alastair's expression was disapproving. "He also asked about the lecture."

Nolan's gut clenched when Beth flushed. But she simply sighed. "The day I met him, I was...unhappy. I'd planned to wait until you were feeling better before telling you about...my summer...but he made me promise not to delay." Beth's face turned redder. "It didn't matter; you dug out the information, anyway."

Nolan's lips twitched. He'd learned early in their relationship that fucking her worked better than any truth serum. And he'd been an idiot. "I see. Okay, then." He met the other Dom's level gaze. "I appreciate your care with my submissive."

Alastair's smile was white in his dark face. "Since you didn't know she's our landscaper, I can understand your concern. I respect how you addressed it immediately."

As they escorted the cousins to the door, Nolan shook his head. Concern be damned—he'd overreacted. Because his first wife had been a liar and a cheat. Apparently, Beth wasn't the only person to have lingering problems bequeathed from an ex-spouse.

Chapter Eight

MONDAY AT NOON, Beth walked out of the hot sun and into the coolness of the martial arts studio. The center of the long room held a few college-aged students counting their push-ups in Japanese. Supervising them, the sensei saw her and gave a formal nod.

When Master Marcus had told the studio's owner about the Shadowkittens teaching themselves self-defense, he'd offered them free space in his dojo—and when he wasn't tied up with his regular classes, he'd assist with theirs. He'd taught them some pretty sneaky moves.

"Hey, it's Beth!" Andrea's voice came from the far side of the dojo. The other three women over there turned and waved.

Beth grinned. It was nice to be back. Carrying her shoes, she walked around the perimeter of the mirror-walled room, inhaling the scents of sweat, the cleansers used on the mats covering the floor, and a hint of sandalwood incense. After tossing her shoes in a cubby, she joined her friends.

"Girl, it's been a long time." Slender, black-haired Kim gave her a hug.

"It really has. I've missed you guys." Beth couldn't stop smiling.

When Andrea leaned down to kiss her cheek, Beth asked, "How go the wedding plans?"

"*Mierda.* The guest count grows bigger and bigger—because *mi abuelita* insists on having everyone she knows, and she knows everyone in Tampa."

"I bet she does." Andrea's tiny grandmother was a force of nature. "You're doomed, honey."

"Oh, I know. We've already had to reserve a larger building for the reception. Cullen says we should fly to Vegas and just '*do it*.'" Andrea's light Spanish accent grew stronger with her obvious exasperation.

"He sounds like Anne. She's been pushing for a quickie ceremony with Ben." Beth looked around. "Where is she, anyway?"

"She was involved in a missing teenager search and couldn't get away," Kim said, "but she'll join us afterward for pizza."

"Oh good." Beth bounced a little. "I want to see the evil Mistress' baby bump."

"She's so cute." With shaggy, strawberry blonde hair and wide, brown eyes, Gabi was Beth's height but much curvier. Perhaps because she was a victim specialist, she gave the warmest hugs. "I'm so glad you're back. And I hear you have changes in your life."

"Oooo, gossip." Sally used her hips to edge Gabi away far enough to give Beth a happy squeeze. "Spit it out."

Before Beth could speak, Gabi said, "We saw Dan and Kari last night and heard that Connor and Grant from the shelter are staying with Beth and Nolan."

"You have the two cuties at your house?" Pulling her brown curly hair up into a twist, Sally tried to talk around the scrunchie in her mouth. "I thought they went home with their mom."

"She's in the hospital. Price said they were searching for relatives."

Andrea shook her head. "Those poor babies. They must be so scared."

"They are. But they're settling in." Beth smiled. "Nolan came home to be with them while I'm here. And since I'm in *fighting* class"—she used air quotes to emphasize the word—"he promised they'd have their own lessons at home. They're thrilled, especially Grant."

"He's quite the little man, isn't he?" Andrea slid down into the splits.

"Oh, he is. Sometimes he acts as if he's Nolan's age." Beth noticed a pretty black woman hovering in the door. "Hey, Uzuri is here. Somebody grab her before she changes her mind." Since the beginning, they'd tried to get her to the self-defense classes, and she'd never come once.

"I'm on it." Sally trotted around the perimeter of the room, avoiding the small class. She latched onto Uzuri's arm and dragged the prankster to the group.

"Uzuri, at last." Gabi hugged her. "I didn't think you'd ever join us. Why'd you finally cave in?"

"Because of Holt." Uzuri pouted. "He's an annoyingly rah-rah Rowdies fan, so I bet him that San Antonio's Scorpions would win the game. Would you believe the Rowdies slaughtered my team last week? Stupid soccer."

"I like that he forced you to be here, though. The new Master is making his influence felt." Andrea waggled her eyebrows. "Is he exerting his efforts in other ways?"

Uzuri's skin darkened with a flush, but she laughed. "No, Ms. Gutter Mind. We're friends—with occasional benefits and scenes—but nothing more. There's no zing. You know, like some guys just...do it for you and make your pulse go rat-a-tat?"

A chorus of agreement came from the other women, who had Doms of their own.

Sally grinned. "Yeah. I've got two of them who do."

"Blondie, I can't even deal with *one* man. Never in a bazillion years, would I sign on for two at once." Seeing the shelves, Uzuri stored her purse and the loose shirt she'd worn over her hot pink tank top. Beth gave her lightweight beige jeggings an admiring look. Trust Uzuri to find awesome workout gear.

"Let's get started so we can get some pizza afterward." Sally pointed at the mat. "Uzuri, stretch out like Beth."

Uzuri sank gracefully down onto a mat and started stretching.

Beside her, Beth pressed her forehead against her knees, feeling the pull in her leg tendons. *Darn it.* She'd lost her bet with Nolan. Last spring, she'd been sure Uzuri and Holt would fall in love. They were so cute, him all biker-tough, tanned, and dark blond, her so stylish, dusky skinned, and black-haired. At the club, Uzuri scened with him all the time. She'd bet Nolan that they'd end up together.

Sir had disagreed. He thought Uzuri scened with Holt because he didn't push her, not because she wanted him as a permanent Dom. And her Master had taken the bet.

Unfortunately, when she'd offered a week of oral sex as the stakes, Sir had laughed, since he could simply say, *"Blowjob, darlin'. Now,"* anytime he wanted. As the loser, she would have to bake two pies every week for a month. So unhealthy. Bad enough she made him cookies all the time. Those, at least, contained oatmeal and nuts. Pies were pure sugar and fat. *Damn sweet-loving Dom.*

"I was rather hoping you and Holt would get together," Gabi told Uzuri. "But I'm glad you and he are on the same page." When Gabi put her palms flat against the floor, her voice grew muffled. "It's not so great if one person is in lust and the other one isn't. I remember when I was head-over-heels for one guy, but he looked at me and saw only the extra ten pounds I can never shed."

Complaints came from the others about the proverbial ten pounds that could never be lost.

Well, at least she didn't have that problem, Beth thought, gripping her ankles. Quite the contrary, which was why Nolan kept pushing food on her. Stretching harder, she stared at her muscular, *bony* thighs. In fact, since he returned home, her Master had been constantly nagging her to eat. Did that mean he didn't like the way she looked? After all, at one time, he'd preferred his women soft and curvy.

Soft and curvy like Alyssa was. Beth's mouth twisted. Yesterday, Alyssa had been at the house for Nolan's therapy, once again when Beth wasn't home.

Had she pressed those big breasts against him? Had he enjoyed it?

No. She was falling into foolish Kyler-induced self-loathing. *Stop.* She'd conquered these self-doubts before. She would again.

As for Alyssa? Nolan hadn't asked her to do therapy; Beth had. His shoulder *was* getting better, so it was a good decision.

Enough angst. Time to kick Cass, as Connor would say. Beth rose. "I'm ready to toss some punches around."

"Over here, Zuri." Andrea pulled her off to one side for beginning lessons while Beth joined the others, working on blocks and kicks.

The blood started to hum nicely in Beth's veins. Grinning, she easily blocked Kim's punch and kicked toward her knee, stopping before she made contact. She'd missed this. Working out with her friends, doing self-defense, made her feel stronger. Braver.

Eventually, though, all of them should work out against guys. Sparring with girlfriends was a lot different from facing down a big guy. When that abuser and his friends had attacked Beth's friends, Uzuri said she'd frozen up completely.

Beth had a feeling she would have done the very same thing.

Chapter Nine

THROUGH HER OPEN door, Beth could hear giggling from downstairs. Candyland had been a hit, and the boys were playing another game while she made phone calls. With a smile, she listened to the private adoption lawyer reiterating how the process would work: A pregnant woman would choose Nolan and Beth out of the pile of prospective parents. They'd cover the woman's bills and hospital fees. Papers would be signed…etc. etc. Lawyers loved all that paperwork, didn't they?

"Thank you," Beth said. "We look forward to hearing from you when there is news."

As she swiped the END CALL, she glanced at the crossed-off numbers on her list. Last night, she and Nolan had seen a baby in the online files, so Beth had called the adoption agency today only to find the newborn already had a waiting list of interested people. Darned if the same wasn't true with every single baby in the Florida system.

She wrote up her notes of the conversations for Nolan and set the pen down. Time for some fun.

Tucking her phone into her back pocket, Beth rose from the desk and frowned at the silence. Facebook had a meme about silent puppies meaning trouble. Over the past week, she'd learned that logic also applied to little boys.

She walked down the stairs and checked the clock. Four p.m. Nolan should be home soon. She needed to get some supper started. This evening, she'd update the scheduling for her clients, including Alastair and Max, and work on a new landscape design for a day spa. Nolan would probably take the boys out for some hide 'n' seek or something.

Juggling work and children made for interesting times. Thank goodness, her job was flexible, and her yard guys had been happy to pick up some extra hours. Nolan had been working shorter days, as well.

But for the joy of having the children around? She wouldn't change a thing.

"Hey, guys." She poked her head into their bedroom. No one there. "Grant? Connor? Where are you?"

No answer.

A quick search showed they weren't in the house.

Frowning, she stepped out onto the covered patio. Empty. No sign of them in the yard. They weren't by the pool or on the dock—which they shouldn't be able to reach anyway. Relieved, she checked her potting shed on the left of the house. No one there. So she crossed to the right.

Voices. In Nolan's workshop.

She opened the door. At the workbench, Connor stood on a small stepladder to be able to see. Grant was pushing a plug into the wall.

It'd turn on the *bandsaw*.

"Stop!"

Grant spun around. Connor tumbled off the ladder onto his butt.

Taking a shaky breath, she told herself to relax. Hopeless. All she could see was her cousin's little finger—missing half because he'd been careless with his bandsaw. Her imagination provided Connor's screams. *God.* She tried to calm herself, and her voice still came out too high and harsh. "You aren't allowed in the workshop without a grownup." She'd told them that when she'd shown them around. "Out."

With a terrified squeak, Connor darted past her. Grant ran after him.

She followed them to the house. *Easy, Beth.* Stay calm. Rational.

Was she supposed to punish them because they'd disobeyed her? *Oh heavens.* Her dad would've swatted her butt, but she'd grown up knowing the rules. What kind of discipline was appropriate when a child was still new to a household? Even a timeout sounded too cruel.

They'd fled to their bedroom and closed the door.

She tapped, waited for a response, and opened the door when she didn't get one.

In the corner, they were using the small table as a barricade. At least they weren't hiding under the bed.

Rather than penning them in, she left the door open and leaned against the wall. "I know the workshop is filled with interesting equipment. But it's not a safe place for children. That's why I asked you to stay out of it."

Connor's chin quivered. His back was to the wall.

She moved forward. "Oh, honey, you're safe. I'm not—"

Grant stepped in front of his brother. "Leave him alone! I won't let you whip him, you-you bitch."

Beth closed her eyes for a second, almost in tears herself. How had this gone so wrong? "Grant, I wouldn't."

"What's up?" The ominous growl came from behind her. Nolan was home. He set a hand on her shoulder. Protectively.

"Don't be mad at them." She blocked him. "Grant's just afraid and is protecting Connor."

"What happened?" His gaze was level.

She didn't answer soon enough, and he turned his attention to the boys. "Grant. What happened?"

Grant's small hands closed into fists. "We went into the workhouse. To play."

"With the equipment?" Nolan's voice darkened.

Grant nodded. But didn't move from in front of his brother. Such a little protector.

"I see." Nolan considered. "Grant, walk with me. Beth, can you talk with Connor?"

"Yes, Sir." Her automatic answer won her a brief tilt of his lips before he motioned to Grant and walked out of the room without waiting. So self-confident. He never doubted someone would obey him.

Grant moved toward the door, although she could see his reluctance. He was afraid to leave Connor with her, and a band of sadness squeezed her chest.

She curled her hand around his arm and slowed him long enough to whisper, "I won't hurt Connor. Honey, I've never whipped anyone in my life, and I'm not going to start now."

When she felt his muscles relax, she kissed the top of his head and nudged him into moving again.

As he disappeared, she took a seat on one bed, studying her bare feet. Giving both of them a chance to calm down.

After a minute, she glanced at Connor. His color had come back. He wasn't flat against the wall. She patted the bed. "C'mon and sit beside me."

Like a terrified kitten, he advanced with tiny, heartbreakingly tentative steps. Then he was on the bed—and didn't run when she carefully tucked an arm around him.

When he leaned against her, her heart started to beat normally. *Oh, Connor.* "I didn't mean to frighten you. I'm sorry, honey." She swallowed. "I got upset because the bandsaw could have hurt you. I was really scared for you."

Eyes the color of dark chocolate went wide. Had any child been more precious? Unable to help herself, she pulled him closer.

"Scared...for me?"

"Yes, for you." She was still shaking, in fact. "Those saws can be dangerous. Let me tell you about my cousin." A story—minus the gruesome details—was the finest way to give a warning and make real the danger.

"Okay." When he rested his little head trustingly against her chest, relief and love tightened her throat so thoroughly she couldn't speak at all.

IN THE GREAT room, Grant saw Nolanman crossing the patio outside. He hurried to catch up.

His stomach felt funny, all shaky, and he wanted to go back to his brother. But Beth had said she wouldn't hurt Connor. She'd said that. And her voice hadn't been loud. Her eyes hadn't been mad...no, she'd almost seemed as if she might cry.

Connor'd be okay.

The air was hot outside and the sun too bright, and Grant's breathing was going all funny, too fast as if he'd been running. But Nolan was mad at him. And Nolan was awful big.

He followed the man down the sidewalk toward the lake. At the fence, Nolan punched in the numbers for the lock, opened the gate, and waited.

Carefully, Grant eased past him, and the gate closed behind them. Nolan walked out on the dock and settled into one of the old wooden chairs. He pointed to the other.

Feeling his chin start to tremble, Grant eyed him.

Nolanman had a hard face, and a big scar down one side. His eyes were black. Not mean like Jermaine's, but not friendly like Beth's, either. Not unless he smiled—or sometimes when he looked like he wanted to laugh but didn't.

He wasn't smiling now. But he wasn't shouting, either. Just...waiting.

Grant edged into the chair and stared at the rough wood of the dock.

At a sound, Grant jumped about a foot, but Nolan was only stretching his long legs out, and with a slow sigh, settling lower in the chair. He was awfully big and had muscles everywhere. Jermaine would look like a…a mouse next to Nolanman.

Grant wanted muscles everywhere.

"Guess you figured out that sneaking into the workshop isn't a great idea." Nolan's voice wasn't mad. It sounded like when he talked about baseball, or how to make a fist, or float in the pool.

Grant opened his mouth. Swallowed. If he spoke, would Nolan get really mad like Jermaine did? Only, sometimes Jermaine got mad even when Grant didn't talk. *"Answer me, you little shit."* Grant gripped the chair arms in case he needed to move quickly.

Nolan eyed him. "The best answer for me—if you agree—is, 'Yes, sir.' If you don't understand, you say, 'I don't understand, sir.'" The long dent in his cheek got deeper, like it did when he didn't quite smile. "I was in the military, so I like a lot of sirs."

Grant sucked in air, like he hadn't taken a breath in a long time. The right words…those were important. To know what to say to keep a grownup from yelling was good. "Yes, sir."

"Very nice."

Grant let go of the chair arms. His fingers hurt, and he opened and closed his hands.

"Later, we'll discuss why I don't want you in the workshop. But first, let's talk about how men treat women in this house."

Huh? Grant frowned and realized he knew the right words. "I don't understand, sir."

"Sometimes a guy loses his temper and shouts at someone. That…happens, although it's not good if you're a lot bigger than the person you're yelling at." A corner of Nolanman's mouth tilted up. "You've got a ways to go before you need worry.

However, no matter your size, I don't want to hear you call any woman a bitch—or any other nasty name."

"But-but Jermaine said it to Mama all the time."

Nolan's mouth flattened. "I bet. But, Grant, did your pa call your mother ugly names?"

Grant blinked. Considered. Shook his head no. Daddy had called her sweet names. *Honey. Sweetheart. Darling.*

"Didn't think so. Even if pissed off, good men—strong men—don't call women nasty names." He paused. "You'd probably rather grow up into a man like your father than an asshole like Jermaine, yeah?"

Grant stared at the wood planks. He'd called Beth a bitch—and sounded like Jermaine. Like *asshole, douche* Jermaine. His daddy wouldn't call Beth a name. Not never. "I want to be like you and Daddy," he whispered.

"Good man."

Fear slid over Grant's skin. Beth probably thought Jermaine was a douche, too. She'd never said anything, but Grant could tell. And just like Jermaine did with Mama, Grant had called Beth a bad name. Would she stop liking him now? His insides felt as if darkness was filling him up. "Will"—he gulped back a sob—"will Beth be mad at me?"

Nolan's dark eyes met his. "Tiger, everyone screws up sooner or later and hurts someone he loves. Time for another lesson." He rose and clapped a hand on Grant's shoulder. "Let's get some lemonade, and we'll talk about the manly art of apologizing to a woman."

Chapter Ten

ON SUNDAY, STORM clouds had rolled in around suppertime and finally rumbled into a pleasant evening rain. As the drops pattered against the roof and window, Beth let herself out of the children's room, closed the door, and indulged in a muscle-easing stretch. Since she'd shifted most of her outdoor work hours to the weekends when Nolan could be home with the kids, she'd spent most of today weeding and planting.

Working on Sundays meant she hadn't been home—*again*—when Alyssa did her therapy visit. The boys had told her how they'd played with their trucks on the patio while the therapist had worked on Nolan's shoulder. Beth huffed a laugh, imagining the lush submissive trying to be seductive with the boys making truck noises a few feet away.

Thanks, guys.

They should sleep well tonight, after a big supper of Nolan's spaghetti, an active game of hide 'n' seek, soapy baths, and story time. They'd conked out halfway through the third picture book.

Tired boys. She smiled slightly. To her surprise, they'd actually been more relaxed since the fiasco of them sneaking into the shop. Maybe because they'd misbehaved and nothing horrible had happened to them. She'd feared that Connor would never trust her again; instead, he'd cried in her arms.

Later, with Nolan beside him, hand on his shoulder, Grant had given her a lovely apology and, chin trembling, whispered, "Don't hate me." When she'd held out her arms, he'd blindly stumbled forward and clung to her, shaking. Hate? Hardly. God, she loved them both.

They were such good boys, and would be good men...if they had someone like Nolan to show them how. Maybe Drusilla would let her and Nolan stay part of their lives?

Heart feeling bruised, she walked into the empty kitchen. The dishwasher was running, and the counters had been wiped down. Nolan must be outside; her Master loved watching the rain.

Quietly, she walked out the French doors to the covered patio, and there he was in a chair, bare feet up on another. The rain-cooled wind whipped at her hair, carrying the faint taste of brine from the Gulf.

He motioned to a well-filled wine glass on the table. "Figured you earned some alcohol. How many stories did you read them?"

"Just two. And a half." She picked up the drink, but frowned at the sandwich beside it. "I hope this is for you. I'm still full from supper."

"You need to eat, sugar. You're still underweight."

"My weight is coming back up." She'd been planning to talk to him about his almost obsessive urging her to eat more. "And I'm not hungry."

"Take a few bites anyway." He shook his head. "I should be horsewhipped for leaving you alone all summer. Fucking stupid of me. I didn't—"

"You did exactly what you were supposed to do." That Sir should feel he'd let her down was intolerable. She worked to keep her voice even. Reasonable. "Raoul asked you to supervise the construction, and it was the right thing to do. They needed you there."

"You needed me here. Protecting you is my—"

"No, Master." His remorse simply broke her heart. She

wouldn't let him feel guilty for being away. Not ever. "I'm not a child. If I have a few nightmares and lose a few pounds, it won't be the first time." Regret lowered her voice. "It won't be the last either." Like with a gravel road, the ruts Kyler's abuse had created in her mind would have to be graded out whenever she had a bad episode.

Nolan leaned his forearms on his thighs and pinned her with a resolute gaze. "I don't think of you as a child, but as your Dom, I have obligations to you."

"Yes, you do. Of course, as your submissive, I have obligations to you, as well. Are you angry with me because I didn't bring you lunch at work on Friday? Or because I was late getting home, and you cooked supper and cleaned up the kitchen afterward? Oh, and you didn't get any sex last night. Should I feel guilty for that?"

His smile flickered before he reached for his beer. "You're so sweet I forget you have a temper that'd put a rodeo bull to shame."

She crossed her arms over her chest. "You, Sir, are evading the issue. I lost weight. You feel guilty. So you're trying to get me to eat. Honey, I'm stronger than you think—and I'd rather you just lose the guilt."

His sexy, rough laugh bounced off the patio walls and rolled out into the night. "Yes, ma'am. I will, ma'am." Filled with his intimidating self-confidence, his deep gravelly voice didn't sound submissive in the least. He held his hand out.

"That's better. Subbie." She haughtily took his hand.

He yanked her right into his lap.

As she curled against him, he was all hardness and heat, his scent compellingly masculine. When he gripped her hair and angled her head to take her mouth, she had no doubt which of them was in charge, no matter how many ma'ams she might hear.

Nevertheless, her Master had listened to her, and if she'd eased a bit of his senseless guilt, she'd call it a win.

Arm supporting her shoulders, he cupped the back of her head, intensifying the kiss, his lips firm, his tongue insistent, a determined assault on her senses. When he growled and tipped her farther, forcing her to depend on him for support, a hum of arousal started low in her pelvis.

Lifting his head, he smiled down at her, undoubtedly knowing her brains had seeped right out of her skull and onto the concrete.

What had they been talking about anyway?

Her hip rested against a wonderfully thick erection. Under her bra, his callused, powerful hand cupped her breast. A shiver ran through her at the dark promise in his eyes. "Master," she whispered.

"Now, about that night of sex I missed…"

Chapter Eleven

O N MONDAY EVENING, the doorbell rang. Perhaps just as well, Nolan thought. Grant was slaughtering him on Xbox to the cheers of Connor *and* Beth. His li'l subbie was going to pay for her disloyalty. Tonight. In a myriad of carnal ways.

Nolan opened the front door, and a wrecking ball flattened his cheerful mood. "Price. What are you doing here?"

"I have bad news for the boys." Price tugged his brown suit-coat straight. "I need to see them."

"What bad news?" Hell. He knew. Every morning, he called the hospital to check on Drusilla. Today, the nurse had warned Drusilla wasn't doing well. He and Beth had discussed taking the kids to say farewell, but seeing their mother comatose, gray-faced, and hooked up to tubes wouldn't be good for the children. Instead, they'd tried to explain how ill she was. "Drusilla?"

"Yes. She died a couple of hours ago." Price glanced at his watch. "I don't have much time before my next appointment."

His next appointment was probably with his supper table. Nolan didn't move. "Can I trust you to break it to them gently, or should Beth and I handle this?"

The asshole's lips thinned. "It's my job."

"Then do your job *carefully*."

By his heightened color, the social worker heard the unspoken threat.

Nolan dumped Price in the formal living room, rounded up

everyone, and tucked the boys between him and Beth on the long couch.

Poor little men. He couldn't imagine a childhood without his mother. She'd cheered her kids through every sport, even while cringing at the football pileups. Admired their art projects and kept the fridge covered with drawings. Helped with their homework, although she sucked at calculus. Cooked the fish and game they caught…if they cleaned it first. Pitched baseballs so well they were never struck out. Endured and babied a true menagerie of pets, including the snakes she feared.

These boys would never have that. Sadness filled him as he slung an arm around Grant's shoulders and tugged him closer.

"Do you guys remember Mr. Price?" Nolan asked. "He's been checking on your mother at the hospital."

The boys nodded.

Seeing Nolan's grim face, Beth closed her eyes for a second, then gently pulled Connor onto her lap.

"I'm sorry to tell you that your mother passed away today," Price said without any build-up. Or emotion.

Sorry, my ass. Nolan's temper surged until he had to grab for control. *No.* This wasn't the appropriate time to beat the crap out of the asshole.

Connor looked up at Beth as he'd been doing more and more when confused. "What's passed? Did she go somewhere?"

"Oh, baby. Remember how we talked about her being ill?" Face soft with compassion, she waited for his nod. "Sometimes when someone is very, very, very sick, her body stops working."

The color faded from Grant's cheeks. "D-did Mama die?"

To hell with treating him like a little man. Nolan scooped the boy onto his lap. "She did. I'm sorry, Grant."

Connor probably didn't know what dying meant either, but he was sensitive to the emotions in the room. His eyes filled with tears. "Does that mean she can't come home?"

"She can't come back to us anymore, honey. Your mama has gone on to the next life and won't be back here. Not ever." Rocking him, Beth kissed the top of his head. "She would never have left you if she'd had a choice."

Connor burst into tears and buried his face in Beth's shirt. On Nolan's lap, Grant was crying silently.

"Well." Price stood. "I need to check their bedroom before I go."

Beth cast him a look of disbelief.

Can't hit him. Best to simply get the asshole gone. Nolan set Grant down next to Beth. When she immediately curved an arm around him, the boy leaned into her, giving her his sorrow.

She was the most comforting person he knew—the children would be all right, exactly where they were. "Let's go, Price."

After Price gave the bedroom a cursory perusal—as if he gave a damn—Nolan escorted him to the front door. "What happens to the children now?"

Price brushed at lint on his jacket sleeve. "We located their grandmother, but haven't talked with her yet. With luck, she'll take guardianship of Grant and Connor."

The boys would go away? "How long will the home studies and background checks take?"

"Not long at all. The process is expedited for near kin. Most of the steps are eliminated."

Nolan stared. "Have the children even met this woman?"

"Doesn't matter." Price shrugged. "I'll be in touch." Without further discussion, he walked to his car.

Frowning, Nolan closed the front door. Dismissing the asshole from his thoughts, he concentrated on more important worries—like where the fuck had Grandma been all this time?

✧ ✧ ✧ ✧ ✧

THAT NIGHT, WITH jagged sorrow filling her chest, Beth tucked the covers around Connor. Her poor, poor babies. Everything inside her wanted to make their hurting stop, to bring their mom back, and there was nothing she could do. How could the world be so cruel to the little innocents?

After the boys had recovered from hearing of their mom's death, she and Nolan had kept them involved in quiet activities—a sunset walk beside the lake to see frogs and tadpoles and then coloring. Connor had asked if he could send his crayon drawing to his mother, and they'd had to explain Drusilla couldn't get mail. The boy still didn't understand exactly what had happened.

Grant hadn't wanted to talk. Not a surprise—he was as reserved as Nolan—but he'd never been farther than a step away from her all night. But she was okay with that. If he needed to, he could stay right there by her side forever. She blinked the tears back.

Oh, Drusilla, why couldn't you have caught a break? Have managed to come back to your babies?

What would happen to the boys now? Would they go to the grandmother Price had mentioned to Nolan? Hopefully, the woman was from their father's side, since Drusilla had been incredibly negative about her mother. A fanatic, she'd called her.

And what if putting them with their grandmother didn't work? After all, they were comfortable with her and Nolan—and, oh, she loved them so much. Maybe…

But this wasn't the time to think about it. "There you go, all snug as a bug in a rug."

Connor's faint giggle was the prettiest thing she'd heard all day.

Gently, she tucked Grant in. Although the boys had chosen separate beds recently, tonight, Connor had crawled in beside his brother.

"Sleep tight, sweeties." She bent to give them squeezes.

Connor, smelling of soap and boy, put an arm around her neck and kissed her cheek. "Night, Beff."

Grant didn't say anything, but his big brown gaze had fastened on her face, and he seemed so lost. Unable to leave him, she sat back down beside him. "Do you know what lullabies are?"

A frown puckered his brow, and he shook his head.

"They're songs that"—mommies—"people sing to children to help them go to sleep. Sleepy time songs." She stroked his hair, still little boy soft. "My M-uh, family used to sing these to me."

Beth's voice was nothing to write home about. On the other hand, neither was Mom's, and her lullabies had eased childish heartaches in an almost miraculous way. *Please, God, let me give my boys the same solace.* "Rock-a-bye, baby…"

Under her hand, Grant's small body slowly relaxed.

Voice quiet, she launched into the next. "Hush, little baby, don't you cry…"

Eyelashes brushed sunburned cheeks.

"Lullaby and good night…"

Connor was sound asleep. Grant's fingers were curled around her wrist.

"Hush little baby, don't say a word…"

Letting her voice trail off, she bent and kissed the sleeping, motherless children. Her heart ached at the telltale wetness on Grant's cheeks. Her own were damp. Dammit, wasn't life supposed to be kinder than this?

The nightlight lit her way to the door where she found Nolan leaning against the frame. His eyes were dark, face gentle. Tucking her against his side, he guided her to the great room…and held her while she cried.

Chapter Twelve

WHEN HE WOKE the next morning, Grant realized his left leg was wet. *Ugh*. Tossing the covers back, he glared at his sleeping brother. "Look what you did."

Connor rubbed his eyes. "Huh?"

"You wet the bed, you little bas-" He broke off, remembering Nolan's talk. Calling names wasn't right. Yet, rage burned like a fire within him. He shoved out of the bed and stomped around the room. "Why didn't you get up?"

Connor hunched into himself until he was a small ball on the bed. "Dunno."

Grant turned away, wishing the...the *brat*...had shouted back. Now the fury inside had nowhere to go, and it rolled around, getting bigger and meaner. There wasn't even anything on the floor to kick.

Was the anger why Mama broke stuff? Because she got all twisted up inside?

Mama.

Grant froze in the center of the room, breathless like when Jermaine'd kicked him in the belly and he hadn't thought he'd ever get air again. Mama wasn't going to shout or scream or break anything. Not anymore. She was *dead*.

Grief filled him again and drained his mad right out, leaving him empty inside. *Mama. Come back, Mama.*

As he saw Connor's white face and red-rimmed eyes, guilt swelled into the hollow places, making them hurt even more. *I'm sorry*. He hadn't protected Mama, hadn't kept her from being with Jermaine or from taking drugs. And he'd yelled at his little brother.

Daddy had told him to take care of Mama and Connor, and he hadn't.

Rubbing his damp eyes, he frowned at the wet bed and Connor's jammies. "We gotta—"

At a tap on the door, Connor grabbed for the covers.

Too late.

Beth stood in the doorway. Silently, she looked at Connor and his wet pajama bottoms and at the soaked bed. And she *snorted*. "Oops. I guess we should've made a trip to the bathroom before bed."

Grant stared. She wasn't mad?

Connor's lower lip quivered. "I'm sorry, Beff."

"No worries. A couple of Nolan's nephews are hit and miss at night, too." She motioned to the bed. "You two strip the mattress down to the plastic cover while I turn on the shower. You'd better have a quick clean-up before getting dressed."

As she walked into the bathroom, Connor stared at Grant with big eyes before tumbling out of the bed.

Together, they stripped the bed.

IN THE KITCHEN, waiting for Beth to rouse the children, Nolan left a message for his secretary that he'd be in late and would leave work early, as well. If having both him and Beth around helped the kids feel more stable, he'd give them that. His staff and crews were getting accustomed to his creative flexing of hours.

Beth was doing her own adjustments, working in the early morning hours before he left and on weekends when he was off. He enjoyed the time with the boys. Hell, the swimming pool had never been so lively.

They'd been playing tag in the pool last weekend when Alyssa had shown up, and no one had wanted to quit while he had his therapy.

His smile faded. Alyssa's behavior was a problem, although easy to identify. Sub frenzy happened when a submissive grew desperate to be dominated. Although more common to newbies, sub frenzy occasionally happened with submissives released from long-term service.

For whatever reason, Alyssa had focused on him as the perfect Dom to handle her needs, and she wasn't listening to reason. He'd explained how her craving to experience submission was fucking up her judgment. He'd been damn clear he was interested in P.T. for his shoulder and nothing more. She wasn't hearing shit. Next session would be the last, and if she didn't listen to him, he'd get Z to chat with her.

The sound of the children's shower broke into his thoughts, and Nolan tilted his head. Odd. The kids usually showered at night.

Not five minutes later, Grant wandered out.

"Mornin', Grant."

Dressed in shorts and a Superman T-shirt, the boy hesitated. Worry darkened his brown eyes. Drawing himself up, he advanced.

Brave little squirt, wasn't he? Nolan tucked an arm around him and pulled him in.

After another hesitation, Grant leaned against his knee.

"What's the trouble, tiger?"

"Nothin'."

"Grant."

He got puppy-dog eyes. "Connor wet the bed. He didn't mean to, he just couldn't…"

Hell, was that all? "It happens." Another shit inequity of life. Not only could women have orgasm after orgasm with no recharging period, but they also stopped wetting the bed a fuck-of-a-lot sooner. When he'd been in the Army Corp of Engineers, he'd known guys who'd *still* had a problem. "Good news is we all outgrow it sooner or later."

Grant's whole body relaxed.

Nolan tapped the thin cheek. "Want to help me make pancakes for breakfast?"

"Really? Pancakes?" His eyes brightened.

"I think we're due."

During breakfast, Nolan studied the kids. Grant's moods were flipping from over-excited to anger to sullen. The little man was trying incredibly hard to be perfect. When he'd poured too much pancake batter into the pan, he'd almost burst into tears.

Perfectionist behavior wasn't uncommon especially in the abused. Beth still occasionally fell into the trap. But he figured Grant was less afraid of being smacked than of being rejected. Thrown away.

Connor, even more sensitive to moods, was clinging, never more than a foot away from Grant. His speech had regressed, the double consonants like "th" disappearing again. A couple of pancakes also disappeared…right into his pocket. Did he subconsciously feel food might be in short supply in the future?

Hell. As if their life hadn't been a mess before, now the boys were completely cast adrift.

Beth, as sensitive as Connor—and for much the same reasons—soothed them without even realizing she was. Hugs and squeezes and pats were dispensed as freely as her smiles and encouragement. When Grant admired the postcards on the fridge door, she'd given him the one with a child standing next to an elephant and handed the lion cub one to Connor, explaining how Nolan had mailed them when he was far away.

Despite the sadness of the day, Nolan enjoyed seeing his little submissive at work. Beth could probably draw the sun out of hiding on an overcast day...because she cared.

She'd be damned wonderful with a new baby.

Having given the kitchen clock a confused study, Grant turned. "Nolanman? Are you gonna work today?"

"Yep. But I felt like having breakfast with y'all. I'm going in a tad bit late."

The sweet smiles from both boys made his heart ache. Good kids. Fine boys. Simply needed some care and attention and they'd be wonderful men. Would they get that care and attention? Could he stand to see them passed around like unwanted kittens?

Nolan eyed Beth. When they'd talked about preferences, she'd said she wanted to start with a baby. But...how old could a *baby* be? Connor would turn five this month. Was that too old?

Chapter Thirteen

ON SATURDAY, BETH turned the air-conditioning up in her truck. Her last client's home didn't have trees tall enough for shade yet, and all the ice had melted in her cooler. *Warm iced tea? Meh.* As long as she was so close to home, she might as well restock and grab lunch before beginning the afternoon.

Besides, she wanted to see how the children were doing. Connor had finally relaxed again and wasn't sticking to Grant like glue. After three nights of bed-wetting, he'd been dry the last two.

Grant, though… His emotions were still pretty volatile. His efforts to be grown up and brave simply broke her heart.

As she walked in the front door, the boys' voices came from the great room.

"Hey, we gots a cop house…Max can work there."

"Yeah. The bridge should have trees.. Put trees right here, Connor."

A train set in the great room, hmm? Well, they'd have more space, and the tile flooring would provide a better surface. Amusement tilted her lips up. And Nolan would play with them. It was a kick to see her so-serious Master on the floor, building whatever the guys decided they needed.

"Beff!" Connor dashed over, followed by Grant. They hit her like small bullets. She couldn't stop smiling. Was there anything nicer than little-boy hugs?

"Beff, we gots a town." Connor pulled her to the construction area where train tracks made a graceful, although incomplete, figure eight.

"You've done a wonderful job," she said sincerely. They were amazingly smart. "Is that a town?" She motioned toward the police station. Next to it, a post office sprouted a tiny flag.

"Uh-huh. Grant's making a bridge there." Connor pointed to the gap, and Grant's tiny chest expanded.

"It's going to be a beautiful bridge." She glanced around. Odd that Sir wasn't here. "Where's Nolan?"

"He's lying down with the lady," Grant said.

"What? *What* lady?" The sharp stab of shock faded when Beth realized the lady was probably Alyssa. Nolan had mentioned the therapist had asked to move the appointment to Saturday—today. "You mean the one who helps him with his sore shoulder?"

A nod from Grant confirmed.

"Can we have a cookie and milk?" Connor asked.

Grinning, she bent and patted his leg, tilting her head to listen.

"Whatcha doing, Beff?"

"Trying to see where you put all this food. Is your leg hollow?"

The ripple of giggles from both boys made her laugh. "Cookies are probably fine, but let me check with the boss first." After a couple of mistakes, she and Nolan had learned to see if the other adult had already told the children no. "I'll be right back." She started toward the patio.

"The lady said it was too hot outside, so they're back there." Grant waved at the hallway.

Oh, really. The temperature was cooler today than it had been for a month. Beth turned. They must be in the small living room. The very *private* living room. Why did the realization set her teeth on edge?

Well, if she were going to interrupt, she'd do it the right way, Beth decided. Maybe she wasn't from the south, but Kim and Gabi had taught her it was mandatory to serve food and beverages to guests. She'd hate to break some Southern law of hospitality, right?

A detour to the kitchen provided a tray with cookies and iced tea. In the hallway, she frowned at the living room. The semi-closed door practically begged to be kicked open hard enough to bang on the wall.

Bad Beth. Abrupt entrances weren't polite Southern behavior. *Bless my fucking heart.*

Through the narrow opening, she could see Nolan, shirtless, and lying face down on the couch. Seated on the ottoman, Alyssa was attired in a low-cut, red tank top and exceptionally short shorts. Her gaze held open lust as she massaged oil into his hard-contoured back. "I missed you at the club last weekend," she said in a silky voice. "I was hoping you'd—"

"Hey, people." Beth shoved the door wide open with her hip. "Are you ready for something to drink?" Nolan wouldn't cheat on her, not ever. Yet, the sick feeling in her stomach was surely jealousy. Maybe because she could see the desire in Alyssa's face.

"Why, how nice." Alyssa's sugared tone made Beth's palm tingle with the need for a good bitch-slap. "You even brought cookies."

"Beth makes great cookies." Nolan pushed up to sit on the couch and smiled at her. "Thank you, sugar."

"Yes, thank you," Alyssa echoed.

"You're so very welcome," Beth said in such a sweet voice that Nolan's eyes narrowed. "Just a little something to show how much I appreciate your efforts to get my husband's shoulder back in shape. I'm afraid he's overdoing when playing with the children."

"I'm sure Master Nolan is excellent with those poor orphans." Alyssa ignored the cookies and picked up a glass.

Beth's lips turned up as Nolan took a cookie. "He totally is."

Alyssa gave Nolan an intimate smile. "When I came here, *before*, you said you built this huge house for a large family. So when are you having children of your own? I bet you can't wait to have a little boy with your gorgeous black eyes."

The words hit Beth hard, like a heavy ice-filled sleet, crushing brittle emotions to the ground. Her shaky inhalation pulled in air filled with Alyssa's musky perfume. "We are—"

"It won't take us long to fill the house with children," Nolan stated firmly.

"Of course." Pursing her pillowy lips, Alyssa laid her hand on Nolan's forearm and gazed up into his eyes. "Someday, I hope to have a Dom so I can give him beautiful babies. So he can see his babies growing inside me." The way her gaze slid to Beth showed she *knew* Beth wasn't able to carry Nolan's children.

Was this what a weed felt like when pulled out of the ground—roots tearing and stem breaking? Alyssa was beautiful. Lush. Fertile. She could give Sir everything Beth couldn't.

Nolan said something that disappeared into the cold fog filling her head. Blinking hard, she took a step back. "Enjoy the cookies. I n-need to get back to work." Turning, she bumped into Grant and Connor who'd arrived in time to block the doorway. Giving them a wavering smile, she edged past and escaped.

✧ ✧ ✧ ✧ ✧

GRANT TURNED AND stared as Beth hurried down the hall. Her voice had been funny, and her eyes were all wet. She was *crying*.

His hands closed into fists. The therapist lady had hurt Beth's feelings. Made her feel bad. He wasn't sure how, but he knew a mean voice when he heard one.

Just like he knew when Nolan was angry.

"We're done here." Nolanman was on his feet, and his face was pissed-off as he stared down at the lady.

"But, Sir." When she tried to grab Nolanman's hand, he stepped away. "You don't understand."

Connor pushed past Grant. "You made Beff cry!"

The lady glared at him. "Why, I did *not*."

Anger swelled inside Grant, red and thick and hot. She *lied*. "Did, too. You're mean. Get out of here, and don't come back."

Her eyes went squinty mad. "Go play in your room. I'm talking to Nolan."

He could still see Beth's tears, and his voice came out all shrill and loud. "*You* go. Go *away!*" He picked up the cookie plate and threw it hard. But the dish went over her head and hit the window.

Crash. Glass flew everywhere.

As the roaring in his ears faded, Grant stared at the shattered window. At the glass glinting all over the carpet. His stomach clenched. He'd busted the window. He'd gone crazy-mad and yelled and thrown things just like *Mama*.

He'd tried to hurt the lady. And Nolan looked really mad.

Fear wrapped around his chest until he couldn't breathe. With a low whine, he darted out of the room and down the hall.

JESUS FUCK. MISSING his grab for Grant, Nolan secured Connor with a hand on his shoulder. *What a fucking mess.*

Alyssa's expression held shock.

He gave her a level stare. "The boys told the truth. Your words were fucking cruel."

"He-he threw a plate at me!"

"He was defending the sweetest woman in the world. And

you made her cry." Nolan gave Connor's shoulder a squeeze. "Perhaps the guys went about it the wrong way, but I'm proud of them both."

The trembling under his hand stopped. Brown eyes stared up at him in wonder.

"I-I'm sorry, Sir." Alyssa's eyes filled with tears. "I guess I was... I miss you, Sir. And I remember how good we were together, and—"

"I appreciate the therapy you did." He kept his voice even. "But, as I told you earlier, my shoulder is fine now. I want you to talk with Z about getting help for what we discussed earlier. Let me see you to the door."

She stared at him as if she couldn't believe he was serious. "But... Yes, Sir."

After he got her out of the house, he asked Connor to play in the great room, sweetening the deal with a couple of cookies. He also had to promise he wouldn't be "mean" to Grant. Loyal brothers; he liked that.

Finally, he hunted for Grant. He hadn't heard the back door open or shut. The deadbolt on the front was locked. The boy was still in the house.

When in trouble as a kid, Nolan would take refuge in his bedroom. But the boys' room was empty. No one in the closet or the bath. Remembering what Beth had said, Nolan checked under the bed.

Grant was curled into a ball in the far corner, tears on his cheeks. Shivers shook his small body.

Hell. And hell was what the kid had lived through with a drug-addicted mother and her abusive boyfriend. Pity twisted Nolan's heart as he sat back and leaned against the nightstand. "Alyssa's gone and won't be back. You and Connor were right. What Alyssa said was mean, and it made Beth cry."

Silence.

He knew exactly why the boys had reacted so angrily. Seeing Beth cry…hurt. And he wanted to go after her right now. But he had his work cut out for him here.

More silence.

Nolan shook his head. *Dammit.* Pretty speeches were his submissive's strength, not his. "As the men in the house, it's our job to keep Beth safe and try to make her happy."

Still silence.

Absently, he considered the picture of flowers on the wall. Nice and generic, but his guys would probably prefer something more interesting. Trains or football. "You did good defending her. Both of you. Your mistake was in throwing the plate." He scratched his cheek. "It's against the guy code to hurt women"—unless they were into it—"so it's good your aim was off."

"Are you mad at me?" The whisper was so low he almost couldn't hear it.

"Nope." He considered the picture again. Yeah, it definitely had to go. Beth should buy more masculine bedspreads, too. "Actually, I'm fucking proud of you and Connor for standing up for Beth. You showed real courage."

A rustling sound came from under the bed. "I didn't mean to hurt the therapist lady. I was…mad."

"Yep. It'll take work to get your temper under control. I had one, too, and I did some stupid shit when I was your age." And he hadn't had the excuse of having crappy examples of how to behave.

Grant crawled out from under the bed. "I busted the window." Tears had left streaks on his cheeks, but he was on his feet and facing Nolan. Like a man.

Pride clogged Nolan's throat. "Guess you'd better help me fix it then."

A second later, he had his arms full of boy.

Chapter Fourteen

THAT NIGHT, BETH hesitated at the door of the Shadowlands. Turning, she stared back at the long, curving drive lined by stately palms. Sunset threw darkness into the contours of the land and gilded the stones of the three-story mansion.

This wasn't exactly the place she'd have chosen to talk with Nolan.

His text hadn't invited discussion. *The Shadowlands. Nine tonight. Kids are going to Dan's. Ben will have your clothes.* Was he angry with her?

Probably...not. She hadn't been rude, merely fled the house like the rabbit he called her. Humiliation washed over her.

Her afternoon hadn't been pleasant—and many weeds had died as she'd worked out her frustration and hurt and anger. She felt so petty to be jealous of Alyssa. To want to be lusher and more like what she knew Nolan liked.

She bit her lip, wondering what he'd planned for tonight. Maybe she could ask him for a quiet chat before the scene? Because...she needed to woman-up. She'd been an idiot and a wuss.

With a sigh, she grasped the heavy wrought iron handle, yanked open the door, and entered.

"If it isn't little Beth." The giant security guard's pleased greeting made her feel better.

"Hey, Ben. How is Anne doing? Is she enjoying working for Galen?"

"Yeah, she loves it. I swear, listening to the two of them—and Sally—could make a guy paranoid. Never knew there were so many ways to spy on a person."

Beth snorted. "Sounds like the beginning of a joke doesn't it? An ex-Fed, an ex-PI, and a hacker walk into a bar…"

"No shit." His rough laugh almost matched Sir's. "Hey, Nolan left a bag for you. Some clothes." He reached under his big desk and drew out a backpack.

"Right. Guess I'd better get dressed." She bit her lip. How angry was her Master?

"Relax. He didn't act pissed-off." Ben gave her a sympathetic smile before motioning toward the locker room. "Get moving now."

A few minutes later, dressed in a boring brown leather skirt and matching halter-top, she walked into the main clubroom. Eyes peeled for Nolan, she crossed to the bar where Master Cullen was serving up drinks, mostly nonalcoholic this early in the evening. Hard drinks were usually a treat indulged in after playtime.

The huge bartender regarded her with a smile. "You're looking healthier, love. Your Master is setting up near the back." He waved his hand, indicating the left rear of the room.

"Thank you, Sir." Without stopping, she headed that direction. As the sounds and scents of the club filled the air around her, she felt the familiar sinking sensation, a combination of excitement and submission as her body and mind prepared her for what was to come.

"Hey, girlfriend." Rainie, resplendent in a bright blue corset that made the most of her abundant curves and highlighted her flower tats, was sitting on a couch beside Master Jake. Without waiting for her Dom's permission, she jumped up to hug Beth. "I've missed seeing you here. Now Master Nolan is back, you'll be in more often, right?"

"I… Probably." If the boys left, she and Nolan wouldn't stay at home as much. Her heart ached at the thought and even more at the thought of the boys facing another unfamiliar house and people. If there weren't any relatives, maybe…would Nolan, maybe, change his mind about adopting a girl first? She put the thought to one side to consider later. "But we're hoping to adopt one of these days."

"So Sally said." Rainie grinned—because Sally was the acknowledged queen of gossip. "Some kid will win the jackpot with you and Nolan as parents." The sincerity in her voice couldn't be doubted.

Rainie got a hard hug. "I totally needed to hear that right now. Thank you."

"Beth. Heads-up, pet." Master Jake pointed toward a nearby scene area. "You should get over there before someone loses patience."

Nolan was at the "spider web," a shoulder-high bondage device resembling a massive hula-hoop filled with intricate rope webbing. Sir's arms were crossed over his chest. He didn't appear happy.

"Oh boy," she said under her breath and heard Jake chuckle.

As she hurried up to her Master, the flutters in her stomach felt like frantic butterflies in a tropical storm. "I'm sorry, Master. Am I late?"

"No, sugar." His features gentled. "Come and give me a hug before we get started."

Oh, she needed his hug really badly. His arms closed around her, pulling her close, and she melted against him. When she'd first met him—this dark Dom with a cruel, scarred face—his big size and muscular body had seemed a terrifying threat. And now? He was still dangerous, no doubt about it, but he was *her* dangerous Dom.

After not nearly enough time, he stepped back and gripped

her shoulders, holding her still as he studied her for a long, uncomfortable moment. "You were crying when you left. And you didn't answer your phone."

She swallowed. "I'm sorry about the way I acted, Sir. I was just having an"—she waved her hand in the air—"an emotion attack."

"Were you now?" Nolan put a finger under her chin and lifted, forcing her to meet his razor-sharp gaze. "Sugar, I've made some mistakes over the summer. Starting with leaving you—although I've already been scolded by my submissive for feeling guilty." His hint of amusement disappeared under determination. "I'd thought the violence at Anne's house was still bothering you, only to learn about the hormone treatments' failure. Today, I figured Alyssa's bullshit about adoption was what upset you, only I'm gettin' the feeling I'm off base again. Not being able to get pregnant will probably always grieve you, but did you have another reason you ran?"

Reluctantly, she nodded. Honesty—this damn honesty was awful hard, especially when her reasons were so ridiculous. Surely, a woman should be past having self-image problems by her age. God, she was such a loser.

"Tell me why."

Her mouth opened, but...what could she say? *Hey, Sir, do you still love me even though I'm way too skinny and have no breasts to speak of?* He did love her. This insecurity had no basis in reality and was her problem. "Honestly, it's nothing you have to handle. It's something...personal and is my responsibility to deal with and nothing we need to discuss."

"I see you believe that." She felt a moment of hope until a corner of his mouth lifted and he added, "But I don't agree." His hand tangled in her hair and fisted, trapping her, sending a shiver of need up her center. "Do you trust me, Beth?"

Her answer was instinctual. "Of course." She did, to the

bottom of her soul.

"That's good, sugar, because I'm going to push you."

She stared up at him as her legs started to tremble. His jaw was hard. Not angry—but with determination. Oh God, what had she let loose?

"Strip down, sugar. The clothing I picked out should be quick and easy to remove."

He had chosen boring fetwear because it was easy to take off? Such a guy. "Yes, Sir."

"Good answer. High protocol begins now."

High protocol. Obedience, respect, silence. "Yes, Master." She remembered the first time he'd demanded it, right after they met.

"If I institute high protocol, you will keep your eyes lowered and speak only when permitted. However, during a scene, I want your eyes on me." He tilted her chin up, met her eyes in a look that seared straight down to her toes. "You have pretty eyes, Elizabeth. Keep them on me."

Did he have any idea how much that compliment had meant to her?

Head bowed, she removed her short leather skirt and top, folded the garments, and set them beside his leather bag. Quietly, she knelt to one side of the scene area.

She studied him as he finished setting up. His long, straight hair was pulled back in a tie. He wore his usual Dom clothes— sleeveless, black muscle shirt, black leather pants, black boots. He could still make her mouth go dry.

He glanced over at her, and warmth lit his dark eyes, making her flush. "Very nice. I like you naked and kneeling." After pulling a wheeled table into the area, he laid out rolls of short, transparent cling wrap.

Alarm took big bites out of her calm. Cling wrap? The stuff was used for mummification. He'd never done that to her—and she didn't want him to now.

He cleared his throat, and her gaze shot to his stern face. *Oops.* She lowered her head and stared at the floor.

The minutes passed too slowly. She could feel each beat of her heart, each too-rapid breath. The music of Bella Morte, "Where Shadows Lie" made it worse. Cries of pain from the adjacent scene area and the sobbing of a slave in a cage ramped her anxiety higher.

"Beth, come here."

Almost relieved to begin—and still terrified—she approached.

"I'm going to wrap you in this." He indicated the transparent film. "Head to toe, except for your nose and mouth." She opened her mouth to protest, but he continued. "You like tight, rope bondage, darlin'. This is just the next level up."

But, but, but. He was right. *But, but, but…*

He was waiting for her response.

She gave him a jerky nod.

Pulling her forward, he caressed her cheek. "I know you're scared, but a lot of submissives love mummification. It can be very calming."

She'd say he was full of it, but being bound in his ropes sent her to the most tranquil place in the world, and he knew it. A resigned sigh escaped her.

His lips curved. "Good girl."

How come, even after being married two years, his approval still filled her with fresh joy?

After backing her closer to the spider web, he wrapped cling around each arm and leg individually. Although the mummification kink had become fairly popular, it had always creeped her out. She even avoided watching those scenes.

Now she regretted her lack of knowledge.

Then he started at her head, beginning the process of turning her into a transparent mummy. At her shoulders, he paused.

"Take a deep breath and hold it." As she inhaled, he positioned thick cardboard circles over each nipple and cling-wrapped her chest, pinning her arms to her sides. Layer after layer went around her until the binding sensation was like a corset. Slowly, he moved downward.

When she swayed, he leaned her against the spider web, which was tilted slightly backward to take her weight.

She tried to help, but couldn't move her arms or hands or anything. There was no…give. Her mouth was so dry she could hardly swallow.

After a moment, she realized he was watching her, silently. Monitoring her reactions.

Okay. Okay. She pulled in a breath and forced herself to relax.

He brushed a kiss over her lips and continued.

Another cardboard piece went over her crotch—and, knowing her Master, it wasn't to hide her private parts.

Towels between her knees and ankles padded the bones as he enclosed her from her waist down to her feet. And then he tied her to the spider web and tilted it back to a forty-five degree angle, so it supported most of her weight.

Bracing a hand on the web beside her head, he leaned in close. His perceptive eyes were darker than a moonless night. "You doing all right, sugar?"

She couldn't even nod. "Yes, Master," she whispered.

"Good enough. Some people spend hours in this, but this first time, you get no more than thirty minutes. I won't leave you, Beth."

Okay, she could do this. Half an hour. That was nothing.

Her poise disappeared when he blindfolded her and added more cling wrap around her head.

"Hey, no, wait." Her arms jerked, testing the limits, telling her she could do nothing. "*Yellow.*"

"Shhh, baby. Take a slow breath. Breathe, Beth. I'm right here." His low gravelly voice was a lifeline of safety, even if he was the one who'd done this to her.

A long inhalation brought her his soap-clean, masculine scent. He squeezed her shoulder. Staying close. She couldn't do…anything…and she was safe.

Something inside her gave up, and her muscles went lax all at once.

"There we go," he murmured and put something over her ears—noise-reducing headphones.

He must have left her ears uncovered so he could reassure her during the preparations. Now the music and noise of the Shadowlands faded to a low murmur, quieter than the internal sound of her pulse.

Slowly, the wrap began to seem less binding and more like a warm, secure hug. There was no sensation on her skin. There was no noise. There was no light. She felt as if she were eternally falling backward. Floating. Rocking in a dark ocean.

NOLAN WATCHED HER go under, pleased to see the tense muscles around her mouth go slack. Gradually, all of her relaxed. Yeah, he'd had a feeling she'd enjoy this. Mummification often sent submissives into a unique kind of subspace akin to the one many rope bunnies achieved.

With luck, being in subspace would lower her defenses far enough she'd tell him what was troubling her. After they talked, he'd play with her a bit. Or not. His goal for this scene wasn't for sex, but for understanding.

In his own focused space, he monitored her breathing, her color, and her faint movements. Minute by minute ticked by.

When the time was up, he brushed his fingers over her lips, bringing her back up slowly, one sensation at a time. The sense of feeling came first. Her tongue ran over her lips, and he leaned forward for a kiss.

Then he removed the headphones so she could hear him. From the slackness of her muscles, he knew she was still more in la-la land than out. Right where he wanted her. He'd like to see her eyes, but she might be more forthcoming if she couldn't view the world.

"Beautiful Beth. I love you," he said.

"Love you." Her words slurred together.

"You were upset today. Because of Alyssa. Part of it was because she talked about our adopting, right?"

Her lips pursed slightly. "Yes?"

More of a question than an answer. "Was there any other reason?"

"Mmm. Pretty. She's so pretty."

What? Nolan leaned in closer. "*You're* pretty, sugar."

Her mouth tipped down. "Skinny. Scr-scr-scrawny. No tits."

"Oh, you have breasts." Ones he wanted to get his hands on, in fact.

"Sir likes big breasts." Her lips trembled. "Likes curves. Soft."

Oh. Fuck. He closed his eyes for a second. *Should have guessed that one, King.* He could actually see how she'd arrived at such a damn fool worry. Knowing the way the submissives gossiped, Beth had undoubtedly learned all his past lovers had been exceptionally well endowed rather than willowy.

His Beth was usually a confident, happy woman, but sometimes, her asshole ex's programming caught hold. What with finding out she couldn't bear children, of course, she'd fall victim to old fears. To top it off, when she'd lost weight, he'd gone overboard with pushing food on her.

In her head, she'd undoubtedly twisted his concern into him disliking her appearance.

Well, hell. He kept his fingers brushing over her lips to help her remember she wasn't alone.

She was deep in subspace, and her defenses were down. Could he make a start at fixing this self-image problem now?

Nolan frowned. He often told her how beautiful she was. Didn't it suck that humans remembered insults far better than praise? As the years passed, his approval would outweigh the ex's derogatory comments. Trouble was, she needed help now.

What would tip the balance? A wealth of compliments? But if his pleasure in her body hadn't weighed heavily enough, maybe...

At the spot where cardboard shielded her nipple, he gashed the cling wrap so he could use bandage scissors to cut a circle out and expose her entire right breast.

Her skin gleamed with sweat, and her nipple contracted with the cooler air.

WRAPPED, TRAPPED, ALL her senses dulled, Beth gasped at the sudden wash of cool air over one breast. Some of the fog lifted from her brain, and she realized Sir was tugging on the clear film. Jostling her. And then her other breast was exposed. The nipple tightened painfully.

She was a mummy...in transparent film...with exposed breasts. The knowledge floated through her mind, not important enough to worry about. She couldn't do anything about anything. And her Master was here. Everything was all right.

He touched her, warming her breast with one big hand, plucking the nipple, and drawing it out.

Long, sizzling surges zipped to her groin, and she tried to squirm and couldn't. Couldn't lift her arms. Couldn't move...at all. A whimper escaped her. Her breasts were naked—available—and she couldn't prevent anything. Lava pooled in her center.

Nolan fondled her casually. "I love these beauties. Love the size, the tenderness, how they sit up on your rib cage—as if begging to be played with."

"But." She stopped as her head cleared slightly. No, she didn't want to tell him that he liked bigger breasts.

"You know, I dreamed of sucking on these when I was gone." His chuckle was dark and sexy. "Jacked off to the thought of you every night."

"Really?" She heard the note of hope in her voice and cringed. "You don't want me to be bigger?"

He snorted. "I'm a man. You have breasts. If I can play with them, suck on them, I'm happy. And when playing with them turns you on as if I flipped a switch? I love it." Obviously to illustrate, he ran his tongue around one nipple.

She dampened immediately.

His blunt declaration almost...almost made her believe. But as he said, he was a man. Men always liked bigger breasts. Didn't they?

His hands abandoned her breasts. "Got one more place to open up."

She felt a tugging at her groin, and air brushed over her naked, wet pussy. The feeling of coolness after the sweltering heat startled her, and she gasped.

He made a rumbling sound of approval. "You're drenched already, sugar. Very nice." After teasing the slick surface of her shaved labia, he pressed one finger between her folds. Her thighs were still tightly bound together by the cling. Only the front of her pussy—and her clit—was accessible.

He found it easily and rubbed lightly, up one side and down the other. Her attempts at wiggling grew more intense, but he didn't stop.

"Master..." Her moan of protest, of arousal made him laugh.

"Shhh, Beth."

She tried, but when he stopped, she actually whined. "Nooo."

"Uh-uh, little rabbit. High protocol, remember?"

She hadn't, exactly. With an effort, she compressed her lips. The exposure of only her breasts and pussy heightened her arousal, as if her buried nerves had to funnel everything through those three bare circles. *Please, let him release me so we can really play.*

"My plan was to take you down and fuck you at this point, but since you don't believe me about how gorgeous your body is—especially your breasts—I'll have to ask for help."

"What?" Her shocked question earned a stinging slap right on her clit. The brief pain and intense sensation rang through her like a bell of need.

But—ask for help? He wouldn't.

Under the harsh electrobeat of Virtual Embrace, she heard murmurs. Laughter. Nolan's voice and others. Male voices.

Someone touched her breasts. Lean hands. Not Nolan's.

She tried to stiffen, to pull back, but nothing moved—and her breasts were right out there, poking through the cling wrap.

The Dom caressed her and teased her nipples to hard, aching points. "I've admired these beauties for years, King. Appreciate you letting me play. They're as delightful as I figured they'd be." With a farewell pat to her tightly peaked nipples, he disappeared.

"Nice." A different, familiar voice, one low and gruff. Who? Why couldn't she think? His touch was rougher than the last man's. He cupped her breasts with both hands as his thumbs circled her nipples. "This is my favorite size, the perfect handful, and damned responsive. You're a lucky bastard."

"Gotta agree with you there," Sir said. When the Dom moved away, Master Nolan touched her cheek. "Let's make sure you're awake, why don't we?" A humming sounded, and a vibrator was pressed against her clit.

Oh, he wasn't even trying for gentle. The hard, urgent vibrations would have brought her to her tiptoes if she'd been able to move. Her body tried to bow upward as the sensations propelled her into urgent excitement. The pressure in her depths grew, her clit hardened, she was...

He took it *away*.

She groaned, loudly and clearly, and heard amused masculine chuckles. So many. *Oh, God*.

They stood there, watching, talking about her, and through the pounding storm of her need, she caught fragments of the conversations.

"...prefer smaller breasts." "Fucking cute set there." "Love the pink color." "Damn, she's got a pretty rack." "...like the littler ones." "...wish I could clamp those puppies."

Hands touched her. Different ones. Some gentle, some rough. The Doms talked to her or Nolan, complimenting her body, her breasts. Some made masculine sounds of pleasure and approval.

Approval of *her*. Of her size and shape and...and her breasts. Each sound of appreciation, each admiring touch raked through her soul, clearing away the weeds Kyler had sown. Leaving her blooming.

Her mind untethered again as inside the steamy wrap, her body grew hotter, needier.

And she got wetter and wetter.

"Time to get you out of this, sugar," Master Nolan finally said. "Your body needs to adjust to being released, so I'll remove everything slowly."

As the covering on her right arm came free, she hazily decided if he didn't want sex the minute she was out, well, she'd—ever so politely—beg.

Chapter Fifteen

NOLAN'S SWEATY SUBMISSIVE had started to shiver, although he'd covered her bared skin with towels as he slowly removed the wrap.

And her pussy was drenched. Someone had enjoyed being played with.

In the beginning, it'd been fucking difficult to watch other Doms touch his submissive, even under his control. If they hadn't had his permission, he'd have incapacitated them. His possessiveness really did go bone deep.

But the Doms had been careful, and he'd realized why Z could let others touch Jessica—because, they were, in a way, extensions of his own hands. Totally under his power.

His cock had hardened at the sounds of her growing arousal.

Even better, all the men's appreciation had made inroads into the crap her ex had fed her. She needed to see herself as the gorgeous woman she was.

The last bit of wrap came free, and he bundled Beth into a blanket. Sweeping her up, he looked for a place for her to rest while he cleaned the equipment.

"Master Nolan." Holding a spray bottle and wipes, Z's little cleaning lady waited at the edge of the scene area.

Nolan frowned. Cleaning a scene area was up to the people who used it.

"Got my orders from Himself." She motioned to where Z was approaching.

Well, damn. "Thank you, Peggy."

As Peggy started to spray down the web, Nolan turned to Z. "Add a bonus for her to my card."

"She'll appreciate it." Z bent, zipped Nolan's toy bag, and picked it up.

Roused by Z's voice, Beth blinked up at him, her blue-green eyes still slightly glazed. One hand had crept out from under the blanket to capture a lock of Nolan's loosened hair.

Z smiled at her before telling Nolan, "I had the thermostat in the Midsummer Night's Dream room turned up if you want to use it."

Interesting choice, in fact, perfect. Nonetheless… "Thanks, *Mom*."

Both Doms laughed as Beth rolled her eyes at the disrespect to the Shadowlands' owner.

Z motioned to a nearby unaccompanied submissive and handed over Nolan's toy bag. "Run this upstairs and leave it in the Midsummer Night room, please."

"At once, Master Z." The chain-clad young man trotted toward the circular stairs in the corner.

At a more leisurely pace, Nolan followed.

Once upstairs, he carried his little submissive to the end of the hall and into the reserved room. Yeah, Z had definitely turned up the thermostat. Newly out of mummification, Beth needed to be kept warm. Still…it felt sultry as high summer. *Jesus*.

"Oooooh." Beth stared at the room. "This wasn't here before."

"Z put it in last spring." The room appeared to be a meadow. The "grass" of a plush green fleece was broken up with "granite" boulders. The right wall mural showed a full moon glimmering through a night forest. On the left, fairies danced over a grassy meadow at night, probably to the faint Celtic harp music on the sound system.

The third wall displayed a moonlit lake. Jessica had wanted a unicorn added to the mural, but since everyone knew unicorns only visited virgins, Z told her the poor thing would get too lonely in the Shadowlands.

There was no obvious BDSM equipment. Multiple posts carved like tree trunks encircled the room, and their branches extended up and across the high ceiling. Above the leafy canopy, pinpoint lights replicated a night sky.

A mural of climbing roses covered the last wall—and pot-pourri near the door filled the air with the scent of flowers.

Keeping Beth rolled in her blanket, he put her down and propped her against a hillock.

She frowned at the irregularly rounded foam rocks around her, all covered in a mottled stone-gray fabric. "Why did Master Z add boulders to this room?"

"I'll show you." He pulled off his shirt.

Watching him dreamily, she smiled. Her hand beneath the blanket moved toward her pussy.

"You touch what's mine, sugar, I'll punish you."

With a start of surprise, she jerked her hand back.

DARN HIM, BETH thought, hugging herself. The initial chill of being released from the cling wrap had worn off, the room was nice and warm, and she was getting hotter by the minute as Nolan continued to undress. Her Master was some serious man candy. His chest and arm muscles were pumped to rock-hardness from carrying her. The faint starlight made shadows over his six-pack abs and between his pectoral muscles. Fully erect, his cock jutted upward.

He took a bottle of water from the toy bag inside the door. After flipping open the snap top, he sat on the knee-high boulder beside her and held the bottle to her lips. "Get this inside you while I consider how much trouble you're in."

She took a sip, and with the first wash of cool water, discovered she was enormously thirsty. After struggling free of the blanket, she took the water herself and gulped half of it down. "Why am I in trouble?"

He lifted one eyebrow.

She frowned as the misty memory of her mummification started to return. Had she actually blurted out she wanted bigger breasts? And...and... "You let other men touch me!"

His chuckle was a low rasping sound. "Well, damn, I did, didn't I?" He tugged her blanket down farther and cupped his hand over her exposed breast. It was still swollen—from all those Doms playing with her. The scrape of his fingernail over an acutely sensitive nipple rippled straight down to her pussy.

"But why?"

"You didn't believe me when I told you I like you just the way you are." He abandoned her breast and laid his hand over her cheek, turning her face to him. "You like my body, Beth. Get hot for me. If I gained weight—or lost weight—would that change?"

Not want him? He could lose...everything...and she'd still want him. "Even when you're a hundred, I'll still lust after you."

"Same goes, little rabbit."

Oh.

The corners of his eyes crinkled. "You know, guys can't fake being attracted." He took her hand and set it on his cock...his quite rigid cock. "Does this feel as if I'm half-hearted about my interest?"

Her mouth went dry. He was huge. Incredibly huge. Almost mesmerized by the heat coming from his erection and how the velvety skin was stretched so tautly, she missed what he said. "What?"

"We're discussing the trouble you're in. Seems like you forgot that in a D/s relationship, even *personal* problems get shared." He took the water, closed the top, and set the bottle on the floor before stripping her blanket away.

She realized her hand was still curled around his thick cock. *More.* On her knees, she wiggled to a place between his thighs, gripped his shaft, and leaned down. She got in one quick lick before his hand in her hair pulled her away. "But...*Siiir.*"

"Nope." With firm hands, he stood her up and held her there beside his thigh.

"What are you doing?"

"Getting ready to turn you over my knees. You're in trouble, remember?" His voice held open amusement...the...bastard.

"A spanking? Now?" She shoved against his hold, and his ruthless grip tightened.

"Yeah. First, tell me why you earned punishment."

Punishment. Thoughts filtered through her head and, slowly, guilt filled her. "Because I didn't tell you what was wrong."

"Bingo. Beth, how would you feel if I tried to keep problems from you? Basically lied to you by hiding my concerns and worries?"

The question was like having cold water dumped over her. One of the reasons she loved him—trusted him—was because he always gave her the truth.

She closed her eyes and summoned her courage before looking straight into his eyes. "I couldn't stand if you hid your feelings. I'm sorry, Master. I was trying to protect myself and messed up what we have between us and let you down." Her throat thickened, and she felt the flush that preceded tears. *No. Don't cry. Crying is cheating.*

His hard expression turned tender. He lifted the hand flattened on her sternum and gently fondled her breasts. "I'm sorry, too." In his dark eyes, the undiminished resolve was as plain as the regret. "I'm going to hurt you. Hopefully, the pain will remind you next time you're tempted to evade a question."

Oh. Damn. Her teeth gritted together. This wasn't going to be a sexy, fun spanking, was it?

With merciless hands, he pulled her down so her pelvis rested against his rock-hard thighs. His erection hadn't diminished, and it pressed against her hip as he ran his hand over her bare ass. "Count for me, Beth."

The first slap hit with a mild sting. It would grow worse. Her Master rarely spanked her for punishment, but when he did, he showed no mercy. "One."

And then he spanked her—hard—his construction-work-toughened palm harder than any paddle. The blows alternated cheeks and sometimes hit the back of her thighs. By the fifteenth, she couldn't speak through her crying, but he didn't stop for another ten.

"Done, sugar. It's over." Gathering her up, he settled with her on the grassy floor, stretching out on his back with her beside him. Holding her as she cried.

After punishment came cuddles.

Cheek against his shoulder, she inhaled his scent. His steely arms held her firmly, and gratitude filled her that she'd found her safe harbor in an uncertain world.

When her sobbing had turned to sighs, he tilted her head up and studied her face. "No more burying your feelings," he said softly.

"No more." Only... She hadn't shared everything. "There's something I've been fighting against."

"Tell me."

"Today, I was worried about being too skinny to make you happy. Partly. But...the rest was Alyssa." God, she still felt petty for being jealous, but...fair was fair. If her Master were ever jealous, she'd want him to tell her. "I hate seeing her touch you. How she touches you."

"Ah. I get it." He was silent for a minute. "And you didn't like sharing how you felt."

He had no idea. When she rubbed her cheek on his broad chest, he stroked her hair, playing with the waves.

"You had a reason for being upset, actually. She was getting...pushy." At the tone in his voice, Beth looked up. His mouth had flattened. "She already knows she won't be returning."

"Really?" She breathed out. Confessing had been much easier than she expected.

"Yeah. Later, remind me to tell you about your li'l protectors."

Uh-oh. What had the boys done?

He gave her a break to clean up in the tiny bathroom—which she badly needed—and when she returned, he was sitting with his back against one of the odd "boulders."

"Better." Smiling, he made a twirling gesture with his index finger.

Her face warmed with a telltale flush, and she turned—quickly—hoping to get it over.

But at his low growl of enjoyment, she slowed. And when she looked over her shoulder, she saw his eyes were half-lidded, his hand fisting his erect cock, his gaze fixed on her ass.

A bolt of lust sizzled up her spine. The way he openly showed his desire for her was so...exciting. As she dampened, the area between her legs tingled with arousal.

"Come to me, li'l rabbit." His voice was rough. "On your knees."

Avoiding the gray boulders, she crawled across the velvety fleece floor to him, her hair bouncing loose over her shoulders. When she stopped beside his hip, he motioned her to kneel up.

His heated gaze burned over her face, her shoulders, her waist and returned to her breasts. "Still red. The other Doms touched you and left marks, but now those breasts are all mine, aren't they?"

"Yes, Master." Her words were barely audible.

"Yeah. Didn't know how much it'd turn me on to watch." He drew her closer. His lips closed over one nipple, and his tongue swirled around. Hot and wet. She was still so sensitive; the sensation expanded outward before zeroing straight to her pussy. He switched to the other breast, rolling the first nipple between his fingers, squeezing hard enough her toes curled. "Next time, maybe I'll tie you to the bar and let them have another go."

Her mouth dropped open. "You wouldn't."

The amused glint in his eyes said he'd do whatever he wanted, and they both knew it.

At least he wouldn't tie her down there for the other Doms to *punish*. "So, am I forgiven now?" To her dismay, he didn't immediately answer yes.

"Hmm. Mostly. I'm still a tad bit angry and so"—his eyes glinted with a look she knew. One that made her shiver—"I'll work out my anger on you. When I get off, you'll be forgiven. Completely."

And she knew she would be. Her friends considered him a hard-ass Dominant—and he was—but he was consistent in his rules. Consistent in what he considered problems. And once an argument or punishment was over, it was done. He didn't hold grudges or keep score, and she loved that about him.

"You wanted to know why Z put fake boulders in here?" Lifting her, he set her on a torso-length boulder next to the fake trees. "Let me show you."

When her tender, abused bottom rubbed over the coarse gray material, she hissed and tried to stand again.

"Sore, darlin'?" He squeezed one ass cheek and grinned at her squeak. "Now, lie down." Setting a hand between her breasts, he pushed her onto her back.

The "rock" was made of firm foam, and dammit, the knee-high thing was tilted exactly enough to have her hips higher than her head. Why did the position make her feel so defenseless?

He showed her why. With merciless hands, he held her thighs apart and licked from her pussy up and over her clit.

"Aaah!" The exquisite sensation sent her to wiggling uncontrollably.

"Squirmy subbie. I'm in the mood to put a stop to that." Ropes were concealed on each side of the "rock," and he clipped her ankle cuffs to them.

God, only Master Z would put restraints on fake boulders.

Using a chain anchored on a tree trunk, Sir secured her arms over her head. His firm lips curved up as he contemplated his work. "You look like a druid sacrifice, li'l rabbit."

The words uttered in his low, rough voice sounded threatening, and in the dim starlight of the room, his face was hard. Almost cruel. His gaze lowered to her pussy, which was now open and exposed and...available.

Her heart started to pound, and need rolled over her in an implacable demand.

"I'd hate to waste a good sacrifice." Smiling slightly, he went down on one knee and kissed the skin of her inner thigh, then rubbed his chin against her skin. The day's growth of beard on his jaw scraped her tender skin, and she shivered.

Slowly, as if he was willing to take all night, he kissed his way to her pussy, teasing his lips over her mound. He returned to nuzzle the crease between her pussy and her thigh before he licked over her labia.

Her pussy was swelling with each touch of his lips, tightening and tingling so fiercely it burned. Ever so lightly, he traced her clit with his tongue, teased around the hood, and rubbed the sides.

Oh, the feeling was amazing. Why did the sensation always seem new and different? *More, more, more.* She lifted her hips up.

His laugh was a low rumble. "Sugar, if you move again, I'll…reprimand…you."

Oh, not good. Her friends had shared their Doms' various punishments. Some, like Master Marcus and Master Z were diabolically inventive. Master Nolan was more straightforward—and scary.

Don't move, Beth.

He hadn't missed a beat. His tongue continued raising her excitement, never exerting enough pressure to get her off. He pressed a finger inside her, adding new sensations. She felt him turn his hand to massage her G-spot. She didn't know where the location was exactly, but oh God, when he rubbed there, her clit expanded a hundredfold.

As the compulsion to come grew, her legs trembled, her nipples peaked—and ached. She couldn't bear it. "Ple-e-e-ze…" Her voice came out barely louder than a sigh, but he heard. *Oh no.*

He sat back on his knees, pulling his hands back. "Bad little rabbit." He brought his callused palm down in a stinging slap directly on her pussy. On her *clit*.

"Ow!" Even as the shock and the surge of heat shot to her core, she realized she'd spoken. Again. *No, no, no.* Her knees jerked with the effort to close and protect her most vulnerable spot.

He slapped her *again*. This swat was harder…right on her swollen clit.

She almost climaxed right then and there. Every muscle quivered—and she needed to come so badly she could hardly think. *Need more.*

He didn't smile, despite the laughter in his eyes. "When I want, sugar." He didn't order her not to come though. He rarely did…maybe because he didn't need to. He knew her body and its reactions so well that if he didn't want her to come he'd simply back off or slow down, leaving her teetering on the edge.

Like now, the rat bastard.

Her lips moved, forming the word *please* without making a sound.

"Ah, that's pretty, li'l rabbit." He lowered his head, closed his lips over her stinging, burning clit, and her lower half tightened into a hard ball of need. When he slid one finger, then two, inside her, and increased the coiling pressure in her core, she had to bite back a moan.

Please. Oh God. Her hands fisted over her head as he leisurely teased her, rubbing her G-spot, licking lightly all around her clit.

When he rose up and pressed his cock at her entrance, she bit her lip in anticipation—and frustration. Her clit throbbed angry demands for his tongue to stay right there.

She wanted everything. And would get only and exactly what he wanted her to have. His unwavering control somehow expanded every action until the sensations overflowed into her mind and soul.

Slowly, slowly, he entered her, his shaft wonderfully thick and long.

Her eyes closed as she savored the slick sensation and the stretch as new nerves were stimulated, as he steadily sheathed himself to the hilt. *Wonderful.* Her back arched at the sensuous slide.

When she opened her eyes, his molten gaze burned into her as he thrust in and out, driving her up and up and—He stopped, and wicked amusement filled his eyes. "You know, I kinda liked your reaction to getting your pussy slapped."

What? No, wait.

Before she could react, he eased out and lightly slapped her pussy—right on her clit—three times. Even as she gasped at the shocking sting, even as the burning sank into her, his shaft drove in. And he was thrusting hard and fast, sending her back up.

He pulled out and three more slaps landed on her pussy.

Oh God. The blows were a thick, hot sensation sliding to her depths, coiling the pressure tighter and tighter deep within her.

And he thrust back inside, his cock thick and hard, pounding her in the way she loved. His hands closed on her swollen breasts, caressing, teasing her nipples, until her entire body was shimmering with hot need.

He slid back out. And paused, his gaze holding hers as his hand rose and stopped.

She tensed, not breathing, poised there at the exquisite edge, powerless to do anything else but anticipate the arrival of the unbearable pain and stupendous pleasure.

His hand came down.

Smack.

And she *came, came, came,* the orgasm so ferocious and blinding that the waves of pleasure threw her into an ocean of sensation, rolling her head over heels. His hum of enjoyment teased her ears before he slapped her clit again, kicking off more intense waves.

The slick slide of his thick cock entering her spawned more explosions in her center. Her vagina spasmed around his penetration, and her whole body tingled at the magnificent feeling.

Before the convulsions had slowed, he was pumping into her with hard, fast strokes. His hands tightened on her hips. She could feel his shaft jerking and heat filling her as he rumbled his own pleasure.

When he relaxed, anchoring her to the squashy boulder with his heavy weight, covering her in heat and safety, she sighed in perfect contentment. Turning her head, she breathed in his clean scent and rubbed her cheek against his shoulder. "I love you,

Master."

"Mmm. I love you, too." Still buried inside her, he growled a laugh. "And darlin', you are now forgiven."

A WHILE LATER, back downstairs, Nolan set Beth on a barstool and leaned against the bar beside her. She'd taken a quick shower upstairs, and Nolan bent to kiss her neck and savor the clean, moist scent of her skin. Eyes heavy-lidded but free of shadows, she practically glowed with satiation.

It'd been a rough then fucking satisfying night. They both deserved a drink.

Near the end of the bar, Raoul was setting beers on a bar-maid's tray. He nodded at Nolan to say he'd seen them.

"Hey Nolan." Dressed in his brown leathers, Cullen strolled over. "Why don't you bring the boys over next weekend? Hector would love them—and they'd get a kick out the jungle-gym."

No shit. Cullen's Airedale loved kids. "Yeah, your mess of equipment"—swings, poles, platforms, bars right on the sandy ocean beach—"would send 'em into a play frenzy."

In fact, it'd be fun to build something similar at home. Connor and Grant would have a blast designing their own playground-gym after seeing Cullen's. He caught Beth's nod of agreement. "Next weekend sounds good."

Cullen smiled at Beth. "Andrea will call you, assuming she survives tonight." With a grin, the big Dom headed back toward the scene areas, lifting a hand to the Drago cousins as they approached.

Nolan nodded at them. "Drago and Drago, good to see you."

"I heard about Mrs. McCormick's death," Max said. "How are Grant and Connor doing?"

Nolan almost smiled. Amazing how two little boys could

turn a hard-ass into marshmallow goo. "Hurting, but okay. We're trying to keep them busy. In fact, maybe you should swing by and help me teach them martial arts."

An exasperated groan came from Beth.

"It'd be a pleasure." Eyes lit with laughter—and without looking at Beth—Max added, "If you want to instruct them in sword-fighting, I've still got some blades. Sharp edges, but short enough for your boys."

"*What?*" Beth jumped to her feet. "Absolutely *not*. Nolan, you—"

Max roared with laughter. "Kidding."

Beth set her hands on her hips. "You-you're evil. I'm going to make your yard the prissiest, formal landscape in the world. All in shades of white and pale blue."

"Christ, woman. That's just mean."

Behind Max, Alastair gave a slow smile. "I think it sounds fine."

"You would, you fucking limey." Still chuckling, Max motioned toward where the unattached submissives were sitting. "C'mon. Let's find a subbie to torture."

As the cousins moved away, Nolan chuckled. Some submissive was going to have an exciting night. He gripped Beth around the waist and returned her to the barstool. "No blades, sugar. But you know the munchkins need to get over their fear of cops."

"Can't they play Candyland with him instead?" She heaved an irritated sigh. "You guys and your fascination with fighting is truly disgusting."

"It satisfies our sadistic natures on the days we can't beat on our women. Good thing for me, I have you." He squeezed her tender ass and grinned at the gratifying squeak.

A grating laugh came from behind him, and he glanced over his shoulder to see Sam Davies taking the empty space. Lean, gray-haired, and one of the Shadowlands Masters, the rancher was in his usual black jeans and black work shirt. "How you doin', King?"

"Been a good night." A damn good night.

Moving with the stiffness of a well-beaten masochist, Sam's submissive joined him. Somewhere in her forties, Linda was curvy, redheaded, fair skinned…and was using a big cotton handkerchief to clean up the eye makeup streaking her freckled face.

Sam's lips quirked. "Don't know why you wear that stuff, missy. It sure doesn't last."

Linda narrowed her brown eyes. "It streaks because every time I wear it, you deliberately set out to make me cry. You wait; I'm going to find some industrial strength waterproof."

"You do that." Chuckling, Sam nodded at Beth.

She smiled at him and moved her legs under the bar to give Nolan more room. Her hiss of pain as the movement abused her tender ass made the sadist snort in amusement.

Sam's glance at Nolan held approval—probably because Beth also had the radiance of a well fucked, well satisfied submissive.

The same glow Linda had.

As Nolan exchanged a smile with Sam, he saw Alyssa approaching on his right. She stepped between him and Sam and flattened her hand on his chest.

Behind him, Beth let out an annoyed growl. He didn't blame her. Submissives didn't touch *any* Dom without permission.

Annoyed as fuck, he brushed Alyssa's hand away. "Go away, sub. I'm not available or interested."

"I don't believe you, Master," she said in a breathy voice. Her gaze was fixed on him. Totally on him. Sub frenzy, dammit. Desperate to be dominated—and fixated on him. Damn well obsessed.

Yeah, she wouldn't believe anything he said at this point.

BETH STARED AT the beautiful, curvy brunette who was still lusting after Sir…even after being told he wasn't interested. *Seriously*?

She saw Nolan's dilemma. If Alyssa had been a male, he'd have swatted the guy out of his life like a buzzing mosquito. He wouldn't put up with being pushed, yet his Texas code didn't allow swatting women—not if it wasn't consensual.

Nolan was a hero; guess it was time for her to get with the program. *Super Submissive to the rescue.* A fetwear cape was going on her shopping list. Beth stepped around Nolan, planting herself between him and the villainess.

Heroes always gave the villains a warning first, right? But Beth's annoyance prevented her from keeping her voice quiet. "Alyssa, I asked you to do physical therapy for my Master. Since his shoulder's healed, your job is done. Leave him be, please."

Alyssa set her hands on her hips and tossed her head. "This is between me and Master Nolan. You shouldn't interrupt. You shouldn't even be speaking without permission. Obviously, he doesn't care enough to train you properly."

The weak insult didn't even hurt. Her Master had gone overboard to show how much he loved her—both her body and her personality. If war was going to be conducted with insults, she could now hold her own.

"You shouldn't be *touching* without permission." Beth's huff of exasperation was loud. "If you knew him at all, you'd know he doesn't say anything he doesn't mean. What part of *'I'm not interested'* did you miss? Honestly, Alyssa, trailing after a Dom who doesn't want you is simply pathetic."

Alyssa stepped back as if she'd been punched.

A second later, to Beth's disbelief, the damn woman tried again to get to Nolan.

Not. Going. To. Happen. Beth blocked her and, thoroughly fed-up, drove the heel of her hand into Alyssa's upper sternum, knocking her back a step. The next move should have been shattering her kneecap, but fracturing bones might be over the top. "Listen, dumbass. Try for him again, and I'll mess you up— yank out your hair, bust your nose, and smash your lips in."

"You-you…"

Feeling evil, Beth stared at the woman's breasts. "And since you have those cow-sized tits sticking out like an invitation, I'll flatten them on my way past."

Mouth open in shock, Alyssa looked around, obviously in hopes of support.

Instead, she collected frowns from everyone within hearing.

Beside Sam, Linda wore the disapproving frown perfected by mothers of teenagers. "Why in the world would you hit on a Master who's not only happy with his submissive, but married to her? What is wrong with you?"

"But, I…" Alyssa took another step back before her pleading gaze returned to Nolan.

He simply turned away to face the bar. "Raoul, how about drinks for me and my Beth?"

When Alyssa still didn't move, Beth leaned forward, her voice menacing. "Go. *Away.*"

The woman did. She retreated two steps and finally turned and hurried toward the door.

Sam's barked laugh blended with Nolan's chuckle.

Beth glared at them both. "Did you think that we were *funny*?"

"Not Alyssa—her behavior is just sad." Nolan drew Beth so close her back was against his chest. "But *you* were fucking hilarious. Thanks for the defense, sugar."

Sorely tempted to shove an elbow into his gut, Beth snuggled against him instead…and discovered he was erect. *Seriously?*

Men. Totally from a different species. Maybe even a different genus. Maybe even a different *planet.*

"Nolan, here you go." Raoul handed over a Corona and set a drink for Beth on the bar top. "You earned this, *gatita.*"

Just what she needed. She picked up her drink and took a sip. Single malt whiskey. Her favorite—it was like getting a war prize. "Thank you, Master Raoul."

He smiled at her before telling Nolan, "You have a most effective guard subbie, my friend."

"Quite effective indeed."

At the grim voice, Beth went rigid. *Oh no, no, no.* Surely he hadn't heard the argument. Her voice came out hoarse. "Master Z."

His unreadable silvery gaze ran over her. "You're back to fighting weight, I see."

Fighting weight. Oh, God, he must have heard everything. "I'm sorry."

Z's lips twitched. "No you're not. But, if you start a fight in the Shadowlands, you *will* be."

Her instinctive retreat pressed her harder against Nolan—and his erection.

"Like I told you, Z, Alyssa needs help," Nolan said. His arm around Beth's waist kept her in place.

Master Z glanced at the path the submissive had taken. "So I see. I doubt she comprehends how irrationally she's behaving. After I talk with her, I'll arrange for some Doms to take her under command and ease her need to be dominated. She'll be fine."

"Thanks. She's a good woman when she's herself."

As Z headed in the direction Alyssa had gone, Nolan picked up his Corona while keeping Beth anchored against him. Leaning a hip against the barstool, he looked down at her. "You know, that day when Alastair made a house call, I had a couple of uncomfortable thoughts about you and him. I understand how much Alyssa bothered you."

At his easy tone, Beth's shoulders relaxed. If he'd been displeased with her threatening Alyssa, it would have been difficult to take. Then his words registered. "Me and Alastair? You were worried? Seriously?"

Okay, she would never want her Master to feel worried or unsure about anything, but maybe there was a tiny bit of delight there. Just a little.

He shook his head in reproof at her uptilted lips. "Seriously. Listen, sugar." He frowned, obviously trying to find the right words. "Yeah, I enjoyed Alyssa back when. But now... I've got no interest in touching anyone else. None."

"Oh." Her breath came out in a soft sigh.

"You taught me the difference between empty fucking and making love." He gave her a slow kiss. "I'm not interested in going back."

To keep from dissolving into tears, she knocked back a good gulp of the whiskey.

He only grinned. "Gotta say, though, I was kinda hoping for a girl fight."

Men.

Chapter Sixteen

PERCHED ON A stool at the kitchen island, Grant finished his super-biscuit-egg-sausage thing that Beth'd made. "Mmm." His stomach felt happy.

On the other side, Beth smiled at him.

Already finished eating, Nolanman was sipping his coffee. "If you're done there, tiger, want to help me build a chair?"

Get to play with hammers and nails again? That's a no-brainer. "Sure." Yesterday, he had helped replace the broken window, pulling out the strips that'd kept the busted glass in place, handing Nolanman tools, holding the glass for him. Seeing the new pretty window had felt...good. It was fixed, and he'd helped make it that way.

Nolan pointed his cup at Connor. "You want to build, too?"

Although Grant had already eaten two sausage things, Connor was still on his first. Mouth full, he shook his head no, frowned, and nodded yes.

"I hired Connor to help me weed the south garden," Beth told Nolan. "But he can work with me for a while and then join you. He's a fantastic assistant, so I know you'll find him useful."

Connor's eyes got big, as if he was thrilled but thought she was lying. Only Beth didn't lie.

It was weird—nice, but weird—to have grownups saying nice stuff about them. Nolanman said he got a kick out of having his own work crew at home. He pointed out mistakes, but he'd tell Grant and Connor whenever they did good, too.

And he never said they were stupid or brats or in the way.

Grant picked up his milk and took a sip. Last night, the cop—Dan—and Kari had said nice things, too. They'd told Nolanman that Connor and Grant had been good kids and could come and play with Zane anytime.

Remembering Zane, Grant smiled and finished off his milk. The kid wasn't even two years old but talked almost as good as Connor did and was always asking, "What's that?" He ran pretty fast but with wide legs because he still wore a diaper so it looked funny. He and Connor'd had fun with Zane and the big dog named Prince.

Now, Connor wanted to ask Beth for a dog, but Grant told him no. Grownups didn't like kids who asked for stuff. Or money.

But they had money now without asking. When he and Connor had helped Beth clean the house, she'd given them each a dollar. The next day, Grant helped rake the yard after a storm, and Nolanman said he was a good worker and gave him another dollar.

He'd earned money like a grownup. And he was a good worker. The funny feeling in his chest came back, all warm and...happy.

After the dishes were done, Grant and Nolan walked to the workshop. Near the lake, Connor and Beth were weeding a flower garden, and Beth was laughing at something Connor said.

She had a pretty laugh. It made him want to smile when he heard her.

Nolan pointed to them. "Sure you don't want to help Beth pull weeds?"

"Uh-uh." Grant stared at his feet. "I like flowers, but I can't tell which ones are weeds." Connor was only a little kid, and *he* could tell.

Nolan ruffled his hair. "Me, neither. Beth won't let me help unless she can sit right beside me and make sure I don't screw up."

Grant checked, but Nolan didn't look like he felt bad about it.

"We all have different talents, tiger. Beth can't build houses like I do; I can't design gardens like she does. Part of getting older is figuring out what you're good at and what you love."

Like Lego pieces, the words snapped into Grant's mind, fitting right into place. It was good Connor had something he did well, 'cause Grant had other things he did better than Connor.

In the building—Nolan called it a shop—they got to work. Grant helped Nolan measure the boards and helped hold them as they were cut.

By the time they had a stack made, Connor appeared. "I heared the saw. Can I help?"

"We're going to screw in the chair slats now." Nolan set a piece of wood on the chair frame. "Line up the holes, put the screw in, then use the screwdriver. Connor can start the screw. Grant, take over when it gets hard to turn."

Grant helped Connor get the screw started. Connor did the first turns, Grant did the harder turns—and Nolan finished.

THE BOYS HAD done a fine job, Nolan thought as he leaned against the workbench and watched. They were on the last slat.

Connor looked over. "We better finish and find Beff. She might have cookies she needs to give us."

"She probably does." Good kids. Grant had a real knack for the wood. Connor, not so much. He mostly wanted to be wherever Grant was.

"Dumb wood." Face scrunched up, Connor turned the screwdriver, but got nowhere. Undoubtedly, the screw wasn't lined up with the second piece of wood.

"It's not in the right place. Let me do it." Grant reached for the screwdriver.

Connor pulled it away. "This is *my* part." He tried again, his frustration increasing as he wiggled it. He jabbed at the screw with the screwdriver.

Uh-oh. Nolan headed for the two. "Connor, stop."

The kid's face turned mulish, and he pushed harder.

"Stop *now*."

Before Nolan could reach the boys, the screwdriver slipped and jabbed into Connor's other hand. Gashed it good. Connor screamed.

Nolan spun back, grabbed the first aid kit off the workbench, and flipped it open as he dropped onto a knee beside Connor. Jesus, he should have stayed closer. Should have caught that the boy was getting frustrated and not being careful. Guilt burned in his gut.

He ripped open a gauze packet, applied pressure, and kept his tone mild. "It'll be fine."

God, he hated seeing the child crying. More guilt slid in as he saw Grant had tears in his own eyes. *Give the boy something to do.* "Can you turn the water on in the sink and fetch me a clean towel?"

Grant nodded and ran across the shop.

Washing the cut made Connor cry harder, but finally, they were done. As the bleeding slowed, Nolan butterflied the edges together and applied a bandage. Wasn't deep, although it'd sure bled enough. It hurt to see an injury on a hand so fucking little.

"What happened?" Beth stood in the doorway, concern in her face.

Connor pulled free, ran over to her, and shoved his face against her. Holding him with one hand, she crooned her sympathy and examined the bandaging. "Hey, you got a cool bandage."

Without moving, Connor nodded.

"Nice job." She gave Nolan a gentle smile. "Of course, you probably get a fair amount of first aid practice on those construction sites."

"It happens," Nolan muttered. But it happened to men, not little boys. Fuck, they shouldn't even be in the damned shop. "You want to give them some lunch?"

Her brows drew together at the flatness of his voice. "Sure." She kissed Connor's head and hugged Grant. "You two head up to the house, and I'll be right there."

As the boys ran out of the shop, she walked over and slid her arms around Nolan, leaning into him, merging her body with his. She was warm from the sun outside, her skin scented with the herbs she'd been working with. "You okay, Sir?"

"It was my fault. I should've watched more carefully." He led her out of the shop—he'd clean up later. "Go feed the kids. I'll be up in a while." When he had his emotions back under control.

"But—"

He shook his head, stopping her protest. As she headed toward the house, he walked down to the lake, leaving the gate slightly ajar behind him. He might need to run up to the house if Connor started bleeding again.

On the dock, he took a seat in one of the two chairs. The boys probably hadn't noticed, but the one they were building was kid-sized. He planned to make two, one for each boy, but damned if he wouldn't finish them himself.

How could he have been so careless? Nolan stared out over the water, blindly watching an egret trolling for frogs and minnows in the shallows. A few butterflies flitted over the yellow canna lilies along the banks.

He kept hearing Connor's scream. Seeing his tears.

The gate's squeak caught his attention. Grant walked out

onto the dock, carrying a paper plate as carefully as if it were glass.

Nolan frowned, and the boy stopped. "I brought you... Beth said you should eat." Grant took a step back. "She did."

Scaring children now. Way to go, King. He made his lips curve up as he took the plate. "She's a bossy wife."

Relief flashed across Grant's face. Yeah, he had scared the kid. And he'd thought he wanted to be a father? Crap job he'd make of it. He nodded at the other chair.

The boy slid onto it halfway, stood back up, and pulled a can of Red Bull from his pocket. He handed it over.

"Thanks." Not hungry. Not thirsty. Feeling obligated, Nolan opened the can, but simply held it. After a minute, he noticed Grant was watching him carefully. "Problem?"

"Beth said you felt bad 'cause Connor got hurt, and so you wouldn't eat." Grant kicked at the legs of the chair and admitted, "I can't eat if...if I don't feel right. My stomach gets all twisty."

The easy sympathy smoothed some of the knots in Nolan's gut. "Yep. That it does."

"You didn't make Connor get hurt. You told him to stop, only he didn't listen."

"Kids don't always listen. I shouldn't have had you two in the shop."

"You're wrong." Grant's eyes fired with anger. "We *want* to learn. To do stuff. I'm your home crew."

"But you can get hurt."

When Grant lifted his chin, he looked uncommonly like Beth. Yeah, the resolute movement was hers. Maybe the next generation wouldn't inherit her genes, but her influence would damn well survive.

"Maybe *you* can get hurt." The kid pointed at Nolan's scabbed knuckles—skinned-up when helping the roofing crew move stacks of shingles. "I guess you better stay home."

Sheer disrespect.

Nolan grinned.

The worry disappeared from Grant's eyes, and he grinned back. Problem solved, he dropped to his hands and knees to peer at the catfish in the shallows.

So young. So fucking fragile. So much like Beth—who had no problem telling him when he got overprotective.

Hell. Grant had a point. Injuries were part of life. A part of growing up. He couldn't shield the boys from everything. Not really. All a man could do was guard the youngsters and try to keep accidents to a minimum. Wrapping them in cotton batting would hurt them more in the end.

It wasn't as if he'd given the children power tools. In fact, his father taught Nolan and his brothers to use hand tools at Connor's age. And they'd gotten banged up some in the process of gaining skill, independence, and patience. Mastering the art of building came with the price of cuts and bruises and the occasional smashed finger.

Life had its own balance. Took a kid to make him remember it.

Took a kid to remind him to call his own father—and offer his heartfelt thanks.

Nolan started eating his ham and beef sandwich, enjoying the spicy mustard...and something else. When they'd first been together, he'd asked Beth what she'd whispered as she spread the mustard. She'd turned an adorable red and silenced him completely with her answer. "*Adding a bit of love.*"

Her sandwiches always tasted better than the ones he made himself.

As he took the last bite, he realized Grant was waiting patiently. "Yeah?"

"Beth said to bring you back when you finished, an' she'd give us cookies—or pie."

Pie? Got a bribe for both of them, did she? *Sneaky submissive.*

WATCHING OUT THE kitchen window, Beth smiled as both guys headed back to the house. From the anticipation displayed by Grant's dancing feet, Nolan had finished his sandwich. Cookies were expected.

"Why didn't Nolan eat lunch wiff us?" Seated on the counter, Connor licked a batter-covered spoon. "Is he mad?"

"No, baby." Beth brushed his silky, soft hair out of his face. "He felt bad because you got hurt."

Connor studied the bandage on his hand. "Like when Jermaine hits me and Grant feels bad?"

Beth pulled in a breath at the thought of someone hitting the child. But oh, she was so proud of Grant. "Yes, Grant is a lot like Nolan. They want to keep us safe, and they get upset if they can't."

"Oh." Connor looked up as the patio door opened, and Nolan followed Grant inside.

Before she could help Connor down, he jumped off the counter, staggered, got his balance, and darted to Nolan. "Don't feel bad. I'm more careful next time. Promise."

Rumbling a laugh, Nolan picked him up and gave him a hearty squeeze. "I appreciate the promise, my man. I'll watch over you more carefully, too."

Beaming proudly at his success, Grant claimed the cookies Beth held out.

Nolan pointed toward the boys' bedroom. "Quiet time for an hour, crew. Then we'll go swimming."

They trotted to their room, exchanging competitive comments about who could hold their breath longer.

Grinning, Nolan entered the kitchen. Without speaking, he backed Beth up against the counter, leaned into her, and kissed the worry right out of her.

When he lifted his head, she laid her hand on his cheek, seeing his eyes were clear again. "You're feeling better."

"You're a manipulative little subbie. I should beat you more often." He kissed her again and murmured, "Grant offered me pie. I take it you lost our bet? Uzuri and Holt aren't a couple?"

"That's right, darn it."

"Well, damn. Apple or cherry?" He didn't wait for her answer, ignored her giggling, and with a hunter's single-mindedness, searched the kitchen for his prize.

A few minutes later—after he'd practically inhaled a third of the apple pie—they settled down in the great room to have a second cup of coffee. As Nolan picked up the paper he'd started earlier, Beth slid off the couch and settled at his feet, leaning against his legs. While he absently stroked her hair and read the news, she drifted into a quiet contentment.

He loved her. And her body. And would go to extraordinary lengths to prove it. Somehow, what he'd done at the club had wiped out the derogatory voice in her mind, the one whispering of her unworthiness. She...liked...herself again. Felt at home in her own skin.

Both Jessica and Kari had called earlier to offer congratulations on smacking down Alyssa. Her lips twitched. How embarrassing. Yet, confronting the submissive had felt good, too. Truly, she wished Alyssa the best—as long as she kept her distance from Sir.

The murmuring of the boys came from their room. Sounded as if Connor was falling asleep.

Grant was probably working on his puzzle. He had a mind that liked shapes, hands that liked putting things together. Connor showed a talent for words...and she wanted to see what he'd do with music. Both boys were going to be amazing men. But...would they get the love and the attention they needed to nurture those gifts?

It was amazing how giving they were with their own affection. And how protective. Beth's heart melted. Nolan had told her how Connor had yelled at Alyssa, and Grant had thrown a dish at her simply because the woman had hurt Beth's feelings.

How could she stand to let them leave? To not know if they were all right?

Frowning, Beth tried to turn her focus to a little baby girl. A baby. Yet, her arms seemed shaped these days to hold solid, sturdy frames. Little boys.

Lord, was she crazy? Darn it, Nolan wanted a girl. But, she'd seen his face when he'd lifted Connor into the air. He was as bound up in the boys as she was.

Plans change.

When she'd joined the Shadowlands after escaping Kyler, she'd known exactly what she wanted—a *gentle*, sweet, tame Dom. But no one had clicked and, to her dismay, Master Z had handed her over to Nolan, the roughest, most dangerous Dom in the club. No, in the state. Maybe even in the country.

He sure wasn't any gentle, sweet Dom. Sheesh, it was like putting in an order for a nice tame camellia bush and receiving a huge, knotty cypress tree.

But love came where it would.

Nolan set his paper to one side. "You're frowning, sugar." His hand was on her face as he studied her with Dom's eyes. "Tell me what's wrong."

Pulling in a careful breath, she put her hand on his and tossed their careful plans to the winds. "I want to adopt Grant and Connor. We can always hunt for a little girl later, right?"

A slow smile appeared on his hard face.

Yes, he was her cypress tree, big enough to shelter the world. And it looked as if their family wouldn't be a well-planned garden, but rather a forest that would endure for generations to come.

Chapter Seventeen

O N FRIDAY, BETH heard the doorbell ring. Price was here.

On Monday, she'd spoken to him about their wish to adopt the boys. He'd been awfully casual, saying he'd make a note of their interest and would review their records. He'd made a point of warning her not to mention their hopes to the children.

After that, nothing. Not a word.

She'd left a voice mail on Thursday.

Nothing.

Half an hour ago, he'd called to say he was coming by. Didn't it just figure? Nolan was off helping Cullen build a deck extension and wouldn't return until later. Price hadn't cared that Nolan wasn't home. If he wasn't visiting to talk about their adopting the boys, then what? To check on the children?

Fixing a pleasant expression on her face, she opened the door. "Good afternoon, Mr. Price. I hope you're here to discuss Nolan and me adopting the children."

"On the contrary, I'm taking them off your hands for a couple of hours." Price glanced at his watch. "Get them now, please. We have someone to meet shortly."

Beth stared. "What? Who?"

"Their grandmother plans to give them a home. She feels it's her Christian duty, even if they were raised for the first few years by her 'dreadful' daughter."

"You're talking about Drusilla's mother?" At Price's nod,

Beth wanted to swear at him. "Drusilla said her mother was a fanatic who whipped her for talking back, for swearing, for anything. She had to read the Bible on her knees for hours. That's why she ran away at sixteen."

"Consider the source of your information. Besides, if Drusilla had remained with her mother, she'd be alive today, now wouldn't she?"

"Maybe. But the grandmother doesn't sound like a healthy choice for—"

"Relatives have priority over foster parents, Mrs. King, even if the foster parents have *influential friends*." His sneer wasn't disguised.

The low-life bastard. He'd probably talked the grandmother into taking the children just to get back at her and Nolan. "I see."

"I would remind you, Mrs. King, not to let Grant or Connor know you want to adopt them. Foster parents aren't allowed to interfere—in any way—in a legitimate placement of the children temporarily placed in their home."

With an effort, she throttled back her anger. Nothing could choke back her growing sense of grief. "I understand."

He followed her to the patio where Connor and Grant were drawing a chalk mural on the smooth concrete.

"Awesome job, guys." It really was. Grant's portion of the creation was orderly, the forest animals cleverly drawn, evenly spaced, everything balanced.

Connor's half was asymmetrical, yet pleasing. She could even distinguish—mostly—which animals were which, although the rabbit was the same size as the horse.

"This is you, Beff," Connor told her, tapping the bunny.

At Price's quizzical regard, she felt her cheeks warm. Connor must have heard Nolan's nickname for her. "Put the chalk into the container, please. Mr. Price is taking you to visit your grandmother."

The two stared at her blankly.

As she'd figured. "Have you ever met your grandmother?"

Grant shook his head as Connor asked, "What's a grand-muvver?"

IN A LONG hallway, Grant tried to hurry after Mr. Price, but Connor was behind him, pulling on his shorts pocket. They were going to see their grandmother. Beth said this grandmother was Mama's mother. Would she look like Mama?

Why hadn't she ever visited them?

Some of the kids in school had grandmothers who gave cool presents. Food. Hugs. Mama had never talked about her mother. *How come?*

Mr. Price walked through a doorway and motioned them to follow.

Inside, the room was a sunny yellow with kid-sized tables, and shelves with books and toys. An old lady in a brown dress sat in a grown-up chair beside one of the tables. Her gray hair made a ball behind her head. The long lines beside her mouth weren't happy ones.

When she saw him and Connor, she didn't smile.

"Mrs. Brun, these are Drusilla's children." Mr. Price set his hand on Grant's shoulder. "This is Grant. And Connor."

"Those aren't Christian names."

Grant's heart kicked inside his chest. Her brown eyes held the same *I-don't-like-you* as Jermaine's had.

"Boys, this is your grandmother. Your mother's mother."

Connor's cold hand closed on his. "Hi."

She looked at Connor. "You may call me Grandmother." She motioned toward the small table. "Sit there and we'll talk."

Grant slid onto one of the chairs. As Connor dragged a

chair closer to Grant, the legs screeched across the floor.

Grandmother's mouth turned down.

THE KIDS HAD been…off…since meeting their grandmother yesterday. Beth sighed as she stirred the gravy on the stove. Maybe she was being too judgmental, though. When Connor had wet the bed last night and she decided the woman must be horrible, Nolan said the boys might react poorly to any change, especially one reminding them of their mother's death.

Of course, he was right, yet to see them sad and fretting filled her with misery.

However, tonight, after spending all Saturday with Sir—who'd undoubtedly exhausted them with chores and games—they appeared happier.

Hearing footsteps, she smiled at Nolan over her shoulder.

Fresh from his shower, he sat down at the kitchen island and eyed her pre-dinner plate of cut-up fruit—*healthy food: what was the world coming to?*—before picking up an apple slice. "How'd your meeting with the Dragos go today?"

She rolled her eyes. "They're fun to listen to, the way they disagree. Alastair prefers muted colors and a formal design, although he's open to random *if* it's mostly symmetrical. Max couldn't care less about the actual design as long as the colors are bright. They're so different."

"An English doc and a cowboy cop who top together." Nolan shook his head. "At least Vance and Galen have similar styles. It'll be interesting to see Max and Alastair doing a scene."

"I know." She dumped the potato water and pulled out the masher.

Without speaking, Nolan made a *gimme* motion with his fingers.

Pampering him was sure difficult. Beth set the boiled potatoes, butter and milk, salt and pepper, and masher in front of him. "But they bicker like family. I guess that makes sense since Alastair did summers on the Drago ranch, and Max lived in London with Alastair and his mom for a while."

"Got it. They're more brothers than cousins." Nolan popped an orange slice into his mouth and started whipping the potatoes.

"Mmmhmm. Speaking of brothers…" Beth raised her voice. "Guys, time for supper."

At the thundering of little feet, Nolan snorted. "I've heard cattle stampedes less noisy."

Cheering, the two tore into the kitchen. When Grant skidded to a stop, Connor bounced off his back and grabbed Nolan's leg to catch himself.

"Sounds like y'all are hungry." Nolan ruffled Connor's hair.

"Grant, can you set the island with plates and glasses?" Beth reached into the cupboard and got out the dishes. "Connor, here's silverware and napkins if you would help, please?"

Both children jumped to their duties as if she'd given them a quest worthy of a Disney movie.

As Nolan scooped the mashed potatoes into a serving bowl, she put the fried chicken onto a platter. *Bad Beth.* She should give her men a nice healthy roasted chicken…but fried chicken was a favorite of her Master.

The boys had their own favorites.

"Mashed-toes," Connor's eyes went wide and happy.

"An' gravy," Grant breathed.

Neither boy nor man commented on the pretty salad. Typical males. She started to sit and realized the big cookie jar was in the way, so carried it to the counter. Odd how light it felt.

A quick check showed three cookies left. Three? Hadn't she filled the jar yesterday? "Guys, I know you like sweets but—"

"Beth."

She turned at Nolan's warning tone. Brows drawn, he tilted his head toward the boys.

Grant stood stiffly beside his chair, worry in his eyes.

Connor, though… Every speck of color had drained from his face, and he was slowly backing away.

Oh, dear. She leaned against the counter in a nonchalant *I'm-not-angry* posture.

He stopped.

"Well, baby, I figure you didn't eat all those cookies, or you'd be sick to your stomach." She held out her hand. "Why don't you show me where you put them?"

His little legs were stiff as he approached her. As he led her into the hall, she heard Nolan talking quietly to Grant and keeping him in the kitchen. Nolan said *divide and conquer* was his parents' favorite system for his brothers and sisters. Figuring his folks knew what they were doing, he'd suggested they use the technique for the boys.

In the bedroom, Connor pointed toward Grant's bed. "In our cave."

She knelt beside the bed, noticing how they'd scavenged boxes and pillows to form an under-the-bed barricade. "You two make the coolest caves," she said in admiration and watched Connor blink.

After pushing a box to one side, she pulled out an ancient lunchbox. "How amazing is this? I bet my mom carried one of these to school."

Upon opening it, she found cookies as well as molding cheese, stale biscuits, and a hot dog. *Ew.* She barely kept from wrinkling her nose at the stench. Food…hoarding, was that the term? *Careful, Beth.* "You know, in colder areas, squirrels will run around gathering nuts to store them away for the winter. You're like a little squirrel, honey."

A tiny bit of color returned to his cheeks. Oh, she wanted to hug him so hard right now.

"But squirrels store food that doesn't need to be kept cold. Eating food this smelly can make you dreadfully sick, Connor."

His thin shoulders hunched again, and tears brimmed in his eyes.

How could she reassure him she didn't care if he hid food, yet prevent him from taking food requiring refrigeration?

Nolan and Grant appeared in the doorway. Grant gave her a wary stare and edged closer to stand between her and Connor, as he'd done after the bandsaw fracas in the workshop.

Workshop. That was *it*. Beth looked at Nolan. "Remember the mini-fridge you bought for my garden shed? I never remember to stock it with drinks. Why don't we put it in here—on Connor's side of the room?"

Nolan's quiet smile held approval. He set his hand on Grant's shoulder. "C'mon, tiger, let's fetch us a fridge."

As they left, Beth held out her hand to Connor. "After we toss this smelly stuff, we'll get fresh stuff for *your* refrigerator. Then, whenever I get groceries, you can do what I do—throw away the old food that's going bad and start over with new. Okay?"

" 'Kay." When he took her hand, she felt as if she could conquer worlds.

THE NEXT NIGHT, Nolan lay in bed with Beth a warm weight on top of him. Her forearms on his chest propped her up—and kept her breasts available for his enjoyment. Within her, his cock was slowly softening. Her lips were swollen from his kisses and a damned fine pre-fuck blowjob.

Her breasts were also swollen, the nipples red and sensitive. He wasn't a real sadist—but what Dom wouldn't enjoy the involuntary clench of her cunt when he rolled a nipple? Yeah, nice. He did the left breast next.

"Where do you get all this energy?" With a laugh, she tipped her head down and sleepily rubbed her cheek against his forearm.

"Clean living." As her long hair pooled in a silky-cool mass on his bare chest, he ran his fingers through it. "Good length, sugar. Keep it this long."

When she rolled her eyes at his order—and an order it was—he smacked her ass. "Don't sass your Master, little rabbit, or your tail will be too sore to sit on."

"My tail is already pretty sore, thank you very much." Her voice was husky, not from pain, but from pleading and her high cries as she'd climaxed. Good thing he'd put in a ton of extra soundproofing when he built the place. He'd have hated to forego the noises his Beth made when thoroughly spanked and thoroughly fucked.

He glanced at the portable monitor on the nightstand. Green lights indicated the children's bedroom door remained closed. With the volume turned up, he could also hear the sound of their even breathing.

Knowing they were planning for children, Z's buddy, Simon, had recommended the kiddy equipment when he was putting in the security system.

Curious about the keypads, the boys had been thrilled when Nolan had demonstrated the alarms. On the past couple of evenings, they'd joined Nolan during his evening rounds, checking everything was safe, securing windows and doors, closing things up for the night. They'd been pleased as all get out to help him "*perfect Beff.*"

Good kids.

Beth's gaze had followed his, and with her uncanny ability to follow his thoughts, she snickered. "If I tossed your monitor in the lake, you'd have to leave the doors open to hear the children—and you wouldn't be able to abuse your poor submissive."

"I'd buy another monitor. I'm not going to give up abusing my poor li'l subbie." He massaged her ass and chuckled at her squeaks and whimpers. Damn, she felt good. Her little ass was rounding out as she regained her weight. Since Connor's stomach growled about every three to four hours, she no longer missed meals.

He studied the way the moonlight streaming in the windows brought out the lighter strands of red-blonde in her hair. "You are so fucking beautiful," he murmured.

Tears filled her eyes.

It was both delightful and frustrating she never saw herself that way. "Someday, hopefully before we end up in a nursing home, you'll accept a compliment without being surprised. You're beautiful, Beth."

"So are you, Master."

Beautiful? "Now, that's purely an insult."

She giggled. A noise came from the monitor, and they listened as one of the children stirred, muttered, and fell back asleep. "I'm going to really miss them if they leave."

"Yeah." Nolan stroked her hair. Losing them would hurt like hell. "What do you know about their grandmother?"

"Just what I told you Drusilla said. Her mom was such a fanatic that Drusilla ran away." She made an unhappy sound as his cock slipped out of her.

"And Price told you to consider the source. He does have a point. Addicts aren't always honest."

"True." Curling up at his side, Beth laid her head on his shoulder. His snuggly submissive. "But what if she told me the truth? After all, the kids were badly shaken after meeting their grandmother."

Connor had gone back to wetting the bed; Grant's moods

had deteriorated again. "Or they simply don't do well with change."

Her mouth set stubbornly. "But Price totally blew off any idea the grandmother might not be perfect. Since she's near kin, he won't do more than a basic background check—and I doubt she's been in jail."

Price was an asshole. No question there. Nolan stuck a hand behind his head and studied the ceiling. "If the grandma is all right, the boys will get to grow up with a blood relation. That'd be a good thing, even though we'd miss them."

"Yes." Beth's low answer held a foreshadowing of grief.

He rubbed his knuckles over her smooth cheek. "Remember *religious* doesn't mean crazy. You attend services off and on. Kari and Andrea are pretty involved with their churches."

"This is true. But Drusilla called her mother a *fanatic*. Said her mom whipped her when she was disobedient. I don't want our boys there."

A fanatic. If true, not good. In pursuit of their unreasoning beliefs, a fanatic would flatten anything in his or her way—including children. How truthful had Drusilla been? "We owe it to the boys to make sure they'll go somewhere nurturing. If Price isn't going to check out Grandma, perhaps we should."

"*Yes*. I'd feel so much better if we knew what kind of a person she is." With a bounce, Beth shot up and planted her hands on his chest. "Hey, tomorrow, Anne is meeting us for lunch after our self-defense class. She'd help."

Anne had been a private investigator and bounty hunter before joining Galen's firm. "Good choice. I'll tag Galen and Vance and get Dan onboard, too." Vance still worked at the FBI; Galen had left the Feds to start a company specializing in finding the lost. As a cop, Dan could access local records.

"Okay." Beth lay back down beside him, and her slender body relaxed. "We've got a plan."

Chapter Eighteen

THE AIR WAS fragrant with the scent of pizza, and Beth pulled in an appreciative breath as she led the way into the Italian restaurant. She took a seat at their favorite corner table. "I love this 'reward' for going to the martial arts class, even if most of us couldn't stay afterward this time."

Anne pulled her chair out, grimaced, and pulled it out farther before sitting. At five months, she finally looked pregnant. "Well, I don't deserve a reward, but I'm going to pig out on pizza anyway. Now the nausea is gone, I'm starving all the time."

"You know, you've got an *I'm-pregnant* glow," Beth noted. "And Ben's got a Daddy glow."

"I swear, he gloats over every fraction of an inch I gain," Anne said. "And when he saw the baby on the ultrasound? He teared up."

"Aww." Sliding into a seat, Sally laughed...but she had tears in her eyes, too. "You've made him so happy, Anne."

Eyes reddening, Anne pointed her finger at the brunette. "Don't make me cry, or I'll sic your Masters on you."

With a flash of dimples, Gabi dropped a pile of menus in the center of the table and took a chair. "At one time, you'd have flogged her sassy ass yourself, Mistress."

Anne sniffed. "That happy day will come again. In the meantime—as Ben constantly tells me—I have to delegate."

Uzuri took a chair and set a market-sized, red-striped tote bag on the floor. Since her visit three weeks ago, the last remaining Shadowlands "trainee" had dutifully attended self-defense classes.

Beth planned to talk with Holt and see when Uzuri would finish the bet requiring her to take self-defense. Another bet might be in order to keep her coming.

Sally noticed the brightly colored tote, and her eyebrows lifted. "Interesting combination of styles, girlfriend."

"This is true." Uzuri glanced down at her impeccably fitted, pale blue suit, bone heels, and matching clutch. The department store executive could have been a model for business clothing. "I brought the bag for Beth's little demons."

"Demons? What say you? My babies are *angels*." Beth's lips tipped up. Last week, the boys had wheedled Uzuri and Sally into playing with them in the pool. She'd never heard Uzuri laugh so hard. "But…what's the occasion?"

"I know Connor and Grant might not stay with you, but there was a back-to-school sale in the children's department—and I get an employee discount. I'm merely human; how could I resist?" Uzuri handed over the bag. "It's a good thing you don't have girls. Their clothes are even cuter."

Beth pulled out sturdy shorts, two adorable T-shirts with stripes, others with cartoon character graphics for Connor and superhero figures for Grant. *How perfect.* "You're the only person I know who can figure out sizes at a glance."

"I started in retail in the children's department." Uzuri patted the shirts. "There's nothing too flashy, and I checked the county dress code to make sure the graphics were okay—nothing immoral, offensive, or unlawful."

"Oh my God, I hadn't even thought about dress codes." More things to study up on. "These are awesome. Thank you so much!" Beth jumped up to give her friend a hug.

"So, how is it going with Connor and Grant?" Gabi asked. "And with you?"

"You're such a social worker." And she'd given Beth the perfect lead-in to what she had to ask. "But I'm glad you asked, because I need a favor from you guys."

Every single woman at the table immediately nodded.

"I haven't even told you what I need." *Don't cry, don't cry.* The thickness in her throat was making it difficult to speak. "Nolan and I want to keep the kids."

"Yes!" Sally shouted. Gabi and Uzuri cheered more quietly. Anne said, "Excellent."

My girl gang. When she'd married Kyler, he'd driven away her friends. Beth had a feeling these women wouldn't have given her up so easily.

"No crying," Anne warned. "You make me cry, and I'll whip your ass. Fucking hormones." Her disgruntled tone made Beth giggle instead.

"So, what's the favor?" Gabi asked. "Who do you need killed?"

"Oh, girl, you're hitting too close to the truth." Beth scowled. "You know that jerk of a social worker, Price? He wants to hand the children over to their grandmother."

Beth laid out the facts, piece by piece, and saw nods of understanding. She finished by telling them, "Price called this morning. The boys will have an overnight with the grandmother on Thursday."

"Who knew old lard-belly could move so fast?" Sally said. "So…you want to know if grandma is a sweet, cookie-baking cuddler or a rabid bitch."

Interesting summary. "Um, yes. Trouble is, I don't know her complete name."

P.I. Anne and hacker Sally exchanged smug glances. They were both employees of Galen's *I-can-find-anything* company. "Not a problem," Anne said. "I'll research her past. Sally, you comb through her finances."

Sally gave her a mock salute. "Aye, Ma'am."

"Digital background checks are good, but for this, we also need personal information. What she's actually like." Anne frowned. "Conducting interviews with her friends and neighbors might be tricky, since you don't want the woman—or Price—to know we're investigating her."

"Considering how much hiring we've done this year, I'm excellent at interviewing," Uzuri offered. "But I don't know how to be sneaky about it."

Gabi smiled. "Actually, this is excellent timing. Some of Marcus' boys are selling cookie dough to get money for their boy's club." The Sensei and Gabi's Dom spent a lot of time with teens needing a helping hand. Gabi continued, "Once Anne gives an address, Uzuri and I and the boys will sell cookies all over Granny's neighborhood and get all the gossip."

"Perfect." Anne looked around the table in approval before her gaze turned to Beth. "We've got your back."

Threats from the Mistress or not, Beth couldn't help herself. She burst into tears.

GRANT TRIED NOT to scowl as he listened to Grandmother's boring voice. He hadn't wanted to visit her today. He'd wanted to stay with Beth; they'd been having fun.

Although Nolan had gone to work, Grant and Connor had talked Beth into playing soccer with them. She was really fun and fast, and she'd showed him cool kicks and said he had a *talent*. But, then, they'd had to stop and get ready for the Price guy to bring them here to Grandmother's house. They had to sleep here tonight, too.

He checked through his eyelashes, wishing she'd stop reading from that book. His knees hurt. Why wouldn't she let them sit on the couch to listen to the Bible stuff?

She kept talking, on and on. Her house smelled funny, too, kind of like the stuff Beth used to get the white towels whiter.

Connor curled his cold fingers around Grant's hand. "I want to go back to Beff's," he whispered.

Grandmother heard him, and when she stared at them, her gray eyebrows came together, and her eyes were like a gator's. She didn't like him or Connor—or Mama, either. She said Mama was bad and had run away. She said they were probably bad, too. And they hadn't even done anything.

Squeezing Connor's hand, he looked down at the floor. She'd told them to keep their heads "bowed."

Connor had started squirming a while ago and would start crying soon.

Grant wanted to cry, too.

THAT EVENING, BETH sat with Nolan at the kitchen island. A stack of paper sat in front of them. Outside, a gull cried shrilly, and low voices came from the lake where the neighbors were twilight fishing. Inside, the only noise was the hum of the refrigerator. The house was too quiet with no childish giggles. No silly bickering. No funny Connor imitations of baaing sheep or mooing cows.

The farm animal toys had been a hit...as were the zoo animals, the racecars, the noisy spin-the-wheel games, and everything else. She shook her head ruefully. The kids' bedroom had already contained toys for Nolan's nieces and nephews. That number had exploded. She and Nolan had, perhaps...*okay, definitely*...overindulged in buying things.

But so had their friends. Linda had swung by with a miniature corral and horses set, saying, "Sam and I saw this and thought of the kids." Or Rainie who'd bought stuffed poodles for their veterinary clinic promotion and wanted the boys to have some.

Kari had delivered a grocery sack of children's books from her school's used book sale. "I thought it'd be an easy way for you to find out what they like." Andrea had appeared with a humungous box of Legos her younger relatives had outgrown.

If the strict grandmother kept the boys, would she let them have all their new toys? The thought dragged Beth right down into the morass she'd been avoiding. Were they truly going to lose Connor and Grant?

"Hey." Nolan pulled her against his solid frame and kissed her temple. "Easy, li'l rabbit. Don't surrender before the war is over."

His gaze held as much sadness as hers and—for him—she managed a smile. "You soldier-boys are sure full of battle analogies."

"On the contrary, sugar, my entire vocabulary comes from X-box games."

Doubtful, since although he loved playing silly video games with Grant, he'd said no war games for kids. After a sip of lemonade to wash away the blockage in her throat, she pulled the papers forward. So many reports. So much time and effort. "We have awesome friends."

"Yep." He scanned the first page. "Sally says there's nothing of interest in the financial area. Mrs. Ada Brun retired a couple of years ago from a secretarial position. She lives on a tiny pension and social security. Has a small savings account. Makes heavy donations to a fundamentalist church and their missionary fund."

"A good church-going woman with time to devote to the children." Beth's heart sank. "We're screwed."

"If she'll be good to the kids, we'll have to be content."

"I know." But, oh, she missed them so much already. Nonetheless, they had to hope the woman was a good one.

She checked over Galen and Vance's report. No criminal record, no arrests, not even any parking tickets. Had borne one child. Husband had died when Drusilla was in the mid-teens, which might be one reason the girl had run away. "Nothing interesting in the Feds' information."

"Gabi and Andrea report the woman goes to church and missionary meetings and prayer groups. She has had some minor squabbles with the neighbors over the years. Has no boyfriend or lover and keeps her house clean."

"She's a saint." Beth's heart sank. They were going to lose the children. She knew it.

"GET UP NOW." The bare overhead light came on.

At the sound of his grandmother's voice, Grant sat up in bed and blinked. The window didn't show any sunshine through the curtain. "Is it morning?"

"Yes. Didn't you hear me calling you?" Grandmother walked into the room. "We will have a Bible reading before breakfast."

Grant rubbed his knees, still sore from the long bedtime prayers.

"What is that?" Her eyes narrowed, and she crossed the room to pick up a roll Connor had pocketed from dinner. "Food is served at meals, no other time, and it certainly isn't kept in bedrooms." Taking the roll, she walked out of the room.

Hoping Connor wouldn't get upset, Grant glanced over at his brother.

Still sound asleep. Last night, Connor had cried for Nolan and Beth for a long time. Grandmother had given them no bath, no story, no lullaby. Just on-the-knees prayers and lights flipped off as she left the room.

Grant was a big boy...but he'd missed having Beth tuck the

blankets around him and kiss his cheek. And sing her lullabies. Listening to her felt like floating in the pool. But now, the thought of her and Nolanman was a painful ache under his ribs. He slid out of his side of the bed. "We gotta get out of bed, Connor."

While Connor was still yawning and rubbing his eyes, Grandmother returned. "I said, wake *up*." She yanked the bedding down and let out an angry scream. "You wet the bed! My good mattress is destroyed. You *horrible* boy." With a grip on Connor's arm, she dragged him out of the bed, slapping his wet bottom over and over.

Screaming in pain, Connor struggled frantically.

"Stop!" Grant shoved her. "Leave him alone, you-you bitch."

She released Connor and spun toward Grant. "What did you call me?"

Grant took a step back—but she grabbed his hair.

Leaning down, she yelled in his face, "My daughter was a tramp with no morals and no decency. Led astray by the world. She ruined you. But I will see you brought back to the straight and narrow. God has given this awful duty to me."

Tears filled Grant's eyes from pain...and from her words. "I'm not ruined."

Her grip hurt as she hauled him down the hall to the single bathroom. "Bad words must be washed away. Open your mouth."

Jaw closed tight, he stared at her until she yanked hard on his hair, and he couldn't stop from crying...and crying harder as she shoved soap in his mouth. Gagging and crying, hurting and spitting, he fought her.

When he threw up, she finally let him go and drove him into their bedroom with stinging slaps.

Crying, he curled in a corner. *I want Nolanman. Want Beth.*

After stripping the sheets from the bed, she shut them both in the bedroom. "Bad boys don't eat. Pray that you learn to be good."

Connor had crawled under the low bed, and Grant could hear his sobs.

Their grandmother was mean. Awful mean. Grant scowled, wishing he'd kicked her. Or bit her. "No wonder Mama ran away from her." His words were a whisper, in case she was still in the house.

Connor snuffled. "I want to run away, too."

Could they? He didn't know where they'd go, but at least they wouldn't be around her.

A little while later, the front door slammed, and the house was silent.

They could leave.

Grant tried to open the door. *Locked.* He kicked the stupid thing. At the window, he pulled the curtains back. No screen. And her backyard didn't have a fence. Yeah, they could run away.

Hopes rising, he shoved at the window.

It didn't move.

She would have locked it; she liked locking things up. But when he dragged a chair over and stood on it, he saw the latch was busted off. Why couldn't he raise the window? On closer examination, he saw small holes around the inside of the frame.

The window was nailed shut.

IN HIS HOME office upstairs beside Beth's, Nolan finished an estimate for a real estate building, stretched, and glanced at the clock. Beth was downstairs, indulging in what she called "comfort" reading, and the boys should be back any time now. Before shutting the computer down, he checked his emails. Ah, one from Anne. He had wondered why they'd received no report from her.

After reading the first paragraph, he went to the door and called, "Beth, Anne emailed us."

Her feet thudded on the stairs as she ran up. "What did she say?"

"We'll read it together." He pulled her down on his lap in front of the monitor.

Anne's initial summary stated she hadn't found anything interesting in the grandmother's background check. However, she had analyzed everyone's data together and written another summary.

Drusilla reported running away from home due to her mother's "religious fanaticism." Ada Brun has no life other than her church, no interests other than religion. Glimpses obtained of the subject's home reveal an altar in the living room with lit candles. Religious artwork covers the walls. Although a small television is present, the only other entertainment is a Bible and religious tracts. No other magazines or books were noted. Her life appears unbalanced to an unhealthy degree.

"Yet it would be difficult to indict someone for being religious," Beth said glumly.

"True. But being overly controlling and strict is a problem when it comes to children. Read this." He pointed to the next paragraph.

Follow-up interviews with the neighbors reveal all squabbles were outgrowths of the subject's complaints about various children who cut across her lawn, played too loudly in their own yards (or on a Sunday), used "foul" language—again in their own yards or on the street. She places high value on observation of "the Sabbath." The subject often criticizes various neighbors' child-raising skills, using Bible references. Although the neighbors mangled the subject's quotes, enough was remembered to find the proper references. See below:

"Whoever spares the rod hates his son, but he who loves him is diligent to discipline him." Proverbs 13:24

"Folly is bound up in the heart of a child, but the rod of discipline drives it far from him." Proverbs 22:15

"Do not withhold discipline from a child; if you strike him with a rod, he will not die. If you strike him with the rod, you will save his soul from Sheol." Proverbs 23:13-14

"Train up a child in the way he should go; even when he is old he will not depart from it." Proverbs 22:6

"The rod and reproof give wisdom, but a child left to himself brings shame to his mother." Proverbs 29:15

Beth stared at Nolan as dismay filled her heart. "And she has our boys?"

"I'm calling Price." He set her on her feet and picked up his cell phone.

Beth curled up on his office chair to listen.

Pacing around the office, Nolan eventually managed to get through to the social worker. "Listen, Price, according to information we received, Connor and Grant's grandmother is a fucking fanatic. She's all about corporal punishment as set down by the Bible."

Beth held her breath. Just once, let Price be reasonable.

Nolan listened to the phone and responded, "Yeah, she believes in that spare the rod and spoil the child shit. Seems like y'all told us corporal punishment isn't allowed."

Price's voice was too muted to hear.

Nolan's jaw turned to granite. "Relatives aren't under the same strict guidelines as foster parents? An action is either wrong or it isn't. For fuck's sake, Price, those boys have suffered enough."

After listening for a minute, he simply hung up.

When Beth wrapped her arms around his waist, she could

sense the rage emanating from him. "What did he say?"

"He was heading out to pick them up in a few minutes anyway. He'll ask the children how it went when they're in the car—it's part of the protocol. If they complain they've been abused, he'll check into things with the grandmother."

"All right," Beth said carefully. "That's a start."

"He also reminded me we're merely foster parents providing a temporary place for the boys until placement. Any interference with a placement will result in the children being removed to a different foster home."

"A threat."

Nolan nodded.

"What can we do?" Beth rubbed her cheek over his worn-smooth work shirt and listened to the slow thud of his heart.

"Wait and see how it went." He sighed. "We have to consider the possibility Anne's conclusions are wrong. Maybe the old lady will adore her grandchildren."

"Maybe."

His jaw turned hard. "However, if the grandmother is abusive, we'll rip their placement system right apart."

Beth felt old fears surfacing. Back when she was the one suffering abuse, she'd dealt with social service systems. Nothing moved quickly, and some people like Price preferred not to rock the boat. Because they just didn't care.

"Beth?" Sir pulled her close and rested his chin on her head.

Even with her arms filled with Nolan, they still felt empty. "It'll be all right."

She knew she lied.

IN THE STARKLY lit dining room, Grant pushed at the food on his plate with his fork. It was a hamburger, but not in a bun, and he'd taken a bite and chewed and chewed. He didn't want any more.

His stomach was all twisty, even though they hadn't had breakfast. He'd been hungry for lunch until Grandmother had read out of that Bible book for…forever…and had glared at him every time his stomach growled.

"Do we go home today?" Connor asked Grandmother.

The lady's mouth pinched together, and her eyes went nasty so she looked almost like Mama when she was crazy-mad. Grant felt sick; he should have told Connor not to talk at all.

Grandmother slapped the table hard enough to make the dishes rattle. "*This* is your home."

Connor shrank in his chair, and tears filled his eyes.

"Eat your food," she said.

Connor shook his head, his chin quivering.

When she started to stand, Grant said really fast, "He'll throw up if he eats when he's crying."

"If you two think tears will get you your own way, you have another think coming." She picked Connor's food up although the plate was still full. "Maybe he'll be hungry again at supper."

Supper? "But…" Weren't they supposed to go home today? Grant didn't ask. *Please let the Price man come back and get them. Please.*

A few minutes later, when Grant couldn't force anything down, Grandmother took his plate away, too and finished her food while they silently watched. After wiping her mouth, she checked the clock hanging on the wall and frowned.

When she walked over to stand between their chairs, Grant felt his body trying to slide down. "Mr. Price will ask you how this visit went. You will tell him you had a wonderful time."

Connor stared. "But we didn't."

Her bony hands latched onto Connor's shoulders. She lifted him, shook him hard, and slammed him back down. "You had a wonderful time." She shook his shoulders again. "Wonderful."

Connor was crying so hard he probably didn't hear anything.

"We'll remember." When she stepped back, Grant put his arm around Connor. His mouth set. He'd tell the Price man the truth. See if he didn't.

"Mr. Price will let me know what you say." Grandmother's eyes were hard stones in her wrinkled face. "If you say anything more than you had a wonderful time to anyone—even your foster parents—I'll know, and *you'll be sorry.*"

Everything inside Grant curled up and died. After living with Jermaine, Grant knew what she meant.

She would hurt him. Hurt Connor.

IN THE GREAT room, Nolan stood beside Price, feeling unsettled. Grant and Connor had run into the house, hugged Nolan as if they'd been gone for weeks, and hugged Beth the same way.

When she'd sat down on the couch, they piled right onto her and clung like terrified kittens.

He studied them with a frown. Hell, if they could have burrowed beneath her skin, they would have. He glanced at Price. "Connor's obviously been crying."

"That's not surprising. Change is unsettling to a child his age, and he's been through a lot." Price's expression was smug. "But they'll settle in nicely with their grandmother."

"What did they say about their visit?"

"They had a wonderful time." Price noted Nolan's disbelief. "Ask them yourself."

"I will."

Connor was in Beth's lap, his face against her chest. Her arm was around Grant's shoulders, and he'd nestled against her side.

When Nolan sat down next to Grant, the boy actually crawled into Nolan's lap in an imitation of his little brother. This wasn't like independent Grant at all, and he sure as fuck wasn't acting as if he'd had a *wonderful* time. "How did everything go with your Grandmother, Grant?"

Grant's face was against Nolan's shoulder, and his voice was muffled. "We had a wonderful time." He used the exact words Price had relayed.

"Did you like your grandmother?"

The tough little boy tensed. His answer was slower in coming. "Uh-huh."

Price clapped his hands. "There, see? What'd I tell you, Mr. King? The children enjoyed their visit." Price walked toward the door. "I'll start finalizing the arrangements so they can move in with their Grandmother permanently. In the interim, they'll visit so they get to know each other. I'll arrange another overnight with her tomorrow."

"MOVE IN WITH their Grandmother permanently." The Price man's words circled inside Grant's mind like a train on a round track. Each time he heard it, he wanted to yell, to scream, to throw things.

But this was their after-lunch quiet time. So, at the bedroom table, he colored a truck picture with long, jagged, black and red streaks. Ripping it from the book, he crumpled it and threw it across their bedroom. "I hate the Price man. And Grandmother, too."

Watching with wide eyes, Connor nodded. After a minute, he quietly put his two cookies inside his fridge.

When Beth had said she had macaroni and cheese if they hadn't eaten lunch, Mr. Price said Grandmother had fed them. As soon as the man left, Connor had asked for something to eat. They'd emptied the plates of macaroni and cheese with carrot sticks, so Beth had given them more, and they ate that too, and then her forehead wrinkled, and she asked if Grandmother had forgotten to feed them. Although she'd smiled, her face didn't look right.

When Connor told her, "We had a wonderful time," even her smile had gone away.

But she'd given Connor two cookies. "One for you, one for Grant. For your refrigerator."

With the cookies put away, Connor closed the fridge door and sat down in front of it. "I don't like Grandmother. I don't want to live with her."

"Me, either." Grant sat on the carpet beside him. "I want to stay here."

"But the man said we can't. He said Beff wants a baby girl, not big, clumsy boys."

The Price man said almost nobody adopted big, clumsy boys. Scowling, Grant held up his hands and checked them over. Was he clumsy? Nolan said he was good at swimming and soccer. But, even if he wasn't clumsy, he and Conner weren't babies. Or girls.

His chin quivered. Why couldn't Beth like them instead?

"Maybe we could make Beff like boys?" Connor said doubtfully. "If we were real nice…"

"Yeah, but fosters get money for keeping *other* people's kids. So if Beth and Nolan keep us forever, they won't be fosters no more, and they won't get money."

"Oh." Connor heaved a sigh.

When the Price man had explained about the money, Grant hadn't wanted to believe him. After all, grownups didn't…always…tell the truth, but he remembered that Rory from school lived with fosters, and he'd said they got money to keep him. And they told Rory they didn't get enough money to buy him Xbox games or a skateboard.

"Would Beff like us if we gave them money?" Connor asked. "I have a dollar."

The momentary hope died. "A dollar isn't much."

Connor's face fell. "Guess we gots to go back to the mean lady." Sniffling, he pushed a suitcase over and crawled under the bed.

Grant pulled the suitcase out farther and started to join him. The darkness felt right—like home.

Home.

He stopped crawling and stared at Connor as hope rose within him, big and strong and sure. "*Mama* had money."

THAT NIGHT IN the great room, Beth held a book unopened in her hands and simply listened to the boys splash in their over-sized bathtub. Their giggles mingling with Nolan's deep laugh soothed her worries.

After the children's quiet time in their room, they'd emerged with smiles. When Nolan said he'd teach them to paddle his old canoe, they'd even cheered. After returning, they'd helped put the toppings on the pizza, creating happy faces from the pepperoni and sausage.

Happy faces.

She'd had to force herself to be cheerful, because, when they'd changed into shorts to go on the lake, she'd seen their legs. Their poor little knees weren't scraped or scabbed in the way a child might get from falling down. She knew—oh, she did—exactly what made those reddened bruised marks. Alt-hough she often knelt for Master Nolan, he insisted she use a cushion if the floor wasn't carpeted. But her first husband? Oh, he'd loved to make her kneel on concrete or hardwood.

Nolan, observant Dom that he was, had seen the marks on the boys, and his face had turned dark, but he'd shaken his head at her to wait. Now she understood why. While helping them shampoo their hair, he'd also assess them quietly for other marks.

Beth glanced at her book and tossed it onto the coffee table. Nothing could keep her interest right now. Honestly, if the grandmother were nice, Beth would grieve at losing the children, but would be happy for them to have a loving relative. But this woman…

How could they let the children go to a woman who wouldn't care for them?

Footsteps. The giggles grew louder. The boys were out of the bathroom. There were thumping noises as they got their pajamas from the dresser and bickered over which superhero print each would wear.

Her smile faded when a grim-faced Nolan entered the great room. "What?" she asked.

"Connor has bruising on his ass. They have some bruises on their shoulders and upper arms." He sat down beside her.

Rage filled her so quickly her vision went red. "She made them kneel long enough to leave marks. And now you're saying she hurt them?" Unable to sit, Beth stormed across the room and back. "They were so hungry she must have starved them, too, didn't she? *Didn't* she?"

"Easy, sugar." He pulled her down in his lap. "Maybe it was her. Or could be Connor fell down. Could be the boys were wrestling and picked up bruises. They wouldn't tell me. Not fucking anything. But we'll figure it out and fix it."

Her body vibrated with anger. "I'll kill her. That'll fix it."

His low laugh rumbled through the room. "Best we find something else. The kids won't want to visit you in prison."

"You're taking this awfully well." She turned to regard him. As overprotective as he was, she'd have thought there would be an explosion.

"I'm a calm man." At her skeptical snort, he sighed. "And I'm going to have to fix the bent towel rack in the kid's bathroom."

Now there was the Dom she knew.

"What should we do?" she asked.

"There's not enough evidence to point fingers, but…we're bound by law to report any suspicion of abuse, so we will conform to the letter of the law. I'll let Price know we're worried."

She thought for a minute. "After you call and report the marks to Price, I'll send a hard copy to his supervisor. Mrs. Molina seemed like a nice person."

"Good idea." He growled. "If the boys won't talk, we can't do much else right now."

"But, Sir, the children go back to her tomorrow morning." Beth felt like crying. "Let's run. Take the boys and run. We can…can go live in South America or something."

His mouth was an unhappy line. "I hear you. But we'd have trouble getting them out of the country, especially since we'd be reported missing. We'll stick to the rules…for now. If the system fails them, then, yes. Our job is to protect them, so that's what we'll do, no matter the cost."

He was right. She hated it, but he was right. Only… "What if she hurts them?"

"Easy, darlin'. We don't know if she did, right?" He trapped her on his lap before she could start pacing again. "But, just in case, I'll hire Galen to put surveillance on Mrs. Brun's house. Using one of those noise detectors, the agent will hear if she makes them cry—and someone can…conveniently…intervene."

"Oh." Both intervention and a witness. "I like the idea." She considered. "I bet Gabi, Uzuri, and crew would be happy to visit the old woman and try to sell her cookie dough."

"There you go." He stroked her hair. "We'll keep them safe. Somehow, we'll keep them safe."

Turning in his arms, she straddled his knees. "I love you so, so much, my Master." She kissed him, gently. Sweetly.

With a huffed laugh, he squashed her against him and took control of the kiss. She could taste his fury.

A giggle broke them apart. Two well-scrubbed boys in pajama shorts stood in the doorway.

Beth wrinkled her nose at them. "So, you think it's funny to see the Nolanman kissing me?"

Still giggling, Connor nodded.

"Okay, buster, that means war." She picked up a soft pillow and fired it at him.

The battle was on.

Chapter Nineteen

While Grandmother was locking the front door on Saturday morning, Grant sidled over to the window and pulled back the curtain to watch the social worker driving away. *Finally*.

Before leaving, Mr. Price had told Grandmother she better not hit Grant and Connor 'cause Nolan had threatened with liabitterly, whatever it was. Grandmother had been really mad at Mr. Price. She was mad at him and Connor, too.

Mr. Price's car turned the corner and disappeared.

As his heart began thumping hard, Grant whispered to Connor, "Are you ready?"

Connor tightened his grip on his small backpack and nodded.

Grant turned. "Oh, *no*. Grandmother, my shirt fell out of my pack. Can I go get it?" Trying to act like he was a *good* boy, Grant pointed through the window at his red T-shirt on the sidewalk. Mr. Price had stepped right over it.

Her lips pinched together like Connor's had when he'd eaten a rotten grape. "That was careless of you. Go get it immediately." She unlocked the front door and opened it.

With Connor beside him, Grant hurried to the door.

"Not you." She grabbed Connor's shoulder.

No. Panicking, Grant lowered his head and rammed her.

She staggered back.

Grabbing Connor's hand, Grant charged through the door

and tore around the corner toward the back. They crossed to the house next door and ran through that backyard and then others, zigzagging through yards and empty lots and across streets. He heard her yelling and kept running.

On and on.

He rejected the first bus stop and hid behind a house while Connor caught his breath.

The second bus stop was too close, too.

On the third, he led the way onto a bus headed for downtown. The driver frowned, but closed the door with a whoosh, and pulled into traffic.

No one paid any attention to them as they found an empty seat halfway back. Once in a seat, Grant held up his hand and chortled as Connor's small hand smacked his in a high-five.

IT HAD BEEN one fucking crappy morning so far. At least in his opinion.

Not everyone's. Nolan watched his cheerful construction crew at work on the ten-story commercial building. The happy guys were scoring some nice overtime with the weekend work.

Unfortunately, his day had started with threatening Price, telling the bastard he'd be held responsible—and liable—if the boys returned with any damage. Issuing the threat had felt good, but probably only succeeded in pissing the asshole off. Once Price had left, Nolan had called Galen to get his man over to Grandma's house.

Still didn't feel like enough. Despite the sunny day, a chill kept raising the hair on the back of Nolan's neck.

He turned his attention to the plans he was checking over for the foreman. The schedule had gotten screwed up last week—the electrical subcontractor had fallen behind—and so his crew had to play catch-up this weekend. His head wasn't in the game though.

Neither was his attitude. When he'd arrived, the crew had taken one look at his face and steered clear.

Mid-morning, after getting the foreman squared away, Nolan was considering heading to the office when his cell phone rang. "King."

"Kouros. Got a problem." Galen's Maine accent sharpened when he was pissed off. "My man's at the house. He's got a laser listening device to pick up sound from the windows. Should be able to hear a mouse squeak. Trouble is, he hasn't heard the kids since he arrived. No talking at all. No playing or crying. There are sounds of someone cleaning, but nothing more."

"Maybe the boys are quiet? Coloring or something?"

"That's what Cam figured at first, but now he thinks he was wrong. A minute ago, Mrs. Brun walked outside and yelled for the kids."

"For the kids? Not at?"

"Exactly. Cam doesn't think they're in the house. He probably got to Brun's house a few minutes after the children were dropped off, but that left a gap."

"You figure they ran away?" *Fuck.* As a nail-gun started up, Nolan paced across the construction site to get away from the noise.

"Ayuh. Or they're hiding in the backyard. I'm going to leave my man there in case they return."

"The kids don't know the area. Where the fuck would they go?"

"It's a long walk back to your place. Easy to get lost."

Nolan shook his head. "Grant's a planner. Reminds me of you, sometimes. He'd figure out what to do." He double-checked his phone log. No, they hadn't called. And Beth would have let him know if they'd called her.

"See if the old woman reported the children missing." Galen

hesitated. "I recommend you visit Brun's house along with the social worker. If your kids are anywhere close, they'll come out for you. If not, the grandmother might have some clue as to where they ran."

"Makes sense. Thanks, Galen."

As Galen hung up, Nolan started punching in numbers. To hell with Price, it was time to bring in the supervisor. Then he'd call Beth and head for Grandma's house, whether or not he had company.

Jesus, where were they?

TWO LADIES AT the bus station had helped Grant figure out which buses to ride to Drew Park. The ticket had taken most of his money. But once they got Mama's money, he could buy a ticket to get home to Beth and Nolan. Connor was little enough he could ride for free.

"How'd you know about buses?" Connor asked when they were safely changed over to the next bus.

"Remember when the pretty shelter lady took us older kids to Busch Gardens? She got us dis…discount cards to ride cheap 'cause we're kids, and she showed us how to pay and get on and off and how to get help." Since Connor was getting older, he added the warning she'd given. "She said if a stranger offers a ride, don't go anywhere with him. And ask for help from at least two people in case one of them lies."

Connor's eyes got big, but he nodded after a second. "Jermaine would lie to a kid."

"Yeah, he would."

"But how do we get back to Beff?" His eyes got all wet. "I don't know where she lives."

"I do." Grant puffed up. "Remember she gave us the cards Nolanman sent her? It has her house number and stuff." He pulled out the postcard with the picture of an elephant. The other side had the address.

"All *right*."

After the next stop, as the bus lurched into movement again, Connor frowned. "You think Beff'll be mad at us? Is Nolanman gonna yell?"

Grant's stomach got tight with the same worry. But brothers told each other the truth. "Maybe."

At Connor's worried expression, Grant confided his hope. "But when we give them money, they'll be happy."

Connor considered and finally nodded. "Everybody likes money."

WHEN BETH WAS little, her family would sing the "Over the River and Through the Woods, to Grandmother's House We Go" song. Beth would bounce up and down in the backseat with anticipation, because Nana had been the sweetest person in the world.

Beth shook her head as she parked behind Nolan's truck and got out. Mrs. Brun didn't seem likely to win any awards for grandmotherly behavior.

On the sidewalk, she paused to consider the house and yard. Some people evaluated others by the contents of their bookcases; Beth used a landscaping yardstick. In this case… The clapboard house's paint was a stark, almost industrial white. The sole landscaping was the ruthlessly pruned Japanese privet across the front. The grass had been trimmed almost too short to survive. No flowerbeds. No color.

Conclusion: the owner was…regimented and lacked both joy and spontaneity. How would this person do with the chaos that came with children?

With an unhappy sigh, Beth walked through the open front

door. The acrid scents of bleach and cleansers almost drowned out the musty, older home smell. The sound of voices led her to the living room.

Price, Nolan, and Mrs. Molina faced a stick-thin woman in a darkly patterned, shirtwaist dress. Her long gray hair was tightly pulled into a bun. No makeup. According to the reports, Mrs. Brun was about the same age as Beth's mother but appeared a decade older.

Beth scanned the room. No children. Her heart sank. "Have you found them?"

Nolan turned, and his grim face softened. With his back to the others, he gripped her shoulders, preparing her. "She says they ran out of the house right after they arrived." His voice dropped. "Before Galen's man got here."

"And she didn't notify anyone?" Beth's voice rose.

Price turned and glared.

"No." Nolan put his arm around her.

Mrs. Molina frowned at Mrs. Brun. "I do wonder why you didn't call either the police or Mr. Price."

The old woman's hands were clasped tightly at her waist. She turned a hostile gaze on Mrs. Molina. "They're *my* grandchildren. *My* business. I'm their grandmother, and Mr. Price said the state keeps families together." She glanced at the wall clock, and her mouth pinched. "They've made me late for church."

Will God strike you dead for being late? Beth bit back the words; a fight would get them nowhere. "Have you checked under their beds?"

Mrs. Brun blinked. "The bed? Why would I? They ran outside."

Beth glanced at Mrs. Molina. "Under a bed is their favorite hiding spot. If Mrs. Brun left the house, the children might've sneaked back inside. Let's double-check the house before searching the neighborhood."

"Good plan." Mrs. Molina nodded.

"Who do you think you are?" The grandmother stared at Beth with cold eyes.

"I'm someone who is concerned for the children's welfare. That *is* what we're here for."

The old woman huffed. "They'll return when they grow hungry."

Mrs. Molina looked appalled. Nolan growled.

"Of course they will." Beth raised her chin. "Just like when Drusilla ran away. No, wait—she didn't return, did she?"

Mrs. Brun's affronted expression was dreadfully satisfying.

Ignoring her, Beth headed toward the back of the house. When Nolan joined her in the kitchen, she put her hand on his arm. "What if they manage to get back to our house? We're not there."

"True. You should return and…" He obviously noted her obstinate expression. "I guess that might be asking too much." Pulling out his cell, he punched a number. "Galen, I know it's Sunday, but—"

Even at a distance, Beth heard Galen's rude retort, "Don't be a dense asshole. What can I do to help?"

"Thanks. We're both at Brun's house, which means if the kids go to our home, no one is there."

Beth could barely hear Galen say, "It's quite a ways to Carrollwood."

"Grant knows how to ride a bus, and they'd earned spending money, so he could afford a ticket." Nolan shook his head. "Any chance you could ask Anne or Sally to housesit till we get back? I'll pay for their time."

Galen said something.

"Thanks." Nolan hung up and told Beth, "Sally's heading for our place right now…and Galen told me where to shove my money."

Oh, she did love her friends. "C'mon, let's do our search."

"You take the bedrooms. I'll check here and the backyard."

Beth pointed to the doors under the kitchen sink. "Don't forget they like to tuck into tiny places."

"Got it."

In the hallway, Beth headed for the first bedroom and halted when Mrs. Molina stalked out of the living room.

Red streaks of anger darkened her face, and she let out a quiet string of Spanish curses Beth hadn't heard since the last time Cullen annoyed Andrea. Upon seeing Beth, she stopped and composed herself. "Mrs. King, please excuse me."

"I totally understand." Beth motioned toward Mrs. Brun's bedroom. "Since I'm not official, you'd better be the one to check her room. Bear in mind, the boys will use boxes to barricade and conceal themselves."

Mrs. Molina glanced back at the living room. "I wouldn't blame them." She stepped into the master bedroom.

Beth took the smaller bedroom. Spotlessly clean, the room held a nightstand, a folding chair, and a single bed covered in a dark blue quilt. Over the bed was a picture of Jesus bleeding on the cross. The other wall had a picture of the Last Supper. No toys, no books. Nothing.

Beth scanned the room again in disbelief. How could the two active boys have tolerated this place?

She opened the tiny closet. Completely empty.

Dropping to her knees, she checked under the bed. Not even a dust ball.

Where could they be? Her stomach tightened, and all she could think about was Connor's tiny hand in hers. About how Grant would cry, so, so silently as if afraid to be heard. The trust in their big brown eyes.

I want my babies back.

As she pulled the curtains aside, she saw Nolan already in

the back yard. She should tell him to search under the porch steps, too. She pushed on the window…and it didn't move.

She checked the lock—no lock—and shoved the window more forcefully. Nothing budged. A closer study revealed someone had nailed the window shut. A chill ran down her spine. What if there was a fire?

"No children?" Mrs. Molina stood in the doorway.

"No." Beth moved aside and pointed to the nails in the frame. "Is this legal?"

NO CARS WERE parked in front of Mama's duplex, and relief swept through Grant. Jermaine wasn't there. With Connor trudging behind him, he walked up to the front door and used his key to get inside.

When he stopped, Connor ran into him. "Grant?" His fingers clutched the back of Grant's shirt.

"It's…ugly." Almost like it was when they'd left. Grant felt sick. Unless she was being crazy, Mama kept stuff picked up, kinda. Jermaine never had.

Grant took another step. Beer cans and frozen food trays dotted the carpet. The room stank like the day Connor'd been sick and thrown up.

Mama isn't here.

Tears turned the room watery. He knew Mama was gone, but…he'd still thought she'd be here.

With a wail, Connor slid down to sit on the floor and cry.

"Hey. It's okay." Swiping his own tears away, Grant hauled Connor up and slung an arm around his shoulders. "Let's get Mama's money before the douche comes back."

Wrinkling his nose as they passed the stinky bathroom, he led the way to the big bedroom. The closet door stood open, and his eyes filled with tears again. Mama's clothes were gone.

The dressing table held only Jermaine's stuff—no makeup or perfume bottles.

Don't cry. After rubbing the wet off his face, he tipped the tall pole lamp sideways and lowered it to the floor. Kneeling beside the lamp, he ran his hand inside the curved, black metal base, unstuck the adhesive tape, and pulled out a baggie stuffed with money.

At Connor's gleeful sound, Grant almost cheered with him. Now Beth and Nolan would keep them.

He stuffed the bag into his backpack and grabbed Connor's hand. "Let's go home."

"To Beff and Nolanman?"

"Yeah."

They'd reached the living room when the front door opened.

Jermaine stepped inside.

QUIETLY, BETH LEFT the house, leaving Price, Mrs. Brun, and Mrs. Molina arguing behind her. It sounded like a nasty battle.

Good job, Sir.

Before leaving to search the neighborhood, Nolan had pulled the supervisor aside and told her about the children's bruises and their worries. Then he'd tossed Price to the wolves, saying the investigator had blown their concerns off. As he walked out the door, Mrs. Molina had called Price and Mrs. Brun over.

Once in her pickup, Beth sat for a minute and tried to think like a frightened child. Their most likely destination was back home.

Or not. She and Nolan *had* turned the kids over to Price. Betrayed them. Guilt felt like lead balloons in Beth's stomach. Maybe they should have taken the children and run. But how would running have helped?

No one believed the children would return to their mother's duplex. After all, Drusilla was dead, and surely the boys knew Jermaine or someone else would be living there.

But…

But she'd seen Grant's duplex key when she'd emptied his backpack to do his laundry. If the boys were running, what better location to hide than in their old neighborhood?

Yes. She started the truck and headed for Drew Park.

With worries about the boys filling her head, she'd gotten partway there before realizing she'd goofed. Nolan would be unhappy—call that royally pissed-off—that she'd left without talking to him. *Oh boy.* Punching a button on the steering wheel, she called his cell phone.

"Hey." His deep raspy voice filled the cab and warmed her chilled skin. "I saw your pickup's gone. You heading home?"

"Uh." He wasn't going to be happy with her. "After a quick detour. I know we decided the kids wouldn't return to Drusilla's place, but I want to check anyway. After all, it's the one place they know, and maybe they have a friendly neighbor or hiding place around there."

"Fuck. It's possible." She could almost hear him scowl. "But I don't want you there. Not in Drew Park, not anywhere near Drusilla's. Stop and wait for me."

Anxiety danced through her. What if the children had gone there? Their neighborhood was a really scary one, especially for two little boys. "I can't wait; I just can't. But I'll only swing by the house—and I'll call the cops if anything seems scary."

He let out an exasperated huff. "You're fucking stubborn."

"Yes, Sir. I'm afraid so."

"I love you, Beth. I'm on my way, so be careful for my sake, okay?"

"I will. And I love you, too."

❖ ❖ ❖ ❖ ❖

As Jermaine pawed through their backpacks, Grant wanted to cry. His chest was so tight he could barely breathe.

He and Connor had tried to run past Jermaine out the door, but the *douche* had shoved Connor across the room. Then he'd ripped Grant's backpack away and slapped Grant to the floor.

As Grant pushed to his feet, his hip and shoulder burned like fire. A few feet away, Connor wiped his eyes and watched.

"Well, look at this!" Jermaine held up the bag filled with dollars. "*Score.*"

Mama's money. So they could live with Beth and Nolan. Hands in fists, Grant took a step toward Jermaine. "You leave our money alone. It's *ours*!"

"Dream on, buttwipe." Jermaine shoved the stack of bills in his back pocket. His brown eyes had turned mostly black. As he kept moving from side-to-side, unable to stand still, Grant knew he was in the crazy place, just like Mama.

Connor scowled. "I'm gonna tell Nolan you stoled from us."

"And the cops," Grant added. "We'll tell Max. And Dan."

Jermaine's face changed—got hard and ugly—and Grant edged away. "You little fucker. I talked my ass off last month to keep from getting busted, and now you're gonna call the pigs down on me? Again? Know what I think? I think the gators'd love to eat two shit-headed brats who—*oops*—fell into the ditch."

Grant's insides started to shake, and he grabbed Connor and backed away. The front door wasn't closed completely. If they could…

Jermaine grabbed Connor's shirt and Grant's hair.

As Connor screamed in fear, Grant kicked at Jermaine's legs. "Let go! Let us go!"

"You bastard!" Like Wonder Woman, Beth charged into the room and punched Jermaine right in the mouth. "Let them go!"

She tried to pry his hand from Connor.

"Fuck!" Jermaine threw Connor to one side and slapped Beth across the face.

She staggered back, hand to her cheek, and her other hand up as if she knew he'd hit her again. Tears were in her eyes, and she was scared. Awful scared.

Beth should never be scared.

Grant screamed at him—"Leave her alone!"—and kicked harder and harder.

The douche shook him by his hair. "Stop it, brat."

"Ow!" It *hurt*. Grant couldn't keep from crying.

Through his tears, he saw Beth's eyes get angry, her mouth tightened—and she lunged forward. She knocked Jermaine's fist away, kicked his knee, and punched him in the nose.

Roaring in pain, he dropped Grant. His hands covered his bleeding nose. "*Bitch.*"

Beth shoved Grant toward the door. "Go!" She turned toward Connor in the corner. "Con—"

Jermaine hit her in the face really, really hard.

She fell.

Grant froze. She was just lying there. Like Mama. His heart pounded like Nolan's nail gun, and his whole body shook, needing to run away. To *hide*.

Protect Beth. Nolanman said. Daddy said.

Standing over her, Jermaine laughed and drew his foot back.

"Noooooo." Screaming in fear and fury, Grant dove at Jermaine, butting him directly in the crotch.

A fist slammed into his head. Pain exploded in his cheek. He crashed into the floor so hard he bounced. Tears blinded him. His hip. His shoulder. His face. *Hurt, hurt, hurt.* Shaking his head, he put his arm up, expecting a blow.

But Jermaine hadn't moved. Making choking sounds, he was bent over, holding himself. "Fuck. Fucking brat."

Crying hard, Connor ran to Beth and yanked on her arm to pull her up.

Run. Grant yelled at him, and no sound came out. He tried to move. *Get up. Get up.*

Only a few feet away, Beth shook her head weakly and, with Connor's help, rocked onto her hands and knees.

Grant struggled. *Get up.* But the floor kept moving and swaying, making him fall down again.

"You gonna die. Cut you, bitch." Eyes crazy mad, Jermaine straightened and pulled a switchblade from his pocket. He flicked it open. "Gonna slice you up, slice up the brats, feed you to the gators."

Connor scrambled in front of Beth. "Leave her alone!"

"No, Connor," Grant screamed.

"Fucking little shit." Jermaine raised his knife and swung at Connor.

On her knees, Beth yanked Connor back, and the blade missed. She shoved Connor behind her.

Grant tried again to stand up. Made it. He staggered a foot sideways and—

Thunderous pounding on the door was followed by a shout. "This is the Tampa Police. Let—"

"Fuck the legal shit," snapped a raspy voice. Grant caught his breath. It was Nolanman. The door burst open, slammed into the wall behind it, and Nolan stalked in.

Max and another man followed.

"*Shit.*" Jermaine stumbled backward, away from Beth.

Nolan's black gaze burned, as he looked Grant up and down. When he turned to Beth and Connor, his face got even darker. Grant shivered. *Mad.* He was really mad.

Turning toward Jermaine, Nolan moved forward, and Max tried to grab him. "King, don't—"

Nolanman hit Jermaine so hard the douche went into the air

and flew backward. The floor shook when he hit, and he slid down the wall, mouth bleeding.

"Dammit, Nolan," the other man said.

Grant recognized Dan. Swearing under his breath, he walked over to Jermaine, pulling handcuffs off his belt.

As Nolan knelt beside Beth and Connor, Max headed toward him. "Dammit, King, you have any idea—"

Grant lurched forward, managing to get in front of the cop. "Leave Nolanman alone. You can't put him in jail. I won't let you."

Max half smiled. "Easy, tough guy." Then his brows pulled together, and he cupped Grant's chin and looked as mad as Nolan. "Who hit you, Grant?"

"J-Jermaine. He hurt Connor, and he hit Beth."

"Just racking them up, was he?" Max muttered. He raised his voice. "Start with three counts of assault and battery, Dan."

"Got it." Rolling Jermaine around like he was a little kid, Dan handcuffed the douche's hands behind his back. Jermaine was swearing, but his lips were kinda smashed, and his words came out all funny.

Shaking so violently he felt off-balance, Grant turned and saw Nolan was on one knee.

He hugged Connor and set him on Beth's lap. With one finger, he raised Beth's chin and frowned. "Sugar, you're supposed to dodge better."

Connor twisted in her arms to glare. "She hitted him so he wouldn't cut us up and feed us to the gators."

"Is that right?" Max's voice got quieter and...colder.

A little worried, Grant backed away from the cop to stand beside Nolanman.

With a long arm, Nolan pulled him closer. "Damn, tiger, you scared the shit out of me." He hugged Grant so tightly he couldn't breathe. And nothing had ever felt so safe and right.

✧ ✧ ✧ ✧ ✧

THE LITTLE BODY in Nolan's arms was trembling fit to break—and Nolan had a feeling he himself was shaking like a fucking leaf as well. Jesus, he'd never been so scared in all his born days.

But his woman and his boys were all right—bruised up, but all right. Hell of a strong crew.

With a protesting creak, the front door swung open farther, and Price and Mrs. Molina entered.

Grant twisted to see them and froze.

In a shrill, terrified voice, Connor shouted at Price. "No! I won't go back to the mean lady."

Pulling in a breath, Nolan tried to rein in his temper and a growl escaped. "You won't go back." His hand fisted, and he started to rise.

Beth closed her fingers over his forearm, keeping her other arm wrapped around Connor. "Easy, Sir," she whispered.

Smothering a curse, he stayed on one knee and held Grant. The brave little man was shaking so hard his teeth chattered.

Price glared at Connor. "That woman is your grandmother, and you will—"

"They won't do shit," Nolan growled. He caught the asshole's gaze.

Price paled and edged a step toward the police.

Mrs. Molina moved forward. "Mr. King, if I might handle this?" Her level gaze promised she had it, so he settled himself to wait.

Before she could speak, Grant squirmed free. He planted himself in front of Max, hands on his hips. "I want our money." Tears had streaked his face, but he stood strong. Hell of a kid. "Jermaine took our money, and we need it. Right now."

Max's lips twitched as he studied the little soldier. "Okay, I'll bite. Where did he put your money?"

"In his pants." Grant slapped his own rear to show where.

One side of his mouth tilting up, Dan rolled the bastard, pulled out a huge wad of bills, and frowned. "Where'd you kids get money like this?"

"It was Mama's." Connor joined his brother. "She hided it, and we came to get it so we wouldn't have to go back to the mean lady."

Nolan glanced at Beth. "You know what he's talking about?"

"Uh-uh. Grant, why do you need money to keep from going back to your grandmother?"

Grant turned, his gaze puzzled, as if surprised they were so slow-witted. "To give you."

"Us? Why would we want money?" Beth asked.

"He"—Connor pointed at Price—"said nobody but the mean lady wants us. Fosters don't want big, clumsy boys 'less they get money. So we needs money to give you to keep us."

As anger found new fuel, Nolan's temperature rose. "You called the boys big and clumsy—and told them we didn't want them?"

Price flinched and backed up another step.

"Easy, King." Max set a cautionary hand on Nolan's shoulder.

Beth said gently, "Connor, if—"

"Mrs. King," Mrs. Molina interrupted. "Might I ask some questions?"

At Beth's nod, Mrs. Molina squatted down in front of the boys. "I think I understand, but let's be sure. Did you come here to get money so you could live with Beth and Nolan?"

Connor nodded.

"What about your grandmother?" She tilted her head. "Didn't you tell Mr. Price you had a wonderful time with her?"

A telling shiver ran through Connor, and he took a step away from Mrs. Molina.

Scared. That fucking asshole. Nolan asked, "Did Mr. Price tell you to say you had a wonderful time?"

Connor shook his head and glanced at Grant.

"Ah. Did your grandmother tell you what to say?" Mrs. Molina asked Grant.

Both boys nodded.

Mrs. Molina looked as if she'd bitten into something sour. "What would happen if you told the truth?"

Grant whispered. "She said we'd be sorry."

"She was mean. She hitted me 'cause I..." When Connor stopped and turned red, Nolan figured he must've wet the bed. He saw Beth mouth an explanation to Mrs. Molina.

Connor backed up so Beth could pull him against her. When she wrapped her arms around his stomach, his little fingers clamped onto her wrists. His own personal security blanket. "She pushed soap in Grant's mouth 'cause he called her a bad word, and he frewed up, and she hitted him." His eyes turned wet with tears.

"She's mean," Grant agreed, trying for defiance and only sounding frightened. "She doesn't like us. She says we're bad. And evil. And rotten to the...something." When Nolan curled an arm around him, he turned his face into Nolan's shoulder, finishing in a whisper, "She hit Connor and made him cry, and I hate her."

Nolan heard the rumble of anger coming from his own throat, and all he could do was hold the boy. His furious gaze met Beth's. Still sitting, she leaned over to rub her shoulder against his in unspoken agreement. If things went sour, they'd take the kids and disappear before that woman could get them again.

Connor turned in Beth's arms and took her face between his hands. "Beff, please keep us. We gots money."

Grant rubbed his face against Nolan's shoulder, and the tiniest whisper drifted up. "Please, Nolanman. We're your home crew."

Nolan looked over Grant's head to Mrs. Molina whose expression was appalled and angry, but she met his regard honestly. And understood his unspoken question. "I take it you would rather have two boys than a newborn daughter?"

"Didn't Price tell you?" Beth's eyes lit with furious sparks. "We made the request last week."

Mrs. Molina turned. Her glare probably shriveled Price's balls to the size of marbles before she smiled at Nolan and Beth. "In light of Mrs. Brun's age as well as her…inflexible…behavior and disregard for basic safety, I don't consider her a suitable guardian. I do believe you two and the boys are an excellent match. I see no reason not to let them know they can relax."

Beth squealed in delight. "Ours!" She pulled Connor down into her lap, raining kisses on his face until he was giggling uncontrollably. "You're *ours*."

Grinning, Nolan looked down and saw Grant's confusion. Cupping his cheek carefully, Nolan met his gaze. "We don't need any money from you, tiger. You're our boys, and we're keeping you. Forever."

Grant's eyes went wet.

Nolan tucked him back against his chest and slid Beth closer, so he could wrap his arms around all three. Around his *family*.

Connor squirmed, and his forehead furrowed. "But what about the baby girl. You wants a girl."

Hell, how could he answer that?

Beth managed. "Remember at the shelter when Lamar stole your coloring book because he thought it would make him happy?"

"It didn't," Connor stated decisively.

"No. Because he loves playing soccer, not coloring. But he didn't know that, at first."

Nolan got where she was going. "Beth and I thought we'd like having a baby girl, but we didn't actually know. However, we do know we love you two and want you for our own."

"You love us?" Grant whispered.

Beth's tears spilled down her face as she touched his cheek gently. "Yes, baby. We love you very, very much."

Snuggling down in Beth's lap like a well-fed puppy, Connor gave them a happy smile. "Okay, you can keep us."

Chapter Twenty

CARRYING A TRAY of finger-foods, Beth walked out onto the patio filled with their friends and was struck by a surge of happiness. Could life get any sweeter?

Once Grant and Connor had fully accepted they were loved and wanted, the last couple of weeks had been wonderful. Even starting a new school hadn't bothered the boys, and each day, they'd returned with hilarious adventures to relate.

She'd never heard Nolan laugh so often.

Today, as a way of celebrating their new family, Nolan had invited everyone who'd helped with the Brun investigation.

Beth shook her head, seeing how the gathering had split along gender lines. Nolan was at the grill—and with him were Master Z, Dan, Vance and Galen, Marcus, and Ben.

Seated in the more kid-friendly area were her girlfriends.

"Have you got your business receipts ready for me?" Jessica called. "It's time to pay estimated taxes, you know."

"Yes, ma'am, Madam Accountant." Beth rolled her eyes. "Didn't Z teach you not to nag people?"

"He taught me not to nag *him*." Jessica grinned. "If you ever gain Z's expertise with"—she glanced at Grant who was sitting beside her—"um, with *implements*, you will escape being badgered."

Beth sighed. The nagging would continue. But she couldn't grumble at her friend, not when Jessica had given Grant such a lovely treat—letting the boy hold five-month-old Sophia in his lap. His grin couldn't get any wider.

Next to Grant's chair, Connor and Kari's son, Zane, were playing with a ball. Behind the boys sprawled Kari's big German shepherd, Prince.

Uzuri, Gabi, and Sally had commandeered their own table and had their heads together. The three "brats" of the club were undoubtedly hatching some mischief.

Good luck with that, girls. Really, they should pay more attention to their surroundings. Anne was seated close enough to overhear them, and her expression was filled with amusement. The good Mistress might be female, but when it came to BDSM, her loyalties were firmly on the Dominant side of the equation. The brats were doomed.

Beth crossed to the grill and set the tray down on a nearby table.

Curling his arm around her waist, Nolan kissed the top of her head. "Thanks, sugar."

"You're welcome, Sir."

After nodding to the rest of the guys, she started to head toward her girl gang, when Master Z blocked her way. "Elizabeth."

"Sir?"

Effortlessly, he held her gaze for a long moment before smiling slightly. "Motherhood agrees with you, little one. I'm pleased for all of you."

She smiled back, feeling tears prickle behind her eyes. "You know, three years ago, you gave me an amazing gift, Master Z." Taking a step back, she leaned against Nolan's side. "When you gave me my Master, you changed my life." Saved her life. "Thank you."

"Hold on, sugar." Nolan gave her hair a mild yank. "Seems like you were a gift for me, not the other way around."

"Did you just compliment Z on his matchmaking?" Galen

tilted his beer at her. "Don't encourage him, pet. Every unattached Dom in the club lives in fear of falling victim to his schemes."

Z simply gave the ex-Fed an amused look. Everyone knew Galen and Vance were blissfully happy with their little brat, Sally.

"I do believe we're running short on single Masters anyway," Marcus pointed out.

"Holt could be a good target." Ben popped a deviled egg in his mouth and hummed in pleasure before taking another. "And Anne says Saxon will probably make Master."

When the doorbell rang, Nolan said, "That should be Alastair and Max." He smiled slowly. "Why don't you pick on them, Z? It'd be a treat to see Alastair lose his composure."

Master Z's expression turned thoughtful. "It would indeed."

Uh-oh. The Drago cousins were done for. Beth headed into the house. Should she warn them? Tell them they might as well start picking out engagement rings and wedding colors?

Nah.

As she led the two Doms out onto the patio, Connor spotted them and let out a squeal. "Max! Doctor." He ran up and skidded to a stop. "You came to the pawty."

"Connor, it's good to see you." When Alastair held out his hand, Connor shook it, beaming at being greeted like a man.

"Hey, buddy. I brought you something for your collection." Max went down on one knee, reached into his pocket, and pulled out a long-necked dinosaur. "This one is called brachiosaurus."

"For me?" Connor examined it with awe and started at a run to show Grant. But when Beth cleared her throat, he remembered and spun around, dancing on his tiptoes. "Thank you, Max." And sped right off again.

Max grinned. "You've got great boys."

"We think so. Welcome to the party." Beth waved her hand

at the small assemblage of guests. "Is there anyone you two haven't met?"

Alastair shook his head. "I believe I've made everyone's acquaintance. Max?"

Max glanced at the men. "I've met the Doms and Ben." His gaze turned to the women. "Jessica, Kari, Anne, yes. Not the three at the separate table."

"Ah, they are the submissives who bear the title of 'the brats'," Alastair murmured.

Max's eyes lit. "Them I need to meet. Let me grab a beer, and you can introduce me."

As the two men greeted the other Doms and were handed drinks, Beth wandered over to the *brats*. "What evil are you three planning now?"

Sally shook her head ruefully. "Nothing, I'm afraid. Gabi was telling us about their visit to Grandma's neighborhood."

"Grandma?" Beth stilled. "Like my boys' grandma?"

"Exactly like." Gabi's lips tilted up. "Since the cookie dough came in, Uzuri and I gathered the troops and delivered the orders."

"I didn't think Mrs. Brun ordered anything," Beth said.

"Oh, she didn't. She was far too stingy." Uzuri wrinkled her nose in dislike. "But almost all of her neighbors ordered. So, as we dropped off the cookie dough, we took our time and had a nice gossip with each one."

"We felt it was our civic duty to warn them to keep their children out of her reach," Gabi said virtuously. She glanced over at her husband. "Of course, with a fussy lawyer for a Dom, I was careful about what we said."

"She's such a disgusting person. Would you believe she told everyone that the boys were nasty and rude?" Uzuri turned a tender gaze to Connor and Grant. "I wanted to march over to her house and slap her."

"We did, essentially. The neighbors had seen the commotion when the boys ran away. When we told them why, people were simply *appalled*." Gabi smirked. "Since some of them belong to her church, I doubt she'll be teaching any children's Sunday school ever again."

"Thank you so much." Beth beamed at them. "We didn't want to put the guys through the trauma of pressing charges, and I didn't feel right about beating up someone my mother's age. It's nice to know she didn't get away free and clear."

Sally frowned. "Brun is handled. But what about nasty ol' Price?"

"Mrs. Molina was so angry, his career probably came to a screeching halt," Beth said. "But, Alastair wanted to ensure Price wouldn't be dealing with children again."

"What did Alastair do?" Uzuri asked.

Beth glanced over at the Doms and smiled at the big pediatrician's resonant, full-throated laugh. "As their doctor, he 'interviewed' the boys. Playing with stuffed animals, they made pretend families and talked about adoption and fostering. And, on camera, the kids told Alastair all about the 'the Price man,' as Grant calls him."

"Whoa, two adorable little boys saying the social worker made them feel unlovable?" Gabi smiled slowly. "Price will be buried."

"For the sake of children everywhere, I'm glad," Beth said. "And thank you so, so much for doing the same to Mrs. Brun."

"It was a pleasure," Gabi said. "Besides, as Sally said, life's been boring. I haven't insulted Marcus in...oh, at least a week."

Sally snickered. "Poor Marcus. I'm sure he's missing beating on you."

"And I haven't sabotaged any of the Masters' toy bags in...forever," Uzuri said.

As Max stopped behind the little black submissive, he couldn't believe his ears. "You got into a *Dom's* toy bag?"

She turned, saw him, and actually cringed back in her chair.

Fuck. Okay, yeah, he was big, and maybe she hadn't expected to see a man looming over her, but Jesus, he didn't have a bloodstained ax or chainsaw in his hands. Her reaction seemed over-the-top. Nonetheless, he took a step back and circled around to stand beside Beth.

A pretty redhead with tats on her upper arms scooted closer to the terrified one. "Easy, girl."

"Hey, Max, welcome to the female side of the patio." Beth put a hand on his arm. "Gabi"—she pointed to the redhead—"Sally"—a motion to the brunette—"and Uzuri"—the timid little mouse. "Ladies, this is Alastair's cousin, Max Drago, who recently moved here. You might have seen him at the club."

"Welcome to Tampa, Mr. Drago." Voice reserved, Sally studied him.

Gabi took the mouse's hand. "Good to meet you, Mr. Drago."

Lotta formal *misters* there. They were pretty protective of their buddy, weren't they? His gaze returned to Uzuri who hadn't smiled at all. Yeah, he'd scared the shit out of her…without doing a thing. *Dammit.*

Moving slowly, Max squatted on his haunches in front of her and held out his hand. "I'm sorry I startled you."

Pity swept through him as he saw she'd retreated as far as she could get. But she wasn't sweating, whimpering, cowering. Not a new fear, an old one—and she'd overreacted. She needed to get herself back up on the horse. Been there; done that. *Beat the fear back, pet, or it'll eat you alive.* He didn't withdraw his hand, just waited.

Eventually, Uzuri realized he wasn't jumping on her…and was waiting for her to get control. Flushing darkly, she edged

PROTECTING HIS OWN   243

forward far enough to give him her cold little hand. The way her fingers trembled in his was pretty fucking heartbreaking.

"It's nice to meet you, darlin'." He tilted his head. "What do I have to do to keep you out of my toy bag?"

She pulled her hand back without answering.

"I'd suggest you don't get her upset." The brunette—Sally—dimpled. That one looked as if she'd be quite the handful. And he loved challenges. "Seriously."

Gabi smirked at him, eyes lit with mischief. Yeah, she'd be a hell of a lot of fun, as well. "Too late. You're doomed."

"I see." He also saw both submissives wore wedding rings. The only single one was Uzuri. He ran his gaze over her. Although, as a man, he could appreciate the wealth of hair, the perfectly done makeup, the impeccable manicure and pedicure, and the stylish clothing, he also recognized the signs of a high maintenance female.

On top of that, she hadn't spoken, and her posture still showed fear. She carried some heavy baggage there.

A wise man hopefully learned from his past experiences of being burned. *Don't be a dumbass, Drago.*

Regretfully—she really was a beauty—he shook his head and issued his own warning, "Best you leave my bag alone, pet. I don't think we're in the same weight class." He rather doubted she'd do anything, anyway. She might talk about sabotaging a Dom's toy bag, but this little mouse would never have the nerve.

She blinked, as startled as if he'd swatted her. A shame he hadn't. He'd bet she had a very spankable ass.

"It was nice to meet you all." He nodded at the others, rose, and went back to the calmer waters of the men's huddle.

IN HIS CHAIR with a baby in his lap, Grant couldn't stop smiling. Jessica was letting him hold Sophia who was the prettiest baby he'd ever seen. She'd even said Sophia liked him and didn't like just everybody.

This was the greatest party—even better than last week when Connor had turned five and had a birthday cake and presents and everything.

Parties were fun. He knew most of the grownups, and even the strangers had known him and Connor. Like the dark-haired man named Galen who'd called Nolan when Grant and Connor ran away from Grandmother's house, so Nolanman could come 'n' find them.

And Nolan had.

Right now, Nolan was cooking on the huge grill—and Grant kind of wanted to help, but holding Sophia was more fun.

"Ga-ba-da." Sophia kicked her little feet and said it again. "Ga-ba-da."

Grant grinned, kept one arm wrapped around her, and held up the fat ring with red and yellow keys. She snatched the toy, making him laugh. "What are those?" he prompted.

"Ba-ba-ba."

"Keys," he said carefully. "Keys."

Agreeing, Sophia waved the keys in the air, almost smacking him in the face.

"Careful there. She gets awfully enthusiastic." Sophia's mama had almost yellow hair. Beth's hair was prettier with all the red, but the sun made Jessica's hair glow. And Sophia had the same color hair.

A crow of laughter came from beside Grant's chair where Connor was rolling a ball back and forth with Zane.

Balls were fun. "How long till Sophia can roll a ball?"

Zane's mama laughed. "Probably another year. To you, babies might not grow fast, but to mommies, they sprout another inch every day."

Did Beth think he and Connor grew fast? She was watching him with a little smile on her face. She did that a lot, and it always made him feel…funny. Happy, like now, only kind of like he wanted to cry, only not.

Connor got up and leaned against the dark-haired lady's knee. Her stomach was amazing big, and Beth said Anne was growing a baby in her tummy.

"You really gots a baby in there?" Connor asked in wonder.

"Oh, do I." Her laugh was almost as low and soft as Beth's. "In fact, there's action in there right now, so you might be able to feel a foot." She took Connor's hand and put it on her stomach.

Connor's eyes got big. "The baby *kicked* me."

Over beside Nolanman, the scary guy who'd come with Anne turned. He'd heard Connor and started walking over. He was awfully big.

As he got close, Grant watched him and frowned, "Is that man gonna be the baby's daddy?" He didn't look like he should be a daddy.

"Guys, this is Ben." As the man set his hand on her shoulder, Anne curled her fingers around his wrist, and her face somehow got even nicer. "Yes, he's the daddy. We'll be a family of three."

"Best thing that ever happened to me," Ben said to her, and when he grinned, he wasn't scary at all. "Hey, guys."

"Nolanman an' Beff are our fambly," Connor told Ben. His brows drew together. "But we didn't grow in Beff's tummy."

Grant tensed. They weren't really a family?

Ben ran his hand down Anne's hair and told Connor, "Families are created in different ways. Sometimes from growing in tummies, sometimes from choosing someone—finding someone you love and want to live with. Doesn't matter which."

Okay. They were a family. Grant relaxed and rubbed his chin on Sophia's silky hair. With a crow of laughter, she pitched the keys down on the blanket.

Connor picked up the keys and a stuffed cat the baby had thrown. This time she snatched the cat. It'd sure be fun to have a sister. If stuff worked like Ben said, a family could get bigger, couldn't it?

Connor held out the keys, giggling when she tried to grab them, too. "I like babies."

"Me, too." Grant bounced Sophia slightly to hear her gurgling laugh. "We could choose a baby. We're big boys. We could take care of a little sister."

NOLAN STOOD BEHIND his two boys and could only stare. Were they talking about what he thought they were?

"Yeah. I want a baby." Connor held a finger out for Sophia and grinned when she latched on with a tiny hand. "If we share a bed, she could sleep in the other one."

"Uh-huh. But girls play with dolls. Our boxes are full of boy stuff." Grant considered. "Nolanman would help us build new boxes, but there's no room for them."

Connor frowned. A few seconds later, a sweet smile crept over his face. "I don't need my 'frigerator. We can put boxes there."

He didn't need the refrigerator…because he didn't have to hoard food anymore. Nolan felt Beth beside him and put his arm around her.

"Okay. We'll pick out a baby, then." Grant kissed the top of Sophia's head and said solemnly, "And we'll keep her safe, like Nolanman does with us."

Connor nodded. "Big boys pertect girls."

Nolan looked down and saw Beth smiling up at him with all the love in the world in her soft eyes. "Yes," she whispered. "That's what they do."

Want to be notified of the next release?

Sent only on that day, Cherise's newsletters contain freebies, excerpts, and articles.

Sign up at:

www.CheriseSinclair.com/NewsletterForm

Have you tried the Mountain Masters & Dark Haven series?

Master of the Mountain

Mountain Masters & Dark Haven: Book 1

Available everywhere

Get Master of the Mountain Now!

I loved it! Every word, every page, every moment until the end! So that is my review in a nutshell…….. OK I can do better than that, but seriously a melt your panties right off, intriguing love story that forces you to turn the pages until the wee hours of the night just to get to the end! How about that!

~ Book Junkie

Rebecca thinks she is overweight and boring. Logan disagrees.

When Rebecca's lover talks her into a mountain lodge vacation with his swing club, she soon learns she's not cut out for playing musical beds. But with her boyfriend "entertaining" in their cabin, she has nowhere to sleep. Logan, the lodge owner, finds her freezing on the porch. After hauling her inside, he warms her in his own bed, and there the experienced Dominant discovers that Rebecca might not be a swinger…but she is definitely a submissive.

Rebecca believes that no one can love her plump, scarred body. Logan disagrees. He loves her curves, and under his skilled hands, Rebecca loses not only her inhibitions, but also her heart.

Logan knows they have no future. Damaged from the war, he considers himself too dangerous to be in any relationship. Once the weekend is over, he'll have to send the city-girl subbie back to her own world. But will driving her away protect Rebecca or scar them both?

Excerpt from
Master of the Mountain

THE SUN WAS high overhead and unseasonably hot by the time the trail descended, leaving the pines behind. He led the group across a grass- and wildflower-filled meadow to the tiny mountain lake, clear and blue and damned cold. Granite slabs poked up through the wildflowers, glimmering in the sun. With yells of delight, people dropped their backpacks and stripped.

Logan enjoyed the show of bare asses and breasts as the swingers splashed into the water like a herd of lemmings, screaming at the cold. As he leaned on a boulder, he noticed one person still completely dressed with wide eyes and open mouth. The city girl. Considering she and Matt bunked together, Rebecca couldn't be a virgin, but from her reaction, she was pretty innocent when it came to kink.

"C'mon, babe," her boyfriend yelled, already buck naked in the lake. "The water's great." Not waiting for her response, he waded out deeper, heading for a blonde who looked as if she had substituted bouncy breasts for cheerleading pom-poms.

Rebecca glanced from the water to the trail, back to the water, where Matt wrestled with Ashley, and back to the trail again.

Logan could see the exact moment she decided to leave. He walked over to block her way.

"Excuse me," she said politely.

"No."

Red surged into her cheeks, and her eyes narrowed as she glared at him. Red-gold hair. Freckles. Big bones. Looked like she had Irish ancestry and the temper to go with it. Stepping sideways to block her again, Logan tucked his thumbs into his front pockets and waited for the explosion.

"Listen, Mr. Hunt—"

"It's Logan," he interrupted and tried not to grin as her mouth compressed.

"Whatever. I'm going back to my cabin. Please move your... Please move."

"Sorry, sugar, but no one hikes alone. That's one safety rule I take seriously." He glanced at the swingers. "I can't leave them, and you can't walk alone, so you're stuck here."

Her eyes closed, and he saw the iron control she exerted over her emotions.

The Dom in him wondered how quickly he could break through that control to the woman underneath. Tie her up, tease her a bit, and watch her struggle not to give in to her need and... Hell, talk about inappropriate thoughts.

He pulled in a breath to cool off. No use. It was blistering hot, and not just from his visions of steamy sex. Nothing like global warming in the mountains. He frowned when he noted her damp face and the sweat soaking her long-sleeved, heavy shirt. Not good. The woman needed to get her temperature down.

At the far end of the meadow, the forest would provide shade. He could send her there to sit and cool off, but she'd be out of sight, and from the obstinate set of that pretty, pink mouth, she'd head right back down the trail in spite of his orders.

Shoulders straight, chin up, feet planted. Definitely a rebellious one, the type that brought his dominant nature to the fore. He'd love to give her an order and have her disobey, so he could enjoy the hell out of paddling that soft ass. But she wasn't his to discipline, more's the pity, since a woman like this was wasted on that pretty boy.

And he'd gotten sidetracked.

With a sigh, he returned to the problem at hand. She needed to stay here where he could keep an eye on her, and she needed to cool off.

"Even if you don't strip down completely, at least take some clothes off and wade in the water," he said. "You're getting overheated."

"Thank you, but I'm fine," she said stiffly.

"No, you're not." When he stepped closer, he felt the warmth radiating off her body. Being from San Francisco, she wouldn't be accustomed to the dryness or the heat. "Either strip down, little rebel, or I'll toss you in with your clothes on."

Her mouth dropped open.

He wouldn't, would he? Rebecca stared up at the implacable, cold eyes, seeing the man's utter self-confidence. Definitely not bluffing.

Well, he could be as stern as he wanted. Damned if she'd take her clothing off and display her chunky, scarred legs. She shook her head, backing away. If she needed to, she'd run.

Faster than she could blink, he grabbed her arm.

She tugged and got nowhere. "Listen, you can't—"

With one hand, he unbuttoned her heavy shirt, not at all hindered by her efforts to shove his hand away. After a minute, her shirt flapped open, revealing her bra and her pudgy stomach. "Damn you!"

She glanced at the lake, hoping for Matt to rescue her, and froze. He was kissing the oh-so-perky Ashley, and not just a peck on the lips but a full clinch and deep-throating tongues. Rebecca stared as shock swept through her, followed by a wave of humiliation. He... As her breath hitched, she tore her gaze away, blinking against the welling tears. Why had she ever come here?

"Oh, sugar, don't do that now." Logan pulled her up against his chest, ignoring her weak protest. His arms held her against chest muscles hard as the granite outcroppings, and he turned so she couldn't see the lake. Silently, he stroked a hand down her back while she tried to pull herself together.

Matthew and Ashley would have sex. Soon. Somehow she hadn't quite understood the whole concept of swinging and what her gut-level reaction would be. But she could take it now that she realized…what would happen. After drawing in a shaky breath, she firmed her lips. Fine.

And if Logan insisted she strip to bra and panties, that was fine too. So what if these people saw her giant thighs and ugly scars. She'd never see any of them again. Ever.

For a second, she let herself enjoy the surprising comfort of Logan's arms. Then she pushed away.

He let her take a step back and then grasped her upper arms, keeping her in place as he studied her face.

She flushed and looked away. God, how embarrassing. She had melted down in front of a total stranger, showing him exactly how insecure she was. But he'd been nice, and she owed him. "Thank you for…uh…the shoulder."

With a finger, he turned her face back to him. "I like holding you, Rebecca. Come to me anytime you need a shoulder." A crease appeared in his cheek. He ran his finger across the skin at the top of her lacy bra, his finger slightly rough, sending unexpected tingles through her. "You think I can talk you out of this too?"

Get Master of the Mountain Now!

Also from Cherise Sinclair

About Cherise Sinclair

Authors often say their characters argue with them. Unfortunately, since Cherise Sinclair's heroes are Doms, she never, ever wins.

A *New York Times* and *USA Today* Bestselling Author, she's renowned for writing heart-wrenching contemporary romances with devastating Dominants, laugh-out-loud dialogue, and absolutely sizzling sex.

Fledglings having flown the nest, Cherise, her beloved husband, a far-too-energetic puppy, and one fussy feline live in the Pacific Northwest where nothing is cozier than a rainy day spent writing.

Connect with Cherise in the following places:

Website:
CheriseSinclair.com
Facebook:
www.facebook.com/CheriseSinclairAuthor
Facebook Discussion Group:
CheriseSinclair.com/Facebook-Discussion-Group

32475813R00147

Made in the USA
Middletown, DE
06 June 2016